Jungle Inferno
(The Phoenix Agency)

By

Desiree Holt

Jungle Inferno

To Josh Felker, handgun instructor extraordinaire and former Army Ranger who helped me bring this book to life. There would be no Phoenix without you.

It is often said that writing is a solitary job, but that's not really true. This book, like so many others I have written, could not have come to life without the love and support of some really great people. You are always there when I need you, and support me even when I hit the proverbial wall. So Margie Hager, Kate Richards, Brenna Zinn, and of course my wonderful children—Amy, Steven and Suzanne—this is for you. And to everyone else, the Belles Femmes Authors, all my wonderful friends in the writing world and my incredible readers, Thank you from the bottom of my heart.

They served their country in every branch of the military – Army Delta Force, SEALs, Air Force, Marines. We are pilots, snipers, medics – whatever the job calls for. And now as private citizens they serve in other capacities, as private contractors training security for defense contractors, as black ops eradicating drug dealers, as trained operatives ferreting out traitors. With the women in their lives who each have a unique psychic ability, they are a force to be reckoned with. Risen from the ashes of war, they continue to fight the battle on all fronts. They are Phoenix.

Prologue

It was raining, a steady thrumming on the broad leaves of the trees and plants that formed a thick canopy over the jungle floor. By the time it reached the thick carpet of dead plants and rotting wood it was more like a mist, a thick curtain of steam that sat heavily on the skin.

Mark Halloran inhaled deeply, the sweet scent of vanilla and sarsaparilla plants mingling with that of the wild orchids. The dense rainforest of the Peruvian jungle held a wild mixture of flora whose perfume teased at the senses and conjured up images. Beneath the heavier perfume of these and other plants like cinchona and cedar was the vague hint of the abundance of orchids growing in wild profusion.

But none so arousing as the scent of the woman in his arms. Light jasmine drifted from the silken fall of her hair and mingles with the sweetness of her body. And the musk of her arousal. He ran his hand over the satiny surface of her skin, feeling every dip and hollow with the tips of his fingers. The indentation of her navel. The crease where hip and thigh joined.

Bending his head he pulled a dusky nipple into his mouth, swirling his tongue around it before pressing it flat against the roof of her mouth. He was rewarded with a soft moan and an arching of Faith's body that pushed the nipple deeper into his mouth. His hand molded the full swell of her breast, loving the feel of its weight in his palm.

His cock had been hard enough to drive nails

Jungle Inferno

from the moment they'd entered the tent that had
been pitched for them. A jungle vacation with as
many amenities as the rainforest had to offer.
They'd nearly ripped their clothes in the urgency to
get rid of them, to feel naked skin against naked
skin. So many months had passed since they'd been
together that he was afraid he'd blow before they
even got started.

*You're Special Ops, asshole. You have
legendary control. Use it now.*

So he'd gritted his teeth and dialed it back as
much as he could, willing himself to take the time to
do this properly.

But just looking at her was enough to ramp up
his simmering arousal. Her naked body was a work
of art, lush hips and breasts, long legs and at the
juncture of her thighs the soft nest of curls that hid
the mysteries of her sex. A wet heat the scorched
him, drowned him with the liquid of her passion.
His only conflict was whether to fuck her first with
his mouth or his cock. He'd barely contained
himself enough to urge her down to the mat with
him, so great was the need to take her where they
stood.

He moved his mouth to the other nipple,
poking at him so temptingly, and trailed his hand
down her body over the soft swell of her tummy to
the familiar wet heat. God, she was always so wet
for him so quickly. How was he supposed to hold
back?

Faith opened her thighs to his touch and his
thumb easily found the hot nub of her clitoris. As he
pulled deeply on her taut nipple his thumb brushed
back and forth against the tiny bundle of nerves,
drawing the little cries of pleasure from her that
turned him on so much.

He lifted his head to brush his lips against hers,

2

gently licking the seam of her lips, teasing at the corners, nipping lightly on the full lower one. He'd always been fascinated by the sensuous swell of those lips, loved kissing them and tasting them. Nipping on them. He thought he could spend hours just making love to her mouth.

When she opened them he slipped his tongue inside, scraping over the edge of her teeth to find the hot slickness of the skin inside. The touch of her small tongue against his sent arrows of heat jolting through him, straight to his throbbing cock and his aching balls.

Slow, asshole. Slow. Show her how much you appreciate her. How you feel about her.

He danced with her tongue, darting back and forth over it's surface while his thumb continues to work her clit in a slow, steady motion. Faith moaned again, the tight little sound echoing into his own mouth. Her hands pressed against his back, pulling him down closer to her.

When she bent her legs, planting her feet firmly on the woven mat, a silent invitation to explore further, he moved his hand until he could slide two fingers into her heat.

Oh, god. Hot! Hot, hot, hot!

She was so very wet, her inner walls slippery with her juices, her flesh pulsing against his fingers.

He tore his mouth away from her.

"I can't wait any longer." His voice was so hoarse he didn't even recognize it.

"Then don't," she urged. "It's been so long. I'm ready for you. Now."

Mark reached for the foil packet he'd dropped beside them, ripped it open with his teeth and extracted the latex sheath. Levering himself to his knees he deftly rolled it on with one hand, ready for action.

But the sight of her wet, welcoming, pink flesh was so tempting, so mouth-watering, that first he had to have a taste. He lowered his head, spread her lips wide with his thumbs and lapped the length of her.

"Ohhhhh."

The long exhalation of pleasure sent another surge of heat through him. God, he loved those sounds. So he did it again. And again. Until he wasn't sure exactly who he was teasing. Licking the sweet/tart taste of her from his lips, he positioned himself, pressing the head of his cock her opening and with one hard roll of his hips.

Oh, Jesus!

Her inner walls clamped around him and it was like being burned alive with the sweetest heat. He gritted his teeth, every muscle in his body tightening with the need for release, but he held himself still, giving himself time to enjoy the feel of her like a hot glove around him.

Faith lifted her legs to wrap them around his waist and dug her heels in at the small of her back, lifting herself to him as she did it.

"Jesus, Faith," he groaned. "I'm hanging on by a thread here."

"I'm ready," she hissed. "It's been so long, don't make we wait any longer. Please."

"I can't wait, either."

Drawing in a long breath he pounded into her, again and again, the slick walls of her cunt dragging at him with each thrust of his swollen shaft. Heat. Electricity. Power. It all flooded through him. Between them. Around them.

He couldn't seem to control himself, slamming into her harder and harder. The muscles around his spine tingled and his balls tightened and at the exact moment he feared he'd have to take the ride without her she clenched around him and they exploded together.

He spurted again and again into the latex as her tight muscles clamped around him, milking him and drawing every last drop of release from him. At the peak of his orgasm he threw back her head and screamed her name.

Collapsing forward, he tried to catch his weight on his arms and rested his forehead on hers. His heart was hammering what felt like a million beats a minute and he couldn't get enough air in his lungs.

Outside the tent macaws screeched and parrots squawked, a jungle symphony underscored by the noise of the howler monkeys. Nature's music that only enhanced the sensual heat of the rainforest that surrounded them.

A monkey screamed again, and sudden pain shooting through his leg wiped away every vestige of the sexual satisfaction that had woven around him. He tried to tighten his arms around Faith but she wasn't there. He wasn't holding anyone.

And the pain that had shattered the dream lashed him again, shrieking through his body.

"So, Captain, Halloran. You call the name of your beloved in your sleep. Perhaps we have made you too comfortable."

Mark pried open his eyes and tried to look around. He was in a tent, all right, but there wasn't anything sensual about it. He lay on jungle dirt rather than soft woven mats, and there was no Faith. No soft woman in his arms. No scent of anything but the stink of sweat and dirt. And an evil looking man who seemed to take great pleasure in causing him pain by prodding his leg. His injured leg, he remembered.

A dream. It was all a dream. He was sweaty and

grimy and his leg hurt like hell. He tried to move it and discovered it was tied at the ankle to a stake.

And then it came back to him. The blown mission. The terrorist cell descending ojn them. His team ambushed and killed. Himself wounded and captured, by the very terrorist and arms dealer they'd been sent to take out. He was somewhere in the stinking Peruvian jungle and no one knew where the hell he was or even if he was alive.

Shit!

He dropped his head back to the dirt and closed his eyes again.

Faith!

Chapter One

Damn!

Faith Wilding stared at her computer monitor in frustration, the screen empty except for the annoying cursor winking at her. The first three chapters of her latest political thriller were due to her agent by the end of the month and she hadn't even written the first word. Not once since she'd sold her first manuscript had she ever been stricken with writer's block. Today, however, it seemed as if something had swept her mind bare, knocking out every word or phrase that might be taking root.

She looked around her den, usually a place of comfort and inspiration. The warm earth tones on the rug that had been her grandmother's were an accent on the polished hardwood floor. The couch and chair, covered in navy denim, showed traces of wear from all the times she'd lain or sat there reading manuscript drafts. The walls were lined with family pictures, faces smiling down on her with encouragement and support.

Usually this room unlocked her mind and opened the gates for her thoughts to flow freely. Not tonight. She could have been sitting in a sterile room for all the good it was doing her.

She rotated her head, easing the tension in her neck and shoulders. Maybe she should fix another cup of her favorite Chai tea. Its energy might kick-start her brain.

I need you.

The familiar voice blasted through her mind.

Mark! Oh God, Mark.

Stunned, she tried to focus her thoughts but a white-hot pain pierced her body, stealing her breath. She clenched her fists against it and as it faded an image of Mark's face, bruised and lined with pain, flashed briefly and was gone.

Faith leaned back in her chair, using the skills she'd been taught to control her breathing and slow her racing pulse. Running her hands up and down her arms she discovered a fine sheen of perspiration on her skin.

Mark!

She tried to recapture the image but it was gone. Then his voice was back.

Need you...captured...

Captured! Dear God. He'd reached out to her from wherever he was, but where was that? Hdsow could she find him? He could be anywhere. She felt as if a part of her body had been severed. Closing her eyes and pushing everything else from her brain, she concentrated on sending a reply.

I heard you. Where are you?

She sat perfectly still, eyes still tightly shut, blocking out everything else, focusing as she'd been taught, to strengthen her message.

Mark?

She waited but the only thing that answered her was the heavy silence. Either his strength had given out or something—or someone—had blocked him.

Finally she pushed her chair away from the desk and headed to the kitchen on legs not quite steady. Tea was definitely in order.

The last time she'd heard from Mark Halloran was two years ago. That time she'd been sitting in a Starbucks drinking a mocha latte and checking her schedule on her PDA when the message hit her. Startled, she'd nearly spilled her coffee and looked around to make sure he wasn't just standing two feet away.

Hello, darlin'.

That whiskey smooth voice had warmed her blood and made her smile. And remember the one long weekend they'd had together before he left on a mission.

Hi. Where are you?

Far away.

An image of him in a helicopter danced before her eyes, helmet securely on his head, rifle and other gear strapped to his body. As a Special Ops soldier, a member of the famed Delta Force, he was always in some far corner of the world on a mission that no one could discuss. Usually he was concentrating so hard on what he was doing there was no opportunity to clear his mind and reach out to her.

Miss you, came the next message.

Me too. You'll never know how much. You still have my heart.

The image changed to one of him naked, grinning, his blue eyes laughing at her. Her body heated and every pulse point had begun to throb. She'd looked around her carefully, sure every eye was on her but everyone appeared to be attending to their own business. She carried that short message and those images with her for a long time.

And now, tonight's message. Shocking in its pain. Mark, stolid and steadfast. Bastion of strength. A soldier with special skills who'd stared at death more times than she'd ever know about. Mark never asked for help. The anguish in his voice filled her with a sense of dread. Fear drenched her and a cold knot of it tightened in her stomach. For him to send her this message the situation had to be out of control.

But where was he? What had happened to him? And what was wrong that the only cry for help he could get out was telepathically to her?

Leaning against the counter, sipping the hot tea, she thought about the first time they'd discovered their telepathic ability to communicate.

* * * * *

"Are you finished?"

Fourteen-year-old Faith sat up so quickly the book she was reading slid off the end of the table. The resulting noise drew several hushing sounds from others in the library. Cheeks flushed with embarrassment she leaned down and picked it up, then looked around. Had someone just spoken to her? Out loud? In the library?

Shaking her head, she bent her attention again to the book in front of her.

Let's get out of here.

She gripped her pen as she looked around again. There. In the corner. Mark grinning at her and winking. How had he done that, sent her that message? Sometimes during the past few years she'd had the feeling that she could almost— almost—hear his voice in her head but she'd passed it off as wishful thinking.

Several times she'd thought about calling Aunt Vivi and talking to her, asking her about it but she knew her parents would have a fit. Her mother's sister was telepathic and she belonged to The Lotus Circle, an ancient society now resurrected and spread throughout the world via the Internet. Its members were people with special psychic abilities, always ready to help each other and provide assistance and comfort when necessary. Despite how the rest of the family felt, Faith stood in awe of her. Did receiving Mark's message this way mean, like her aunt, that she might be a telepath, also? The thought made her both anxious and excited.

Faith closed her eyes and built her reply in her head. Just to see if she could do it.

Leave now?

She opened her eyes to see Mark dip his head.

A tiny thrill skittered through her. Clearly she had the same gift as Aunt Vivi. But Mark! Where had he come by this? Who in his family had this special gift that had filtered down to him?

Faith closed her book and shoved everything into her backpack. Mark had already left the large reading room and she followed as quickly as she could She found him outside sitting on one of the broad stone steps, the quirky grin still on his face.

"It worked," he told her.

"How did you do that?" She lowered herself to the step beside him. "How did you know you could do it?"

He shrugged. "I don't know. A feeling. I kept hearing bits and pieces of people's messages in my head. Strangers. I wanted to try this for a long time, to see if I could actually send a message to someone." He grinned. "I wanted it to be you."

He reached over and took one of her small hands in his. At sixteen he already had the structure of a man. Tall body just filling out. Large, warm hands. Eyes full of mischief and a face on the verge of being rugged. All topped with a thick head of inky black hair.

To fourteen-year-old Faith he was the man of her dreams. The invisible bond between them had been forged the day they met, when Faith and her family moved next door to the Hallorans. Her parents now lived in a condo community and Faith had her own house but she still considered he Hallorans family. The shy six-year-old was nervous about entering a new school and meeting strangers. Until the eight-year-old boy held out his hand and said, "I'll take care of you," and helped her onto the bus. Something passed between them, as sharp as a bolt of lightning yet more comforting. Secure. Faith had raised her eyes to Mark's, warmed at the sight of his smile and they'd been a team since then.

As they got older, on warm nights they sat outside counting stars and sharing dreams. When Mark dated now and then, Faith felt an unreasoning rush of jealousy but the thread that bound them still remained as strong as ever. And none of the relationships, even beyond high school, ever lasted.

For herself she had no desire to spend time with other boys. Assuming, of course, her parents would ever lift the restrictions and allow her something beyond group activities.

They'd always been able to read each others thoughts, even as tiny children. This had to be just a natural outgrowth of that. Didn't it? Faith frowned. Or did she—and Mark—have a connection far beyond the ordinary?

"Heavy thoughts for a small person," he teased, squeezing her hand.

She looked up at him and smiled. Even at fourteen the sight of him could make her heart stumble and her blood race. "Just wondering if we could do that again. You know. Talk without talking."

"Maybe. It would be a nice thing when I leave for college in another year."

Mark had been accepted at Texas A&M and planned to become a member of their elite ROTC Corps. Then into the Army.

"It would save on telephone bills," she joked.

"Tell you what. Let's try it tonight when we're at home. Maybe before we each go to sleep."

"A-all right." Talk to him while they were in their beds? She shivered.

"Cold?"

No. I'm having forbidden thoughts about you.

"Come on." He put his arm around her and drew her close to him, giving her a quick squeeze. "I'll drive you home. Don't forget about tonight."

As if she could.

She could hardly wait for evening to come and darkness, so she could test this new phase of their relationship. At ten o'clock she climbed into bed, prepared to lie awake until whatever time Mark might send her a message. Knowing him it could be as late as midnight. But she had barely settled her head on the pillow and tried to clear her mind of any obstacles when she heard him. Sharp. Clear. As if he was standing beside her.

Hi, Tidbit.

His name for her since he'd shot up to his present height while she remained at a tiny five foot one.

Hi. An image flashed across her brain like a flickering movie. Mark, on his bed in nothing but his boxers. The same grin on his face. Faith slid down and pulled the blanket over her head, cheeks hot with teenage embarrassment.

For a long moment silence filled the room. Then faintly, she heard, *'Night.*

Then the image was gone and so was the lingering sound of the message.

Faith turned over and hugged her pillow to her body. Was it possible to fall in love at fourteen?

* * * * *

Faith stood in the shower, letting the hot water beat down on her, hoping it would sweep the clutter out of her mind. She'd tried three more times to reach Mark, focusing her message, making her mind a blank except for that one image of him. Nothing. Now so many images of Mark were crowding together she couldn't separate them from the latest one, so full of pain it hurt her just to think about it.

Lord, she missed him. More than she ever admitted to herself. The men she'd dated in college and beyond were merely pale imitations of the man who held both her heart and her soul in the palm of his hand. But so much separated them, things that kept getting in the way. College. The Army. Even her career to a small degree, although she could write anywhere. But Mark's military assignments were so secret and required such focus he made the choice not to be distracted by her nearness.

Except for that one weekend. The weekend she kept tucked in her mind like a precious gem, pulling it out to warm herself in private. She thought of the one long weekend they'd had together. Unexpected and unexpectedly hot and sensuous. Who had known that their friendship would open up to a mind-blowing sexual connection. But that was the only time they'd been able to communicate in person. That left only the telepathic messages but to Faith they were more special than anything. A means of sharing that shut everyone else out. Words. Images. Enough to keep them going.

They both knew phone calls and brief contact would only leave them wanting more, so by unspoken agreement they pushed everything to the back of their minds.

For now.

Until Mark felt he had honored his commitment to his country and they were both ready to think about the future.

Until tonight.

She closed her eyes and ran her hands over her

body, remembering how it felt to have Mark's hands on her. His mouth on her nipples. His fingers molding her breasts. She slid her soap-slicked fingers down through the softness of her curls and touched herself, softly the way he'd done, just enough to tease her at first, then increasing both tempo and pressure until she was practically begging him to be inside her.

He'd laughed, a slow, sexy chuckle, and told her, "Don't rush me. I'm planning on taking my time. I never thought we'd get to this point, so I don't want to miss anything."

And he hadn't. Not one single thing. She realized suddenly that her fingers slipping into her sex were a very poor substitute for Mark's thick, hard cock. The tremors making her inner walls quiver were a pale imitation of the spasms that rocked her when Mark fucked her.

Deliberately pushing the memories from her mind, she turned off the shower, and reached for a thick towel to wrap around herself, another one to squeeze the excess water from her long hair before using the blow dryer.

I can find him. I'm a writer. I know how to do research.

But this was a little more complicated than delving into a politician's life for romantic political thrillers. She wouldn't be able to find people willing to talk. Or even acknowledge that they knew Mark Halloran or anything to do with his assignments.

She'd start with his parents. Maybe they had a tiny glimmer of where he'd been sent. At least the general region.

But first she'd call Aunt Vivi and go talk to her. If there was another telepath where Mark was being held who was erecting shields to block his mind, she'd need help to get around them. And to strengthen her own abilities to send her messages to Mark.

She slipped into bed and turned out the light. All those years from the time they were children, forging a relationship that outsiders couldn't pierce. Being there for each other. Was it love, what they had? They'd hardly spent enough intimate time with each other to know. Whatever it was, though, it was unbreakable.

"We'll always be there for each other, right?" That's what he'd said the last time she'd seen him.

She'd nodded. "Always. If you need me, I'll come to you."

"Same goes, darlin'."

How could they even imagine he would be the one asking her for help?

As she always did at night she closed her eyes and willed Mark's face to come to her. But tonight it wasn't the one with the rumpled black hair and laughing vivid blue eyes. Tonight it was the one with deep ridges of pain and anguish that darkened the blue almost to black.

Tidbit.

She sat bolt upright. *I'm here, Mark.*

I... you. Please...kill...

Faith felt shock race through her. Kill? Whoever captured him was going to kill him? Her heart banged against her ribs like a jackhammer. She lay back down and forced a calmness she didn't feel. With an effort of will she directed all her energy into the message.

Tell me where you are. Please.

But no matter how long she lay awake, straining her senses, the only thing that answered her was silence.

Chapter Two

The morning did little to ease the tension left from the night before. First thing, Faith took care of things hanging fire with her agent and her publicity person. Then she deliberately shut down her computer, ruthlessly driving her mind away from the latest book she was trying to start and swallowed the last of her coffee. It was time to talk to her aunt.

"Of course you can come and see me," Aunt Vivi told her. After a brief silence, she added, "Is this personal or professional?"

Faith swallowed a sigh. "Both."

"All right. Come over about ten. The house is quiet by then."

Aunt Vivi opened her front door the moment Faith pulled into the driveway.

"Have you been watching for me?" Faith gave a small laugh.

"Yes." Vivi nodded. "I felt the tension in your voice and sensed your trouble." She put an arm around her niece. "Come in. I've made some tea. I want to know what's troubling your mind and shutting down your inner person."

They sat at the kitchen table, scene of every important conversation Faith could remember, inhaling the fragrance of the vanilla tea that Vivi liked.

"Mark contacted me," Faith said at last.

Vivi raised one eyebrow. "That's nothing new. The two of you have been sending each other telepathic messages since you were teenagers."

Faith shook her head. "This is different. It frightened me."

"Oh?" Vivi frowned. "How so? I can't imagine

Mark doing anything to scare you."

"He's in trouble. That alone scares me. Mark has always been the solid, indestructible rock." She raked her fingers through her hair. The two of them had one unbreakable commitment to each other. No matter where they were, if one of them needed the other, they'd come. At once. And she would, if she could only find out where he was. "And I got such an image of pain. Of agony. And I felt it too."

Vivi took her niece's hand. "Remember I told you a long time ago, when you first came to me to talk about this, that you might also have some empathic abilities too? That, in the right circumstances, you could sense other people's feelings and emotions. And pain."

"Yes. I remember." Faith picked up her tea cup. "But I've never felt it as strongly as this." She forced herself to look directly at Vivi. "I felt as if the pain was mine. You know?"

"And that's because of the relationship between you and Mark." Vivi sighed. "I've always wondered why the two of you never moved forward with what I knew you felt for each other."

Faith shrugged. "Time. Circumstances. Not wanting to ruin a friendship with something that might not last." She shook her head. "Now I wish we had."

"If wishes were horses." Vivi quoted her favorite saying. "I hope you'll both acknowledge your feelings once you're together again."

"If only. Aunt Vivi, it frightens me to think what he must be going through. And I don't even know where he is."

Vivi rose and refilled their cups. She squeezed Faith's shoulder, a gesture of warmth. "You have no idea if your messages got through to him."

"No. None at all. And I had the feeling his were

being shut down on that end. That's why only bits and pieces come through."

Vivi nodded. "That's entirely possible. If they have a telepath among them he could be closing the psychic door."

"I keep hoping that in one of these messages he'll be able to give me some kind of clue as to where he is. If he even knows. Right now I don't even have a starting point." She ran her finger around the rim of the cup. "And I have to be able to tell him I got his messages to me." She looked up. "That's why I'm here. I can't do this myself, especially if they have a psychic blocker."

"All right." Vivi put one of her hands over Faith's. "I think for this we need other members of the Circle." She leaned over and kissed her niece's cheek. "Don't sweat it. We'll get this done."

Faith went to stand at the big window overlooking the back yard. The abundance of flowers always soothed her, calmed her nerves when she was jittery. Right now she could have used a truckload of them. The thought of Mark somewhere in danger, wounded, maybe dying, terrified her in ways she couldn't admit. If that was the case, the last thing she wanted to think about was all the years they'd wasted. Years they could have been together instead of off chasing dreams.

No! She wouldn't think about that. Somehow she would let him know his message came through and she was on it. Finding him. She rubbed her hands up and down her arms, as if the very friction could dispel the cold that had settled inside her.

She heard Vivi speaking softly on the phone, then come to stand beside her. "Sarah and Emily will be here in about an hour. Then we'll see what we can do."

Something quick, I hope.

* * * * *

The sun was a globe of fire creeping up in the sky, turning everything below it into an oven. It was barely nine o'clock in the morning yet Mark Halloran was sure the temperature was already close to triple digits. The humidity was as thick as a rainfall. The roar and grunt of the howler monkeys was already splitting the air as they leaped from tree to tree feasting on the canopy leaves.

How the hell did people live in places like this? Or work in them.

And this appeared to be a permanent camp, with tents, lean-tos and crude buildings. It also boasted a campfire pit and other amenities they wouldn't have taken the time for in a transitory situation, unlike the temporary setup where the meeting had taken place. Where they'd been told the Wolf was going to meet with Escobedo's group. A friend of former Special Ops soldier Rick Latrobe's, was deep undercover with Escobedo's group. He had risked his life to get the message out that the Wolf was going to make a personal appearance. Unusual for him but this shipment was so large and involved so much money, Escobedo insisted.

Not at his camp, however. Not even the Wolf would be privy to its location. A meeting place not far away was set up. For the Wolf it would be in and out. Just like that. He would arrive with the shipment, Escobedo would bring the money. As soon as both parties were satisfied with the goods, the transaction would take place and that would be that.

Mark had gone to his commanding office, Major John Gregorio, with the information. The major had passed it up the chain and the word had come down to act. The United States government had waited a very long time for a chance at the Wolf. To make it a two-fer upped the ante.

A simple mission. Get in. Take out the bad guys. Get out. One less group of Al Qaeda plotters to worry about. And the arms dealer meeting with them. That was the key. That's what he and his men had been told. It was a chance to clean out a viper's nest and take out a key arms player at the same time.

With the weakening of the Tupac Amaru terrorist group and the decline of Shining Path, Al Qaeda had been recruiting heavily and spending big money to rebuild Peru's terrorist structure. Another foothold in South America for the promised Islamic world.

But someone had leaked the mission, Escobedo's group was waiting for them and now most of his men were dead. After burning the bodies of Mark's men they'd cleaned up every trace of what had taken place and moved what Mark reckoned was about ten miles away. All of them including the Wolf,

He grunted, trying to shift to a more comfortable position. The tent gave him little protection him from the ruthless sun and having his ankle chained to a stake barely two feet away severely restricted his movements. For maybe the thousandth time he wondered what had gone wrong and landed him in this abominable mess.

And God, what a true mess it had been. One minute they were finding their positions to take their shots, carefully hidden, the target painted. The next they were the targets instead. The noise of the AK47s still echoed in his ears, along with the stench of the blood of his dying men. They'd even gotten the comm guy they'd left at the insertion and extraction point with their gear.

He'd forced himself to look when they dragged the bodies into the center of the camp, piled them together and set them on fire. They stood watching with arrogant, evil grins on their faces, then opened bottles of whiskey to celebrate. Mark was sure it was a sight he'd never forget.

He knew what they wanted—the name of the man who had betrayed them. They could kill him and very well might but the source had to be protected at all costs.

Yet as much as they tortured him, for sport and pleasure as well as information, there were things he hung onto that kept his sanity intact. For one thing, despite his wounds he kept himself alert and counted the bodies. One was missing, Joey Latrobe. The kid. The sniper. Rick's brother, who'd brought them the information. Mark was convinced he wasn't dead or they'd have found him. No, badly wounded or not, he'd found a way to hide from them. Now if Mark could only be sure he got away.

Of course he had no idea what shape Joey was in, or even if he could give his rescuers, if there were any, information about the camp. Which, by his reckoning, was now at least ten miles from where it had been when he was captured.

But the thing that gave him real strength was his connection to Faith. God. Beautiful Faith. The woman of his dreams. How stupid was he to walk away from what they could have had to play soldier? No, not that. To defend his country. His sense of honor and patriotism was stronger than almost anything. But now, if he died here in this godforsaken hellhole, the only memory he'd have would be that long weekend they'd shared before he was deployed the first time.

And the erotic dreams that came to wipe away

the pain.

When he closed his eyes she was in his arms again, her lush body naked against his, her breasts pressing against his chest. His hands coasted over the satiny feel of her skin, fingertips exploring every dip and hollow.

"It's a good thing you aren't around when I'm planning a mission," he murmured, his lips against her throat. "I just look at you and my cock gets so big I'm afraid my pants won't contain it."

Her laugh was throaty and musical, and her fingers drifted down to close around his thick erection. "Good. That's the way I like it."

She moved her hand in a slow pumping motion and he groaned at the heat that rushed through him. Lowering his head he closed his lips over one taut nipple, pulling it into his mouth. It hardened even more at his touch and when he dragged his teeth over it lightly her grip on his shaft tightened.

"Easy." He released the nipple and lapped around the edge of it. "We don't want the dance to end when the music has just begun."

"Ah, but we can always dance again," she reminded him.

He tasted the skin in the valley between her breasts, doing his best to take control of the situation even as her fingers continued to stroke the hard, thick length of him. Light movements that teased him and heated his blood.

But then just being near her did that.

He drew tiny circles with his tongue in her navel, feeling the heat of her body scorching him. He inhaled, drawing her scent into his nostrils, her own perfume mingled with the musk of her arousal. His cock flexed in her fingers.

His tongue followed the sweet indentation where her thigh and hip joined, just a light, flickering touch. She whimpered a tiny sound that pierced him like a bolt of lightning. With a swift movement he lifted her hand from his shaft, rolled her to her back and spread her legs wide. Enjoying for a moment the sight of her sex glistening with her juices, he bent his head and licked her slit end to end, giving the tip of her clit a tiny caress with his tongue.

God, she smelled and tasted so damn sweet. Better than any drink he'd ever had. Better than the fancier dessert. He took his time lapping her, sucking in every drop of juice on her tender flesh. His cock ached unbearably, the need to slide into her so great he shook with it. But he refused to deny himself the pleasure of her taste, or her scalding response to it.

Faith cried out, tunneling her fingers in his hair and clutching at his head. Her juices bathed his tongue, making her passage slick as he thrust his tongue inside her. He always tried to slow down but just touching her ramped up her hunger to such a level that he had only a thin veneer of control

Capturing her clit with thumb and forefinger, he tongue-fucked her in earnest, with hard, steady strokes, her cream coating his tongue. Her inner walls fluttered, then clenched.

"Oh, please," she begged.

He pinched her clit, hard, and she came with an explosion of desire, her body sucking his tongue in and locking it in place. Her hips bucked as he lapped and sucked and drew every last quiver from her. But when she lay back, limp, he rose to his knees and reached for the condom he'd tossed onto the mat beside them. Positioning the head of his cock at her entrance, with one hard movement he drove himself home.

She tightened around him, her breath hitching

as he wrapped her legs around him and locked her ankles at the small of his back. Sliding his hands beneath the soft firmness of her ass, he thrust into her again and again and again. Even as her aftershocks were dying away new spasms began to ripple though her. She matched his rhythm, listing herself to her as he slammed into her over and over.

The climax caught them both at once. As the walls of her pussy milked him she cried out his name again and again. He collapsed on her, both of them covered with sweat, hearts beating hard and erratic.

God, he loved this woman. Loved being with her. Loved fucking her.

He buried his face against her soft shoulder.
Faith!

He opened his eyes to find himself still in the ragged tent in the stinking Peruvian rainforest, anchored to a stake. His leg and his head throbbed. But so did his cock, images of the dream still dancing in his head like some kind of erotic butterflies.
Faith!

Had she gotten his message? Since they discovered their shared ability in their teens, their telepathic communication had been a fun thing for them, a way to shut everyone else out and communicate only with each other. But the Army had learned about his special skill and had people work with him to develop it even more. Hone it. Refine it. One of the men on this mission was also a telepath. And Chase Wohlmann could construct psychic shields. That meant he could put invisible walls in place to prevent strangers—or enemies—from reading their message. He could also protect them from assaults on their minds.

But Chase was dead. Burned in the mass funeral pyre. Mark nearly vomited every time he thought about that horrific scene. He opened his eyes to find himself still in the ragged tent in the stinking Peruvian rainforest, anchored to a stake. His leg and his head throbbed. But so did his cock, images of the dream still dancing in his head like some kind of erotic butterflies.

Faith!

Mark knew one of the men in the camp was a telepath. He'd felt it when he sent the first message. The slamming shut of the mental barrier. Preventing a message from Faith from getting through. He'd have to be very careful.

"Well, Captain Halloran."

The acquired British accent punctured his thoughts. Mark looked up at the man who'd come into the tent, the arms dealer who should be dead now instead of standing in front of him. Tall and lean, aristocratic in bearing, his disdain not only for Mark but for the men who bought his merchandise was evident. Mark knew he'd be long gone by now if not for the information he was seeking. Each time Mark was dragged to the center of the camp for whatever torture the men devised, this man stood watching with eyes that glittered, a tiny smile curving his lips.

"No cheery greeting?" the man asked, then kicked the open cut on Mark's leg.

Mark gritted his teeth and forced himself to show as little reaction as possible. So far he'd been able to keep from saying anything to his captors. They could kill him and they very well might but he'd never open his mouth.

"Ah, well. No matter. I'd really love to be gone from here but unfortunately you have information I need." He deliberately stepped on the injured leg.

26

Mark ground his teeth and swallowed a scream.

"You could save yourself a lot of pain, you know. I will use whatever means the men devise to find out how you knew about this camp and who organized this little mission of yours. This could seriously jeopardize plans already in place, not to mention affecting my business enterprises." He nodded toward the open flap and two men entered. Unshackling Mark from the stake they lifted him by his arms and half-walked, half-carried him outside.

"Oh and by the way," the man called after him. "We counted the bodies carefully. One of your men is missing. Wherever he is, we'll find him."

Please, God, keep Joey safe.

Then Mark concentrated on clearing his mind of everything but an image of Faith and projecting one short message before they shut him down.

Come...need...

* * * * *

Vivi had brewed a fresh pot of lotus tea, a herbal tea blended for meditation and wisdom. Faith loved the scent of fresh flowers that lingered over the pale golden infusion of white lotus, chamomile, chrysanthemum and linden. She had kept her own supply ever since her aunt introduced her to it.

They were seated at the kitchen table again, this time joined by Sarah Winston and Emily Ross, the two women Vivi had called. They were the first members of The Lotus Circle Faith had met besides her aunt and had helped her enormously as she struggled to grow into and control her power. As two of her guides when she became a member of the Circle, they had come today without hesitation.

"I can't thank you enough," she told them,

27

nervously stirring her tea. "Mark and I have never done anything with our...ability...except communicate with each other. I know you think we wasted it but it was a very private thing with us, something we chose not to share. Or use in a way that included others."

Sarah put her hand on Faith's arm. "That is your choice, sweetheart. Being a telepath doesn't mean you have to do anything with it except what you feel comfortable with. The Lotus Circle is only to help people expand their powers fully and teach them how to direct them. And be here, like today, when we're needed."

"Have you had any more messages?" Emily asked.

Faith shook her head. "I told Aunt Vivi I'm sure someone's blocking him. He can't—"

Rrunning out...time....

She gripped the edge of the table, Mark's voice out of nowhere sharp and clear in her head. A sharp, stabbing pain in her ribs followed it, almost doubling her over.

"Faith, honey?"

Vivi was beside her at once, arms around her, pulling her into the jasmine scent that always surrounded her.

"I heard him." Faith could hardly get the words out. "And felt the pain again. Oh, Aunt Vivi, he's in agony. Something terrible's happening to him. Right now."

"All right, sweetheart." She wrapped Faith's hands around her cup and helped her lift it. "Sip your tea, just a little to calm you. We won't get anywhere if your nerves are jangled and interfering."

In a few moments Faith felt herself relax a little but a fine line of tension still ran through her body.

"Faith." Emily leaned forward. "You must try again to get through to him. If you can't, we'll work on something else."

"All right. I'll do my best." She closed her eyes, still holding her teacup and did the mental exercises she used to clear her mind. Finally, when she was ready, she brought up a clean image of Mark, a happy image. "I'm here. Can you hear me?"

"Let's all do this together," Sally suggested, when it was apparent there was no response. "We'll all focus on the same message."

"Wait." Emily put down her cup. "We need to increase our strength." Motioning to the others, she indicated they should leave their seats and form a circle around Faith. "Join hands, please. Left palm up, right palm down, hands interwoven to create an energy ring."

In the thick silence filling the room, Faith absorbed the power the women were infusing into her. She called up an image of Mark and focused her mind on it.

"Mark. I'm here."

After five minutes the lack of response was a strong indication someone had erected a thick shield that prevented Mark from hearing her. Or answering her. The energy ring wasn't piercing the shield.

"Five more minutes," Aunt Vivi said.

When the words broke the silence Faith jerked, startled.

You. Come...South America... in South America.

Mark! Give me a clue.

But it was obvious the barrier was in place again.

"All right." Vivi refilled everyone's cups as they took their places at the table again. "We need to have a plan." Vivi stirred her tea and looked at her friends. "Ladies, we need to figure out how we can pierce that shield and help these two exchange messages more clearly. Honey, Sally, Emily and I will work on that. You've never stretched yourself to that level and you might only be a distraction."

"I can't do nothing," she protested.

"I know you've just started a new book," Sarah began but Faith interrupted her.

"Forget that." She waved her hand. "The book is on hold until I find Mark. For him to ask me for help means he's in serious trouble. Right now that's the only important thing." She looked at her aunt. Don't make me sit on the sidelines and wait."

"Of course not." Vivi gave her a warm smile. "You need to keep sending that message. Do it on a regular basis. Clear your mind and focus. And, my dear, you're going to use abilities you possess that we don't. Your skills as a writer."

Faith wrinkled her brow. "I don't understand."

"I want you to start your own investigation. We have a general geographic location. Use all your contacts to see if you can find out what Mark's last mission was. And get that research assistant of yours busy on digging up anything she can on hot spots in South America, or rumors of dangerous activity, that would require a Special Ops mission."

Energy surged through Faith and for the first time since Mark's first message she felt she was doing something positive. "I'll start right away."

Chapter Three

Faith stared at the pad of paper in front of her, the top page filled with notes in her neat handwriting. As soon as she'd arrived back at her house she seated herself at her desk and begun to make lists.

Who to call? That was the big question. With Special Ops you couldn't just pick up the telephone and ask if the Army had misplaced one of its teams. Because that's what she had to find out first. Mark never operated alone. He was always as part of a team. Four years ago he'd become a team leader. Although he said little about it, she had a feeling he was considered among the elite. But that only meant he got the most dangerous missions. The jobs no one else could be trusted with.

The men tapped for Special Ops were considered "Special warriors, thoroughly prepared, properly equipped and highly motivated, at the right place, at the right time, facing the right adversary, leading the Global War on Terrorism, accomplishing the strategic objectives of the United States." Gathered from the ranks of the Navy, the Army and the Marines, they were the point men in the war on terrorism. This was all Mark had wanted from the minute he entered the Army.

Faith let her eyes travel to the picture of him in his dress uniform taken the last weekend she'd seen him. Their very long, very physical, very emotional weekend together before his first deployment six years ago. Tears pricked at her eyelids. They had taken so much for granted, stupidly assuming life would wait for them.

Why hadn't she protested when he said he didn't want to tie her down? That seeing each other more often would only make it worse. That he had a job to do for his country and he needed to focus on it and not feel guilty about always leaving her. That she had a life she needed to live.

"I don't want you sitting at home waiting for bad news, darlin'," Mark had told her. "This way you have the chance to move ahead with your life."

As if she could. As if she'd ever do anything but sit and wait for word. Just as she had for these past years. It had taken that weekend to show her just how much she loved him. And teach her that she needed to keep it to herself until Mark felt he was ready for that kind of commitment.

If...no, when...she got him out of this mess, there would be some changes in the rules. That was for damn sure.

She wiped her eyes with the heels of her hands and pushed her hair back behind her ears.

Okay.

First, the Hallorans. She knew Mark kept in touch with them, through letters or phone calls. Maybe both. And on the rare occasions he could squeeze in a weekend, he always found time to spend a day with Faith.

"Can't lose touch with special friends," he always told her.

Friends! Since that one weekend they'd spent together, when friendship had been tucked into a corner, she'd wanted a whole lot more. And he might deny it but she was sure in her heart that Mark did too. Then he'd been deployed for a long time and now those years had passed.

She'd made it a habit to stop by and say hello to the Hallorans, even for a moment, whenever she had a chancce. They were her connection to Mark when mental messages couldn't get through.

Sometimes she thought for all the excitement

she had in her social life she could still be living at home but her parents had pushed her out of the nest with firmness and affection and a door always open.

"Time to grow up," her father teased.

With her first big royalty checks she bought herself a tiny house in northwest San Antonio, not too far from either the Hallorans or Aunt Vivi. While she'd been writing her political thrillers she'd also been honing her telepathic skills, an activity she never discussed with her parents. Aunt Vivi and The Lotus Circle had helped her and also provided a respite from her hectic life as a writer.

Faith shook herself. Letting her mind wander wouldn't get her any place. Concentrate. The Hallorans.

Did... hear me?

Faith dropped her pen.

Mark!

Yes. I heard you. Can you hear me?

She held her breath as the silence stretched unbearably. Then, just as she felt frustration grip her again, one word.

Yes.

She wanted to laugh and cry. He'd heard her! He knew she'd gotten his message.

I'll find you, Mark. Wherever you are.

More silence but she forced herself to wait with as much patience as she could manage.

South America in ....

Faith wanted to scream in frustration.

Where, Mark? Where in South America? Help me. It's a big continent.

Hurry...

Somehow she knew this silence wouldn't be broken. The invisible wall had slammed into place again. He was obviously trying to time his messages when the telepathic captor was otherwise mentally occupied. No problem. At least they'd made the connection.

Hurry, he'd said.

She'd hurry as fast as she could. Picking up the phone, she dialed a still familiar number.

* * * * *

"Faith, it's so very nice to see you, sweetheart Come in, come in."

Dinah Halloran reached out and pulled Faith in through the open doorway. In a moment her arms were around the younger woman, hugging her tightly.

"I was just telling Frank the other day how successful your new book is. I hear people talking about it everywhere. And that television show you did must have boosted sales. Come on into the kitchen. I know you're not a big coffee drinker but how about some sweet tea?"

"That would be wonderful. Thank you."

They walked through the living room where every inch of the fireplace mantel and a round side table were covered with pictures of Mark—in his high school football uniform, at his college graduation, in uniform, receiving awards. She was in many of them and the memories of those years swamped her.

The picture that made tears burn at the back of her throat was of Mark when he was accepted into Delta Force and began Special Ops training. War had already etched lines on his face and his eyes were far too old for a man of his age. But he stood tall and proud, his muscular body evident beneath the uniform. Pride stamped on his face. And his mouth split in his familiar killer smile.

Please, God, keep him safe until I can help him.

She allowed herself to be propelled into the big room where she'd eaten many meals with the Hallorans, at the table where she and Mark had often done their homework. Usually she felt warmed by its familiarity. Today she had to work to conceal her tension.

She forced herself to sit quietly while Dinah busied herself getting out glasses and pouring tea. Mark's mother was aging gracefully, her figure still slender and well-toned, her skin smooth, her graying hair pulled back in a clip at the nape of her neck. She's really ageless, Faith thought.

"Well." Dinah sat down across from her. "So what brings you by today?"

Faith sipped her iced tea, collecting her thoughts. How to approach this. She didn't think Mark came home and blabbed classified secrets to his family, no matter how close they were. Honor and country first, that was his motto.

"I was looking at a picture of Mark today," she began, "and realized I don't have any recent shots of him. How's he doing? It seems ages since we saw each other."

Dinah smiled at her. "I know."

"Anyway, I just wondered what you hear from him."

"Well, not too much, as you can imagine." Dinah fiddled with her glass. "The stuff he does is so highly classified he can't talk about it much."

"Oh, yes, I know." Faith made her voice as casual as possible. "I just wondered if he ever talked about the countries he was sent to. You know, just in passing."

Dinah looked at her with eyes that scrutinized. "Faith, what's this really all about? You know Mark can't share any information. More than anyone

35

 the secretive nature of what he
does. So what are you really asking?"

Faith swallowed, weighing her words. "I just... I guess I just had a sudden fit of worry about him. That's all."

The older woman looked at her with the wise eyes of a mother. "Have you ever told Mark how you feel about him?"

"Excuse me?" Faith jerked back.

"Dinah smiled. "Don't kid a kidder. I'd say you've been in love with my son for years. And I may be telling tales out of school but I'm convinced he feels the same way. You know, Frank and I had always hoped the two of you—"

"Maybe one of these days." Faith cut her off. Too much of that and she'd burst into tears. "I just wondered what part of the world he was in these days. Which danger spot he was in. Maybe if I knew that I'd worry less."

Dinah shrugged. "Or more. Anyway, Mark would never say a word. You know that." She sighed. "Not that I'd worry less if I knew where he was. Probably more."

"Oh, Dinah." Faith tried to think outside of herself for a moment. "This must be so hard for you. And Frank."

"You've no idea." Her lips turned up in a crooked smile. "He is, after all, our only child." She sat up straighter. "But one we're definitely proud of."

And one you can't give me much information about.

But she did have the one tiny clue. South America. It beat having to scavenge the entire world.

Faith finished her tea and stood up. "I hate to run but I have a new deadline looming. I was close

36

enough to you that I had to take a minute to stop by. Please tell Frank hello and give him a hug for me." She kissed Dinah's cheek. "And if you hear from that handsome son of yours, tell him I said to watch his back."

"Will do. And you come see us again, okay?" She watched from the door as Faith walked to her car. "We miss you. You're family too, you know."

"I will. Promise." She waved as she backed out of the driveway, anxious to be gone to nibble on the tiny scrap of information she'd happened on. And she'd have to stop by and see her parents or there'd be hell to pay.

Faith wasn't surprised the Hallorans had no information to share. Mark knew the meaning of 'classified'. But she'd had to give it a shot. Even though she still had nothing more than a continent to go by, at least it was a starting point.

An idea was forming in her head. Maybe her sole attack of writer's block had been for a purpose, more than just to clear her head for Mark's message. "Call Tess Ferguson," she told her cell phone that she had sitting in its holder. She'd get her research assistant on this right away. There had to be something about terrorism in South America they could find.

The phone rang and then went to Tess's voice mail.

"Hi. It's Tess. Sorry I'm not here. You know what to do."

"Hey. I know I said you could have the rest of this week and next off but can I exchange the promise for a two-week paid vacation down the line? I need you to meet me at my house in about two hours. You bring your suitcase. I'll bring Chinese."

She had barely disconnected when Tess called

back, laughing.

"I'll hold you to that two-week paid vacation."

"I'll put it in writing."

When the call ended, she finally felt as if she had a purpose.

* * * * *

"He's still in a coma."

The two men, one thin, one heavy, were at a table in a corner of the quiet restaurant, an alcove that insulated them from the other diners. To the casual eye they were two men sharing a business lunch, discussing whatever—investments, a corporate negotiation, the art of the deal. If anyone had an inkling of the real nature of their conversation they'd run for the nearest newspaper.

"Listen, G—"

The heavy-set man held up a hand. "No names."

The thin man's eyebrows rose. "Not even when we're alone?"

His companion shook his head, "We need to get in the habit of using other names, so we won't forget and slip when we're in a place where we could be overheard. You'll be Mr. Brown and I'll be Mr. Green."

"Fine." Mr. Brown blew out a breath of disgust. A thin man, with salt and pepper hair, he resumed cutting his steak into small, precise pieces.

"Do they think he'll come out of it?" The heavyset man, Mr. Green, frowned as he twirled pasta around his fork.

"Don't know. Right now it doesn't appear likely. It's a damn good thing. You need to keep in mind it's only by the sheerest accident of luck that I discovered who he was and where he was found. If he wakes up and starts talking..."

Mr. Green put down his fork. "We'd both better start praying he doesn't. Right now everyone just thinks the mission went down wrong. No one had any answers. If Latrobe starts talking, we could all be in deep shit, including or maybe especially our boss."

Mr. Brown swallowed half of his iced tea. "I still don't know how he managed to crawl to where he did with three bullets in him. Damn lucky, I say, not to be discovered."

"Yes, he was. Not us, that's for sure. We'd be better off if they'd left him to die."

Mr. Green took a large swallow of his wine. "They were all supposed to be dead. Every one of them."

"And I'm sure they thought this man was too. After all, they weren't counting noses."

Mr. Green grunted. "They should have been. At least the one they captured alive is the leader. And they're keeping him alive to get information from him. Like how anyone knew about the meeting and the group to begin with. No one's ever been able to find out before in spite of the fact they've been scouting the Wolf for months."

Mr. Brown carefully buttered a roll. "You'd think I'd have been able to find that out, considering the position the head honcho of this cluster-fuck is in. But Spec x Ops has locked down information now tighter than a drum."

"It's a damn good thing they didn't before."

Mr. Brown nodded. "But we're not out of the woods yet."

"We'd better hope Escobedo's men get the name of the traitor from Halloran. That's a leak we need to plug right away."

Mr. Brown made a face. "Men like him never

break. And it would be political suicide for this government to even admit he's a captive and trade for him or go after him. Supposedly this little nest of vipers was cleaned up long ago."

Mr. Green sighed. "We have to make this go away."

"Oh, right. And exactly how do you propose we do that?"

A shrug. "You're the one always talking about how smart you are. Figure it out. First of all get rid of the one in the coma. You've got the doctor under your thumb but that won't last. This kid has family. Someone will wonder why they haven't been notified. You can't keep that Top Secret classification on his hospital file forever."

Mr. Brown leaned across the table. "Listen, you jackass. I can't just spirit a wounded soldier out of a hospital and make him disappear with no questions. Or wipe out the other problem."

"Yeah? Well, you'd better figure it out or the man we work for will hand both of us our heads and it won't be pleasant. Is that what you want?"

"I can't believe this kid even escaped detection."

Mr. Green shook his head. "Rotten luck, that's what. Somehow he dragged himself back to the extraction point after our friends had moved on. His good luck and our bad that he was there when the extraction team arrived. Now we're in the position of hoping he dies or figuring out how to make it happen ourselves."

Mr. Brown's jaw tightened. "How the hell did we get into this, anyway?"

Mr. Green snorted. "Money. What else?"

* * * * *

"Okay." Tess Ferguson wiped her mouth delicately and sat back in her chair. "You bribed me with Chinese food and dangled a paid vacation in front of my eyes. Ready to tell me what this is all about?"

Faith cleared the debris from the table and stuck the dishes in the dishwasher. After dumping everything else in the trash basket, she took two legal pads and a coffee mug full of pens from the counter and set them on the table.

"Project time," she announced.

"Project?" Tess cocked an eyebrow. "You already have one. I just finished the research for it. Remember?"

Faith pasted a smile on her face. "I've decided to put it on hold and go with a great idea that just came to me."

Tess's jaw dropped. "Are you crazy? You have a deadline. Your publisher won't be happy if you tell him to just chill out."

"No problem." Faith pushed a legal pad across the table. "I'm calling my agent in the morning, pitching my new idea and she can tell Adam to chill out."

"You are nuts, girl. Nuts. You want to start all over when you have a book ready to go?" Tess shook her head. "You've never done this before. Especially not with your deadline looming."

Faith nodded. "Then it's time for me to break the rules. John will buy it when he hears the plot. Now pay attention."

"Are you at least giving me some idea of your brainchild?"

"Yes. It's about...oh...let's say an Army Special Ops guy, who's on a mission that has political ramifications." She doodled on the pad of paper. "But the mission falls apart because someone leaked it to the bad guys. Almost everyone but our hero is killed." She chewed on the tip of the pen, screwing her face into a picture of concentration. "We have to figure out who the leak was and why." She waved her hand in the air.

"There are a zillion possibilities," Tess pointed out. "Just open the newspaper and pick a story. Is this about drug cartels? Overthrowing a dictator? Terrorists? Take your pick."

"It needs fleshing out," Faith agreed, "but we can outline the plot together."

"Outline the plot together?" Tess put down her pen. "Faith, you never ask for help with plots. What the hell is going on?"

"Tess, I just—"

The pain that lanced through her leg from ankle to knee brought tears to her eyes. She gripped the table, holding her breath against the intensity until it passed.

"Faith?" Tess leaped up from her chair and was at Faith's side in an instant, kneeling beside her. "What is it? What's wrong?"

Help me... Need you.

His voice sounded so wracked with torment it frightened her.

Mark? I hear you. I'm here. I'm working on it.

The image assaulted her, Mark's face so tortured his muscles were almost in rictus, followed by a picture of lush green jungle foliage heavily spattered with blood.

And then it was gone, his voice and the pain.

Her face was covered with perspiration and she rubbed at it with the hem of her t-shirt. She had to swallow hard not to vomit.

Tess was still beside her, worry etched on her face.

Faith drew in a great breath and exhaled

slowly. "I'm fine. Really. Just a muscle spasm."

"Yeah?" Tess's voice was skeptical. "That was some spasm."

"It's gone now. Done." Faith picked up her water glass and drained it, giving her time to collect herself. She certainly didn't need to frighten Tess half to death. When her heart rate had slowed, she picked up her pen and tore off the page she'd been scribbling on.

Her assistant gave her a searching look. "If you say so." Her voice was doubtful.

"Let's drop it, okay?" Faith got up, filled her water glass again and sat back down at the table. "Now. I think the mission should be set somewhere in South America. You know, lots of thick tropical plants and trees and remote, hidden locations. Besides, Iraq and Afghanistan have been done to death. Africa too."

"Something to do with drug cartels?"

Faith frowned. "Not sure yet. Maybe terrorists but we'll leave that open. But it's a fact too many countries down there have become havens for terrorists and the cartels run more of the continent than the governments do. I'd say with everything else, something on that continent makes it an ideal choice."

"You got that one right. Okay. South America. Somewhere." Tess sat back down in her chair and made notes on her pad of paper. "So where do you want me to start?"

"First scour the internet for anything you can find on any kind of military missions there. Special Ops. Anything that's been reported after the fact. Or even something the media are sniffing around right now." She gave a short laugh. "You know how they manage to sniff out just about anything."

Tess nodded, making notes in her own brand of

shorthand.

"Check all the countries," Faith went on. "And check blogs as well as newspaper and magazine articles. You know those people talk about anything. Use that fertile imagination of yours. Oh and dig up whatever you can about Special Ops."

Tess looked at her for a long time. "Faith, what's this really all about? Why are you suddenly off on this kick, with a plot totally different from anything else you've written?"

"It's a political thriller, just like the others. Just with a different twist."

"Uh-huh." Tess was silent for a long time. "Okay. I guess when you're ready you'll tell me. Meanwhile, any particular South American country you're interested in?"

Chapter Four

Faith pushed her hair away from her face, tucked the ends behind her ears and picked up her mug of tea. Her eyes ached from hours of staring at the computer monitor. She knew more about Special Forces operations now than she did about her own family and it still wasn't enough. She had the basic structure and the chain of command. Even the location of SOCOM—Special Operations Command—at MacDill Air Force Base in Tampa, Florida. But that was as far as she could get. And Mark could have been deployed from there or Fort Bragg or Fort Lewis, or any one of a number of other bases where the highly trained Delta Force teams trained.

Still, she was amazed at the amount of information out there for just anyone to find.

"We might as well hand our enemies a blueprint," she snorted to herself. "Why do we ever try anyone for leaking secrets. All they need is a computer and the ability to Google anything."

She finished the last of the now lukewarm tea and leaned her head back against the chair. She needed a few minutes to clear her mind before tackling anything else. She also had a list of questions for Aunt Vivi and The Lotus Circle, which she'd call about in the morning.

She closed her eyes and tried to empty her mind but an old memory rose to the surface.

* * * * *

"You look gorgeous, Faith."

Mark's deep voice was like a caress and she shivered as it wrapped itself around her. They were moving in place to a slow ballad, jammed with a hundred other couples on the dance floor.

"Thank you. I'm glad you think so."

He brushed a kiss against her forehead. "I've always thought so, Tidbit. Even when you were a skinny little rabbit afraid of everyone and everything."

She smiled up at him. "But you always took care of me."

"And always will."

She closed her eyes and leaned her head against his shoulder, inhaling the fragrance of his citrus cologne mixed with his special male scent. "I still can't believe you came home to take me to my prom. I know how busy you are at college, with finals coming up and all."

"I wouldn't miss it for the world," he murmured.

So slowly she was barely aware of it, he danced her out of the room and through the French doors to the patio outside. Away from the ballroom he took her hand and led her down the broad, stone steps to a secluded area among some trees. The night air was crisp and sharp, the music like a faint symphony serenading the stars overhead.

"This is more like it."

Mark cupped her face with both hands and lowered his mouth to hers. They'd kissed on and off over the years, tentative, exploratory kisses but nothing as sensual as this. Mark's tongue danced along the seam of her lips, pressing lightly until she opened for him. When his tongue swept inside her mouth, heat spread through her body. Her nipples tightened and her panties dampened. Pulses she didn't know she had began an erotic drum beat.

God. What's happening here? This is Mark. My best friend Mark.

46

This was far from a friendship kiss. He held her head firmly in his palms, plundering her mouth, the kiss one long, sensuous mating. She felt his tongue everywhere, tasting the roof of her mouth, the inside of her cheeks and her lips. Tentatively she pressed her own tongue against his and the jolt of electricity that shot through her ignited every inch of her body.

At last he lifted his head and looked at her with heavy-lidded eyes. She saw desire there, heat and...something more. Then it was gone.

"Mark..."

He silenced her with another kiss. This time his fingers slid down the bare skin of her arms, touched her waist, then moved up to cup her breasts through the silky material of her dress. His hands, large and warm, held the weight of her flesh in his palms and his thumbs brushed across the tingling nipples.

"You are exquisite," he breathed when he broke the kiss. "So beautiful. Jesus, Faith, when did you grow up like this? I'd love to strip you naked right here and feast on your body. You have no idea how many nights I've dreamt of just that. Of the things I'd love to do to you."

She flushed at his words, a tiny drop of arousal trickling along the inside of her thigh. "Y-you have?"

"Oh, yeah." He blew out a long breath. "But my God, you're only eighteen years old."

She scowled at him. "Oh and you're such an old man? You're only two years older than me, Father Time."

He grinned. "Nearly three." His face sobered. "Not only that, I've known you most of my life."

She wiggled her arms up through his and clasped her hands around his neck. "What does that matter? If we feel this way about it, why should we deny ourselves?"

He shook his head, a rueful smile twisting his lips. "Because you're still so naïve. So innocent. I can't take advantage of you this way. Though God knows I want to."

"We have tonight," she told him. "I know you have to leave tomorrow, but let's at least have this." She closed her eyes and leaned her head against his shoulder. "You say you've dreamt about me? Well, I've done the same. I think I've loved you since we were kids."

"You aren't much more than that now," he chided."

She looked up at him, trying to put everything she felt into her eyes. "I'm a woman. And I know what I want. Every female wants the first time to be with someone special. I want mine to be with you."

"Shit," he groaned, and his entire body tightened.

"You aren't going to make me beg, are you?"

"What about your folks? Won't they expect you home? And I'm damn sure not going to do this in the back seat of a car. You deserve far more than that."

"Prom night is traditionally an all-nighter. You know that." She looked up at him and grinned. "Besides, I'm with you. They trust you."

"Jesus, don't remind me."

For a long minute she thought he was going to refuse again. Then the music stopped and instead of taking her back to the table where they'd been sitting, he led her to the door and out into the parking lot.

"Where are we going?" He was walking faster now and she had to hurry to keep up with him.

"The cabin." His folks had a cabin in the Hill

Country where his father went to hunt. And Mark, when he'd gotten older.

They said little to each other on the drive. When Mark pulled into the copse of trees next to the cabin and shut off the engine, he turned to her.

"Last chance to change your mind, Faith."

But she was so sure of this. She shook her head. "I won't. I don't want to."

Inside he turned on a small table lamp and the ceiling fan to stir the stale air. Faith stood in the middle of the room, unsure what to do next. Then Mark came over to her, put his big hands on her shoulders and bent his head to kiss her. His lips were warm and firm, soft and rough at the same time. He traced the seam of her mouth with the tip of his tongue and she opened for him willingly.

When he plunged inside streaks of heat shot through her body and the crotch of her thong became suddenly very damp. The pulse in her womb set up a low beat that echoed in every nerve and muscle. She opened her mouth wider, eager for more, and Mark took everything she offered.

He spent a long time on the kiss, seducing her, teasing her, rousing feelings in her that she'd tried to ignore for so long. Lightning sizzled through her, making her weak with a desire unfamiliar yet so strong she wanted to cry out. All the nights she'd dreamed of this, all the times she'd masturbated herself to completion with Mark's face in her mind—none of it could compare to his actual touch and to the responses he was coaxing from her body.

When his hands slid down her back to the zipper on her dress, a tiny thrill ran through her and the tiny sensitive nerves in the walls of her sex sparked in response. The dress was strapless with built-in support so she hadn't needed to wear a bra. When the fabric fell to her waist she was naked to his touch.

It excited her to hear the intake of his breath, and then to feel his hands on her bare skin. Long, lean fingers each imprinted their individual brand until there was no mistaking who she belonged to. He stroked her back, the same fingers dancing along her spine and the line of her shoulder blades, before moving to her sides. He never broke the kiss, his tongue everywhere inside her mouth, licking and tasting. She dared to thrust her own tongue at him and the thrill of contact raised her heat level even higher.

When he cupped her breasts, weighing their fullness in his palms, the throb of her pulse kicked up another notch and her legs trembled. His thumbs rasped her nipples, chafing them into hard points. Sending streaks of fire straight to her cunt. And still he kept kissing her.

Desperate to feel his bare skin against hers, she grabbed the lapels of his jacket and tried to wrestle it from his shoulder. He laughed into her mouth and took a step back.

"I'll do it." His voice was deeper and rougher.

He shrugged out of the jacket and tossed it onto a chair. His shirt and tie followed. Then he pulled Faith back into his arms.

The instant contact of her breasts against his chest, the hard wall of muscle covered with a soft pelt of hair, made her quiver, and the spasms that rode through her when she pleasured herself— always thinking of Mark—raced through her now, only stronger. She clutched at his arms, barely able to stand. And when he lowered his head to take one nipple in his mouth she moaned in pleasure. She could do nothing but hang on while his mouth and tongue and teeth pleasured each taut bud until she was screaming for more, more, more.

It was almost a relief when he tugged her zipper the rest of the way down and pushed the dress to the floor. She stepped out of it, kicked her shoes to the side, and stood before him naked except for the tiny thong.

"Jesus," he breathed, his voice filled with awe and something close to reverence.

His eyes were so dark they were almost opaque. She knew it was desire and it filled her with a sense of power that she could make it rise in him like that. He kept his eyes on her while he unfastened his trousers, then they were gone along with his boxers, socks and shoes. She couldn't take her eyes away from him, from his lean, muscular body, strong thighs, and most of all his incredible cock rising proudly from the thick nest of curls.

"I want you." His voice was almost unrecognizable.

"I want you, too."

"You should have candlelight and roses and soft music," he told her.

"As long as I have you, that's all I want."

Then she was lying on the bed beside him and he was kissing her again, his hands learning every inch of her body, all the dips and curves and crevices. When he slipped his fingers into her thong and traced the line of her slit, tiny explosions burst everywhere in her body. Mark captured her mouth again, his tongue both soothing and arousing.

He took a long time with her, using his mouth and his fingers on her nipples, the swell of her tummy and at last her sex. She was trembling when he stripped away the thong and put his hot mouth over her wet flesh. And when he licked her, flicking at her clit with the tip of his tongue, she screamed and another mini-orgasm gripped her. Everything fell away except this man and the things he made her feel.

Mark knelt between her thighs and held her while small tremors shook her. Then he began again, using his tongue and his teeth everywhere on her core, driving her higher, rousing her more. At last, when she was screaming with need, he pulled a foil packet from his trousers and sheathed himself.

"This will hurt a little," he warned in a soft voice. "I've tried to arouse you enough to make it easier and you're very, very wet. That's a good thing. But after that first pinch of pain, I promise it will get better."

And he was right. Faith held her breath as he entered her slowly, not daring to breath as he pressed against the thin membrane inside her, biting her lip at the pinch of penetration. And then she was floating on black velvet, suffused with a sensation that invaded even her pores.

"Okay, Tidbit?" Mark brushed his mouth against hers.

"Yes," she whispered. "Don't stop."

And he didn't. He paced himself, his big body taut with the obvious effort at control. But he took his time, building her again, bringing her to where she needed to be, holding her gaze as he increased his tempo. The steady in and out pumping of his cock sent every nerve into orbit, driving her body to a level of pleasure she hadn't even known existed.

When she didn't think she could wait a moment longer, when she was hanging right on the edge of the cliff desperate to take that leap, he finally gave her what her body was begging for. Thrusting into her again and again, he took them both right over that edge. She exploded and spun out, everything falling away except the unbearably pleasurable spasms gripping her. Her inner walls clenched and clenched, and if she was aware of anything it was of Mark's swollen cock filling every inch of her greedy sex.

A long while later, when reality slowly returned, Mark eased gently from her body. She lay there in the dim light as she heard him in the bathroom, disposing of the condom and running water in the tiny sink. Then he was back, cleaning her with a warm cloth.

"Take a long, hot bath when you get home," he ordered, before giving her another of those drugging kisses.

She did just that, lying in the tub with the feel and taste of him still on her body. The next day he was off to A&M to finish college.

"We'll keep in touch," they told each other.

"I'll always be here for you," he said.

"Me, too."

"One of these days the time will be right and we'll be together again."

She reached for him and drew his head down. "I love you, Mark."

He kissed her, a butterfly touch. "I love you, too. Faith."

* * * * *

She was drifting somewhere between dreaming and wakefulness. The memories of the dream still clung to her and she swore she could still feel Mark's lips on hers, his hands on his body.

Why hadn't she argued more with Mark, protested that she'd save her innocence for him, that what they wanted to do was more than all right. Damn him and his reasoning anyway. They'd emailed all the time, but there hadn't been another opportunity for them to be together. A situation that he told her more than once dogged him as much as it did her.

She wished now she'd found a way to make them move forward, explore the relationship, see what they actually had between them. She knew it was powerful and she was sure he did too.

Head resting on her arms and her eyes still closed, she called up the image of him from that night, overwhelming in his tux, his eyes heated with desire for her. And the long hours in the cabin, where he'd pleasured her over and over until she didn't know if she'd ever be able to move again.

They didn't need a phone to send each other messages, only their minds. And some of his messages made her blush. Then right after graduation he'd left for basic training. She was a junior at Texas Tech University and hot to graduate. To pursue her *career. There'd always be time. Later.*

But they never stopped their messages. During the four years after that, when she least expected it, his voice would echo in her head and he'd be there. It was better than email, Instant Messenger or a telephone, because they could be any place and still communicate.

Even when he was first deployed they'd managed to keep the thread in place. It was like an invisible pipeline, immutably intact.

Trying to hold on...

The words pierced her foggy brain like a knife.

Was she still dreaming? Faith sat bolt upright, shaking off the images that had danced through her mind. She had fallen asleep dreaming of Mark, then thinking about the night of her prom. So did she now just imagine his voice or was he sending her a message again?

You there?"

There! She heard him!

The sound was sharp and his voice had a painful edge to it. The unexpected white-hot pain in her leg slammed her again, taking away her breath. She grabbed her leg, rubbing it and tried to still her pulse.

"I'm here, Mark. Please tell me where you are?"

Silence.

She shook off the heavy tentacles of the dream and forced her mind to focus.

Come to me, Mark. Answer me.

Can't...

Mark? Can you tell me where you are? I know you're in pain. Her throat tightened. *Please give me more.*

Silence again. Her stomach knotted with fear and anxiety but she knew she had to block her emotions or she'd never get a message through.

Help!

The word was almost a scream and an intense feeling of pain wracked her entire body.

I will. Oh, Mark. Help me find you.

But instead of hearing his voice a sense of menace swept over her, of unrestrained evil. Fear pressed down on her with a heavy weight.

The other telepath. The menace. Whoever he was, he knew Mark was reaching out to her. He was not only blocking her but sending her his own message. Malevolence and death. Suddenly she felt as if hands were squeezing her throat, choking her.

She leaped up, the chair crashing to the floor, sweat pouring from her in rivulets. Her heart raced and she shook all over. Then, as suddenly as it came, it was all gone and she collapsed in a heap on the nearby armchair.

God. What horrible things were happening to Mark? She had to find out where he was. And quickly. Her inner senses were telling her loud and clear there wasn't much time left.

Faith swallowed two aspirin and dragged herself off to bed. She finally managed to fall asleep but it was fitful and anxiety-ridden. She tossed and turned, now awake, now barely asleep. One minute she recaptured bits and piece of her dream about the prom,. She could almost feel Mark's mouth on hers, his hands on her skin. The whisper of his breath against her mouth.

But then that awful scream would intrude and a red mist would hover over her, carrying evil and danger. Her mind would be invaded by such visions of horror they'd frighten her awake. A warning, she was sure but one she had to ignore if she were to find Mark.

How could she have been so stupid as to waste all this time?

When she finally pulled herself out of bed, her body ached as if she'd been pummeled and her head throbbed. She stumbled into the kitchen, brewed a pot of lotus tea and dialed Aunt Vivi's number.

"I need help." She failed to keep the trembling from her voice.

"Oh, sweetheart." Vivi's warmth reached out to her through the phone connection. "I was afraid of this. Come right over. I'll call Sarah and Emily to come at once."

Faith showered only enough to wake herself up, threw on jeans and a t-shirt and headed for Vivi's. The women were waiting when she arrived.

"The stranger is assaulting your mind," Vivi guessed.

Faith nodded. "Not with words but with...his presence."

Vivi sighed. "We never taught you to build shields because we never thought you'd need them.

The connection was only between you and Mark so it wasn't a problem. But now, if other people can attack you..." She gave Faith a reassuring smile. "We'll see what we can do."

The session was energizing. Faith couldn't believe how much better she felt when she finally left. During the process she'd visualized building a wall brick by brick to block out the intruder. At once she'd felt the pressure ease. And the energy that flowed from the other women had strengthened her determination. She would get this done. She would.

"Oh Mark. I wish we hadn't wasted all these years."

The thought popped into her head unbidden. Even when they'd had their long weekend together they'd never talked about the future, what might have been or what might be. The danger was what brought it all to a head, made her take an honest look at her feelings for him.

South America...terrorist camp...moving...

Faith swerved the car, jolted by Mark's voice. Steadying herself, she pulled off onto the shoulder of the road.

I hear you, Mark. I'm right here.

She waited but nothing else came through. The feeling of evil returned bringing the same pressure on her chest as the night before but she closed her eyes and brought up the image of the brick wall. The menace began to recede.

Mark?

Then Mark's voice came through to her again. *Mission...all killed, except...*

Except who? Someone besides you? Please tell me more.

But this time she was sure he was gone. The sense of his presence faded away.

She pulled out her cell phone and dialed Tess.

"Hi. Just wondering if you've had a chance to pull anything together yet."

Tess laughed. "This must be some book running around in your brain. Usually you give me at least twenty-four hours."

"Yes, it is. I'm really anxious to get started on it."

"Well, lucky for you I couldn't sleep last night, so I've made serious inroads in what you asked for."

"Great." Excitement nipped at her. "Could you meet me at my house? I...had to run an errand but I'll be home in about fifteen minutes."

"Sure." Tess chuckled. "What else would I do with my life?"

"You are a gem and a treasure," Faith told her. "See you in a bit."

Chapter Five

Tess was waiting at the house, sitting on the porch swing, when Faith pulled into the driveway. She picked up her briefcase and followed her into the garage.

"I've been busy, boss," she grinned. "Just like I said."

"I didn't mean for you to stay up all night," Faith told her. "Come on in. I'll make tea for me and—ugh—coffee for you and we'll see what you've got."

Tess sat at the kitchen table while Faith set everything to brewing, then opened her briefcase and took out a thick folder of printouts. "I swear, I don't know why anyone goes to jail in this country for leaking secrets. Most of it is on the internet for anyone to find."

"I guess it's the secret secrets they're guarding." Faith gave her a wry grin. "Come on. Let's see what you found."

Tess's hands stilled over the papers for a moment. She let her gaze roam over Faith, taking in her strained face and disheveled hair. "Are you all right? Because you look like the devil's chasing you and he's waiting right outside the door."

Not so far from right.

"I'm fine. Really. I just needed to run out in a hurry this morning." She pulled a rubber band from her pocket and smoothed her hair back into a pony tail. "All right. Let's have what you've got."

"I started with Special Ops, first, because believe it or not, that was the easiest." Tess pulled out four sheets of paper and spread them in front of the two of them. "I found some good information on how SpecOps, as they call themselves, operates."

She giggled. "They even have their own website."

Faith raised an eyebrow. "There really are no secrets, are there? But good for me. Everything we find helps."

"That's the truth."

Faith dug deep for patience. Tess was thorough in her research but then took a long time getting it all out. "So what did you find out?"

"If you're looking for an exciting background for the book this is it. SpecOps, according to their website, 'plans, synchronizes and as directed, executes global operations against terrorist networks. They use men from the Army, Navy and Air Force, all working together.' That should give you plenty of latitude for framing your plot." She shuffled one of the sheets of paper. "Oh and all missions are planned and executed from there."

Faith tried not to let her voice show the panic she felt at the mention of terrorists. "Bad stuff there." But then, what had she expected? She knew Mark hadn't joined the Army to sit around somewhere in safety. "All right. Go on. What else does it say? What kinds of missions are they assigned?"

"Actually the site has quite a history of some of the things they've done. They've been assigned to break up terrorist cells out in the mountains or the jungle. They've captured people like Noriega in Panama and taken down key government people in Haiti when it was overrun with corruption. Stuff like that. Dangerous stuff." Tess fanned herself and grinned again. "Man, I could really get my arms around one of these alpha men after reading what all they do."

Faith had to grit her teeth to keep from shouting at Tess. This was Mark's life they were talking about. Then she reminded herself as far as her assistant was concerned this was fiction. A story conjured up out of her mind. The research was to try to give her a clue where in South America Mark might be held. And what his mission might have been about. But as far as Tess was concerned, this was merely to give her book the accuracy for which she was famous. She needed something to keep her focused.

"While you're salivating, I'll pour our drinks. But keep talking."

She busied herself at the counter. The remnants of last night's dream and the red menace still clung to her. She was sure the more she learned the more afraid for Mark she'd be. She filled one mug with coffee for Tess and another with tea for herself, stirring sweetener into her drink.

"Can't I drool just a little?" Tess teased. "Never mind. I know you. When you're in book mode all fun goes away."

Faith couldn't help chuckling. "I didn't realize I turned into such an ogre. I'll try to do better." *But I need to find Mark, so let's get on with it.*

"Okay." She pushed her papers to the side and accepted the coffee from Faith. "You could say they're the stealth force of the military. They get the stuff no one else can do. Or probably is capable of."

Faith already suspected that. The last time she'd seen Mark he'd looked like the poster boy for the battle-hardened warrior. And he'd had a look in his eyes that frightened her. For the first time in their long relationship they'd made love—long, erotic, exciting love. But Mark had had a sense of desperation about him, as if he wanted to fill himself up with as many intimate memories as he could. While their time together thrilled her, it also frightened her, a fear that had nested in the back of her mind ever since. And now was coming out full blown.

"I know they operate in units," she commented. "I've read up on it some in the newspapers and a little bit for my other books."

Tess nodded. "They do. Each unit reports to a commanding officer, either a captain or a major, depending on the rank of the unit's senior officer. Their missions are handed down from headquarters at MacDill."

"Good work." Faith took a sip of her tea. "I, um, don't suppose you had a chance to search any newspapers? Maybe see if there's something particular the media is lusting after?"

"As a matter of fact..." Tess shuffled through another stack of printouts and pulled out what she wanted. "There's a lot of ink right now on Peru and Argentina."

Faith nodded. "But mostly Peru, now that I think of it, because Shining Path has both terrorist and cartel ties."

"You got that right." Tess flipped through her notes. "Okay. Here it is. There's a lot of chatter on the blogs about missions failing because information leaks out. Or because someone sells it. But you've come across things like that for your other books."

"I guess that corruption just keeps spreading."

"Well, the news services have people digging around in Peru right now and I'm trying to find out what kind of tips they got. What they're actually focusing on." She dropped her notepad back on the table and leaned back in her chair. "But about that time I decided to spend what was left of the night trying to get some sleep. I'll keep on it, though."

"Tess, you've done a great job." Faith gathered up all the papers on the table. "I'll start a file with these, maybe do a little poking around myself. Why don't you go home and take a nap?"

She started to rise from her chair, when the stabbing pain hit her leg again and it buckled under her. This time it was so sharp it stole her breath.

"Faith?" Tess was beside her at once. "Faith, you look like shit and you're white as a ghost. I'm calling the doctor."

"No!" Faith nearly shouted the word. "No, don't. It's just that spasm again."

"Uh-huh." Tess's eyes were filled with concern. "Tell me another one."

"Really. If you can just help me over to the couch so I can lie down a minute I'll be fine." Sweating, she managed to hobble to the sofa and stretch herself out. But just as the pain reached manageable proportions it hit her again, like a knife slicing through flesh.

* * * * *

Mark clenched his jaw and tried not to show how much the agony got to him. Escobedo, the group member who seemed to be running the little band of terrorists, had strolled into the tent and as casually as tapping his foot against wood kicked Mark viciously in the leg. The open cut where Escobedo's knife had sliced him from knee to ankle the day before began to bleed again and the pain nearly made him pass out. One of the men had put a crude bandage on it but Mark was sure infection was setting in.

He waited, sweating, until the worst of the pain subsided, forcing himself to breath evenly. They could kill him but he'd never give them the satisfaction of beating him.

"*Hola, capitan.* You do not look so chipper today."

I'll chipper you, you asshole. Just give me one of those wicked knives and five minutes and you'll be filleted cleaner than a fish.

But he held his tongue. He knew his silence disturbed them and to reply would mean he'd give them an edge. It frustrated them because they got no sound from him except for the screams he couldn't hold back. He still hadn't figured out why they kept him alive. He'd given them no information, answered none of their questions, yet still they gave him enough food to keep him alive while they tortured him for sport.

He knew the arms dealer was still hanging around. That wasn't usual for him. His habit was to show up where and when he needed to only long enough to transact business, then leave. Certainly this rough jungle camp was far from his normal fastidious surroundings. Mark had seen pictures of the man's home in the Caymans. A virtual palace, built with blood money. But he wanted the leak plugged so it didn't come back to haunt him again.

Escobedo took a thin cigarillo from the pocket of his shirt and lit it. Smoke curled in a thin spiral up past his dark-complected face with its high cheekbones, past the deep-set black eyes and the thick head of black hair, touched at the edges with grey. To Mark he looked like a well-heeled businessman on a jungle vacation but he knew the man was a vicious, cunning animal.

El Serpiente, they called him. The snake.

"Our...*guest*...would like to be on his way. But he must be assured no one in your government has information about him they shouldn't. The question of how you knew about the meeting to begin with must be answered. We cannot afford to have this situation disrupted."

He wants to make sure anyone who knows

64

about this group can be silenced. And that his movements remain secret. Well, they can kill me before I tell them anything. God, just help me to last.

"You're being very foolish holding out this way. You know we'll get the information out of you eventually. It's imperative we find out who knows about us before we can move forward with our plans. You could die a much less painful death if you'd just be sensible."

Mark wanted to spit in Escobedo's face but he controlled himself. He had to buy as much time as he could. Antagonizing the man further wasn't the way to do it.

"Still nothing to say?" Escobedo nudged the leg again, a little more viciously and his mouth turned up in a malevolent smile. "But you speak in your mind, do you not? A little secret you thought to hide from us."

Mark tried to control the anger he felt. Their man had obviously caught the psychic waves when Mark and Faith exchanged messages and been doing his best to interfere. Someone had told them about it but who? That was classified information that very few people were even aware of. But these people would have had to be aware of it for their man to concentrate on intercepting him.

God, he could certainly use Chase Wohlmann now, the poor bastard.

"Felix tells me you have the same ability he does. Somehow he knew when he laid eyes on you that you were a telepath and he's been listening for your messages."

A name to go with the man attacking his mind. He tucked it away in his brain, knowing that putting a name to the person could make them more vulnerable. He would have to study Felix every chance he had, try to figure out how to get around the mental roadblocks the man kept setting up. Try to remember how Chase constructed the shields. He'd been training for it but they'd only just begun their work.

"Unfortunately we only have incomplete fragments of what you are sending. And we do not know who you are sending to. So now we have one more piece of information we need from you. You become more valuable to us each minute." He shook his head. "It will be a shame to kill you. And if you have managed to tell anyone—anyone at all—what happened here or where you are, we will have to take steps to, shall we say, eliminate that problem."

Don't think of Faith. Don't picture her. Think of something else. Like the bastard you suspect of leaking this mission. Someone in bed with the arms dealer.

He'd had plenty of hours to go over everything in his mind, reviewing the prep for the mission and the names of the people who knew about it. The circle was small. Delta Force missions were devised at the highest level, filtered down through Joint Special Operations Command (JSOC) and through the commanding officer to the specific team. Then the team went into isolation to make their plans. Only they and their immediate CO knew the details.

But the terrorists could only have been waiting for them if someone who knew the details had told them about the mission. Mark had finally narrowed his suspects down to two or three, one of them so high up he would be untouchable without complete proof. If he ever got out of this hellhole he'd take the man down. But first he needed to get away, impossible by himself with his wounds and as weak as he was.

"Is this person you're reaching out to someone in your government that you foolishly think can get you out of here?" Escobedo gave a malicious laugh. "I hear your people have a special unit for those with this ability but your government is weak and run by too many politicians. No one would give this out. They would certainly be unwilling to call attention to a failed assignment, whose very nature would bring them unwanted publicity." He spat into the dirt. "They have left you here to rot like a dead animal. Tell us what we want to know and let us get this over with."

Mark kept his eyes open, focusing on a point past Escobedo's head. He knew how it angered the man for Mark to treat him with a lack of respect. It almost always brought on torture of some kind. But he couldn't allow even one clue to Faith's identify to become known.

"No answer?" One corner of his mouth turned up in a grin that was anything but humorous. "Perhaps Felix will be able to pluck the identity of this person from your mind. He is good at breaking through what you call mind barriers. Very good."

Mark watched the man study him through hooded eyes. Waiting, he knew, for Mark to show some sign of suffering. To grab his leg. To do something. But Mark would swallow his tongue before he would give this bastard any satisfaction at all.

"If you will just tell us what we want to know, *Capitan*, we will make your death swift and merciful. If not..." Escobedo shrugged. "You choice. Perhaps tonight Felix will come and visit you and see what's churning in that clever mind."

I will not let him into my mind. He can go to hell and take me with him.

As Escobedo walked out of the tent he brushed

the point of his boot across Mark's open wound.

Mark closed his eyes and in his head he screamed as loudly as he could.

* * * * *

They were eating lunch again, Mr. Brown and the heavy-set one. The restaurant was actually the dining room of a country inn, a quaint, out-of-the-way place not frequented by any of their associates. Neither of them looked as if he was particularly enjoying his food, which was, indeed, the truth. The elephant in the room with them was enough to kill their appetites.

"Escobedo has not been able to get any information from him," Mr. Green said.

There it was, the apprehension that someone had knowledge of their duplicity and could bring everything crashing down about them.

Mr. Brown buttered a roll with slow, precise strokes. "I don't know what exactly he expects to get. Why doesn't he just kill him and be done with it?"

"There's apparently a problem." Mr. Green stirred sweetener into his iced tea.

"A problem? With an injured prisoner? What could that possibly be?"

Mr. Green shifted in his seat. "It appears the man has telepathic abilities and is sending messages to someone."

Mr. Brown put down his fork and stared at his companion. "What the hell nonsense are you talking? Sending messages how?"

"I told you. He's a telepath. He communicates with his mind. Like one of Escobedo's men, Felix."

"Bullshit." Mr. Brown began eating again. "I don't believe any of that psychic garbage and neither should you. Escobedo is working an angle and we have to figure out what it is."

Mr. Green took a drink of his wine and patted his mouth with the snowy white linen napkin. "Listen to me. This is not something to blow off. Psychic ability has become so important the military even has special units made up of men who have it. If this man is sending telepathic messages to someone, we need to know who it is. That person could be right on our ass any minute."

Mr. Brown leaned across the table. "And exactly what do you think he could tell this mysterious person? He doesn't know anything."

"Now there's where you're wrong. With one exception he's the sole survivor of his unit. He's bound to know something was leaked and he may even have figured out who leaked it."

"Are you crazy? There's no way to figure that out. Get hold of yourself."

They ate in silence. Then Mr. Green put down his silverware and took another sip of wine. "Mark Halloran is not a stupid man. He's been around a long time and he knows far more than he should. If anyone can figure this out, he will."

"Then they should just kill him, like I said."

"Not until we know if he's communicated anything dangerous to whoever his psychic partner is. And until he gives up the name of the person who pinpointed the meeting between the Wolf and Escobedo."

"Then they'd damned well better find out who these people are. And let us take care of it."

"And then, of course, there's that other matter."

Mr. Brown fixed his companion with an icy stare. "Ah, yes. And exactly what are we supposed to do with that?"

He stomach roiled at the message the angry

voice had imparted on the phone. "Get rid of him, what else?"

"In a hospital room with people walking in and out all the time?" Green had asked.

"Damn it. I don't pay you to ask me questions. Figure it out."

"What if he knows something?" Brown asked now, as Green repeated the instructions. "Like maybe there's another man still out there unaccounted for, another one besides Halloran that Escobedo and his men also missed. That's not important to find out?"

"Then we're to move him first." His own anger had reached the boiling point. "This thing has fallen apart and if we don't fix it we'll all be marching through the gates of hell."

Brown swallowed his own irritation. "Fine. We'll take care of it."

"We'd better do it soon. He's waiting for my call."

Chapter Six

Faith managed to get rid of Tess at last by taking two painkillers and letting her assistant help her get into bed. She swore to the woman she'd call if she felt any worse. Tess left with great reluctance, promising—no, threatening—to check on her often. Faith finally told her she appreciated her concern but it was time to go to sleep.

It took a long time for the pain to disappear. When it subsided enough for her to move, she fixed herself something light to eat and got back into bed. The evening hours ticked by as she focused her mind and tried to reach out to Mark. This time she didn't want to wait for him to speak first. But shortly after midnight she fell asleep without making any contact at all.

When she awoke in the morning a heavy feeling of dread gripped her and a sense that time was slipping by too quickly. She'd have to figure out how to move Tess along faster without giving herself away.

First things first. Put off the book currently due, pitch the one she'd conjured up to use as a cover story to her agent and buy herself some time. No way could she concentrate on a fictional plot when a real one was consuming her life. She sat at the desk in her den and gathered her thoughts before speed-dialing a familiar number.

"Why do I think this can't be good?" Abigail Loudon asked when she heard Faith's voice.

"That's because you have a naturally suspicious mind," she tried to joke. Flipping a pencil back and forth between her fingers, she did her best to put enthusiasm into her voice as she attempted to cajole her hard-working agent. "Abby, I know we have a contract in place for the next book in the series but just listen to me. I've got a great idea that I can't put aside. You know how I am when I need to get something out of my head and on paper right away."

"And you know I get hives when you get that tone in your voice." Abby's words held a mixture of humor and exasperation. The two women had worked together for seven years now.

"But this story is too good to just sit," Faith told her and proceeded to outline her proposal. "The other one will still be timely even if it waits for a year. Political garbage in Washington doesn't change, unfortunately. But this other is hot, current stuff."

"I don't know." Abby was silent a moment. "How will you even get people to agree to let you interview them? A lot of this is classified stuff."

"Have I ever had a problem before?" Faith tossed the pencil down and picked up a paper clip. Her hands wouldn't keep still.

"No but I say again. This is a different ball game." A heavy sigh made its way over the connection. "All right. They'll probably go for it because this stuff is all over the news right now. I'll do the dirty work with your editor. Send me a proposal so I can get your contract done before they decide it's a bad deal. And if they give us the green light, you'd better get yourself busy before they change their minds."

Faith blew a kiss over the telephone. "Abby, you are worth every penny you wring out of me. I'll make it up to you, I promise."

"Make this one a dynamite bestseller. That's payment enough."

Faith replaced the receiver in the cradle and tossed the now-bent paper clip into the waste basket. So now she had some breathing room, at least as far as her deadlines went. But Mark's situation didn't allow for any such luxury.

On impulse she picked up the phone again and dialed the Halloran house, a number she knew by heart.

"Oh, Faith, I was just thinking about you." Dinah Halloran's voice was warm and welcoming. "It was so nice to see you the other day. And just last night Frank and I were commenting on your last book and wondering when the next one would be out."

Faith worked to keep her tone casual. "Probably a little later than expected. I came up with a new plot and I haven't finished the research yet. In fact, that's what I'm calling about."

"Oh? Sweetheart, I can't imagine what we could tell you to use in those political thrillers of yours."

"Actually, I was wondering if you'd heard anything about Mark since we talked. You know, if he was coming home soon or anything. I wanted to interview him."

Dinah laughed. "I'm sure you won't be surprised when I tell you Mark is the sphinx himself when it comes to stuff like that. You'd better think of someone else you can talk to."

"But have you heard anything?" she persisted, trying to keep the pressure out of her voice.

"Not a word." She paused. "Faith, is there some other reason you want to know about Mark? Something you aren't telling me?"

Faith's laugh sounded false even to herself. "No, no. Just thinking how nice it would be to see him again. That's all."

"Well, at the risk of repeating myself I have to say this. You two ought to take a good look at how you feel about each other before too much more time passes. Life can be a lot shorter than you think."

No kidding.

"We're fine, Dinah. Honestly."

"Uh-huh." She chuckled. "Okay. I'll mind my own business. And if he calls, which he usually does when he's back from wherever he was, doing whatever it is he does, I'll be sure he gets in touch with you."

"Okay. Thanks, Dinah. I'll stop by again soon."

Well, that went nowhere.

Sighing, she opened a blank document on her computer and began writing a synopsis. Once she had the contract for it, that would give her more leverage—more legitimacy—to get in to see some of the people she needed to talk to. Then she'd start making a list of exactly who those people were.

* * * * *

Major John Gregorio hung up his telephone and ran his hand over his military-cut, graying brown hair. Some days he wondered why he'd never taken up his father-in-law's offer to work in the construction business. He might have hated it but at least he wouldn't have sleepless nights over the men he'd sent to be killed.

He pounded his fist on the desk in helpless frustration. Three days since the extraction team had returned to the rendezvous point, found only Joey Latrobe's badly wounded and near-lifeless body. The gear was smashed and there was no trace of the rest of the team. They'd gotten him back to US soil but the young sniper still lay in a coma in Walter Reed Hospital in Bethesda, Maryland. They had no idea what happened to the rest of the men. Except for one small scrap of information. When they'd gotten Joey on board the helo, before he passed out again he'd managed to get out three words. "Took the captain."

When they reported this to Gregorio he swore them to secrecy. If Mark got away and was somehow trying to complete the mission on his own, he didn't want the traitor to find out. If, instead, he'd been captured, the major had to figure a way to find him and get him out without starting a war. The politics of the situation boggled his mind. He could never understand why preserving a political status quo with a band of murderers was more important than retrieving their own people.

Probably why I'll never run for office.

Since then he'd been doing his damnedest to get information that would tell him what happened to one of his top teams but with little success. He had the feeling someone knew and had slammed shut every door, covering his tracks. For a moment he wished for Mark Halloran's ability to communicate mentally. Maybe he could pick up someone else's brain waves.

Colonel Frank Ryan, his superior officer at SpecOps Command at MacDill AFB, was tearing out what was left of his own hair. He'd been on the horn to JSOC and everyone else he could think of without any luck at all. No one seemed to know anything. No, worse. No one wanted to know anything.

Then, finally, the order came down from the Pentagon not to mount a search and rescue mission. The considered opinion was that Joey Latrobe was the only survivor and it would be political suicide to go into that particular area of Peru and look for dead men. Well, hell, there wasn't any proof they were all dead. And somehow Gregorio knew that Mark Halloran would have found a way to stay alive, captured or not.

"I know it's tough, John," Ryan had told him. "I have a special feeling for Mark too. For all the men. But if we go rogue on this, after the order's come down, we'll all be in deep shit. If he's somehow still alive—if any of them are—we have to pray they can find a way to contact us. Then we'll see what we can do."

Not good enough, Gregorio thought to himself. If only Latrobe would regain consciousness and give them some kind of additional information. Beyond that Gregorio needed to figure out what had gone wrong. The information had come, at great peril, to a member of the unit. Unusual since it wasn't your everyday soldier who usually got info like that. But there was a relationship with Joey Latrobe's brother and he was the one who brought it to Gregorio. So it had worked it's way up the ladder, touching as few people as possible, with as much secrecy as possible, waiting for the go ahead to plan the mission,.

Once the order came down from the top, only the head of SpecOps, Ryan himself and his team knew it was a go. Not even the other Delta Force teams were aware of it. It sickened Gregorio that someone highly placed in the military would betray his country and his men but he didn't know what else to think. There were only so many places the leak could have sprung.

Bringing his computer to life, he entered his secure password and began to call up the records of each man in Mark's unit. Not that he wouldn't personally vouch for each and every one but you just never knew when a tiny slip might send a signal to someone. Even the knowledge that one of them might be unreachable for a while could trigger something if the wrong person was looking.

But an hour later he had to admit it was a futile

exercise. He and Halloran had personally chosen each member of the unit together. If his own instincts might be getting a little rusty, Mark's certainly weren't. So. No answers there.

He leaned back in his chair and picked up his mug of cold coffee, grimacing at its bitter taste. Staring at the corkboard over his desk an unpleasant thought dropped into his brain. Whoever these people were, would they try to eliminate Latrobe, believing he could give out information about what happened? And where any survivors might be?

That at least was a situation he could do something about. He picked up his phone again and dialed a familiar number.

* * * * *

The Wolf was prowling. Only an incredible amount of learned self-discipline kept his growing anger in check. He smelled disaster in the making and he didn't like it. *That's what I get for dealing with savages*, he told himself.

But of course these savages had spent millions with him, not just their money but the orders they continued to funnel through from other groups. It pissed him off royally that Escobedo always insisted on a face to face to complete the transaction but for the money he made from them he put aside his distaste. This time, however, Murphy's Law ruled.

It was bad enough that he had to have his helicopter bring him to this miserable tent camp in the Peruvian jungle, with none of the conveniences he was used to. For twenty four hours he always managed to make do but this had been going on for four days. If they didn't resolve the problem soon he might shoot them all himself.

"Contemplating your millions, Lobo?"

He hadn't heard Escobedo walk up on him. A bad sign that his senses were being compromised by his rage.

"Thinking about ways to strip the skin from your body if you don't get results with the American quickly."

He pulled a thin cigarillo from his pocket and lit it. He'd noticed that Escobedo had taken up smoking them too. Copycat. What you smoked didn't make the person you were. This man would always be little more than a savage, no matter how high he rose in the organization, how many places he blew up, how many enemies of the jihad he killed.

"You must have patience. They do not send weak men to do jobs like this. Breaking him is not an easy process."

"I've run out of patience," the Wolf snapped. "You're the one who insisted on this damned meeting here in the middle of nowhere. I never do this."

Escobedo gave him a nasty smile. "But you wanted the money, eh, *lobo*? For that even you will soil your hands a little."

"I must be leaving here. I have other business to attend to. But you know how imperative it is to learn who rang the bell on us and who the prisoner is sending messages to. My hands are tied until I can be assured no one is coming after me. I cannot jeopardize my other clients. Or myself."

"Some things cannot be rushed. We don't want to kill him, before we get our information."

"Just do whatever you have to and get what you need. How the hell did they find out about us anyway? I've managed to keep a low profile for years."

78

Escobedo took a swig from the bottle of beer he was holding. "Perhaps you haven't been as invisible as you think."

The Wolf gritted his teeth, barely stopping himself from the smashing the arrogant face of the man in front of him. "This is on your head. If word of this meeting leaked, it's because someone is tracking you and your people."

"There are other problems here, I told you." The jungle fighter's voice had an edge to it. "An unexpected hurdle."

Yes, yes. The mind thing." The Wolf spat into the ground. "I'm not sure I even believe that."

"Believe it. Felix has the same abilities. He will break whatever shields this man has been able to create and find out who he's been sending messages to."

"When he does, I will make arrangements to dispose of that person. We can leave no traces, do you understand?"

"Of course, Lobo." Escobedo's face wore a disdainful look. "There's nothing wrong with my brain. I'll do my part. You do yours."

The men looked up at a slight shuffle of sound, each going instantly for the weapon he carried.

"*Hola, Serpiente.*" Escobedo's second in command approached.

"*Quien sabe?*"

"We have the prisoner softened up a little more. We thought you might want to take over. Felix says he thinks only a little more pressure and he can crack the mind."

"Fine." He swallowed the last of his beer. "Let's go."

The men were all gathered in the clearing where the campfire was. Mark was hanging by his wrists from the branch of a tree. His shirt had been stripped from him and his body was a series of fine little cuts, blood running in rivulets from neck to waist. When he heard the men approach he raised his eyes.

Escobedo looked into them and nearly shuddered at what he saw. The men were wrong. This man was far from breaking. He had a core of inner steel seen only in rare instances. Behind the look of pain was a message—give me the slightest chance and I'll cut out your heart while you're still alive.

Unwilling to let the men, especially the egotistical Lobo, see how he was affected, he raked his nails over the cuts on Mark's chest.

"These men are amateurs," he said in a soft voice. "Now it's my turn. I promise you this will not be pleasant but in the end, you will tell me what I want to know."

Mark turned his head and spat on the ground.

* * * * *

Faith's head ached and her eyes were about to roll back in her head. She'd sorted everything Tess had given her into separate piles and made folders for them. Then she'd made a list of what she needed to search for herself. But three hours later she had to admit defeat.

She didn't know what she expected. A list of the men who made up the Delta Force? Yeah, right. She had to snort at that one. *Get real, Faith.* Tess's research had given her the information that the Special Operations units were made up of men from Delta Force, SEALs, Recon Marines and elite members of the air force who had trained with Britain's famed SAS. From what little she'd learned from Mark she knew that everything they did was top secret, so how stupid was she to think she'd find anything on the internet about it except whatever had been sanitized for public consumption?

She rubbed her forehead, wishing the headache would disappear, finally deciding to take two aspirins. As she pushed her chair away from her desk sudden fire consumed her body from her neck to her waist. She felt as if a thousand knives were sticking into her at the same time. If she hadn't known better, she'd have sworn she was bleeding all over her upper body.

Mark!

Oh, God, what were they doing to him now?

She drew in deep breaths, trying to ride through the pain but the deeper she breathed the sharper the pain became. If someone poured gasoline on her and set her on fire she didn't think it would hurt worse. Sweat poured from her skin and her heart raced. The pain was so intense she couldn't even move from her chair. She sat doubled over, arms wrapped around herself, the air around her a red haze.

She had no idea how long she sat huddled in the chair, her body consumed with the fiery pain, her brain unable to function. But when the pain suddenly disappeared it frightened her even more because it left nothing behind. No feeling. Nothing.

Oh, God, is he dead?

Mark! Oh, please, Mark. Can you hear me?

She strained for any response, panic stealing her breath as much as the pain had.

Need you...

Oh, thank God. Thank God. He was still alive.

I'm here, I'm here. Please can you help me find you?

A long silence, then "*...moved me...try to hold on...*"

She waited and waited but that was the end of it. No matter how much she focused there were no more messages to hear.

She called back to her mind the one other time they'd managed to be together. Splinters of scenes. Her lying naked on the bed. Mark's body looming over hers. His eyes dark with passion. His hot, thick cock pressing into her. More, more, more. Finally filling her. Stretching her. Bringing down the little tremors that shook her just from feeling him inside of her.

Wrapping her legs around him to pull him in deeper.

The pull and thrust of his movement`

The crashing orgasm that always shook her and made her bones melt.

Mark!

Traces of panic still clung to her. Whatever was happening to Mark it was getting worse and worse. She knew he was mentally tough but even Mark couldn't hold out forever.

Maybe it was time to contact someone who could give her some answers, like his commanding officer. Somewhere in all her notes she'd written down the information from one message he'd sent her—where he was stationed and who his commanding officer was. She could use the book as a cover in an attempt to pry information loose from him.

Not that she expected him to be very forthcoming but she'd be grateful for any scrap he fed her at all.

She dragged herself upstairs and rummaged in the bathroom medicine cabinet for aspirin. She popped three in her mouth and washed them down with tepid water, then sat on the closed lid of the commode until the worst of the shaking subsided.

When she felt somewhat functional, she stripped off her clothing and tossed it in the hamper. She turned the shower jets on full force and waited until the enclosure was filled with steam. Then she stepped into the spray and let it pound over her body, trying to wash away the vestiges of pain.

Mark. Don't give up. I'll get you out. Somehow. I promise.

* * * * *

Joey Latrobe lay silent and unmoving, the beeping of the monitors and the rise and fall of the sheet covering his body as he breathed the only signs he was still alive. The doctors had hustled him into surgery the moment they took him off the chopper, removing one bullet from his arm and two from his leg. And pumping enough blood back into him to counteract the massive amount he'd lost while he lay in the jungle.

"How is he doing?" Green asked the nurse changing the IV bag.

She shrugged. "As good as can be expected under the circumstances.

""He hasn't regained consciousness at all?"

She shook her head. "No. We're doing everything we can for him but he was in pretty bad shape."

"We may be moving him to a long-term care facility. Government orders." He opened his badge wallet and flashed his identification.

"Goodness. He must be somebody special. Special classification and now the possibility of the move."

Green and Brown looked at each other. "Yes. Someone special indeed. Well. We'll get out paperwork together and make the arrangements."

The two men followed the nurse out of the room, neither of them noticing the fluttering of the patient's eyelids or the sudden acceleration of his heart rate.

Chapter Seven

"I need answers, damn it."

John Gregorio slammed the telephone down, ready to bite nails. The impossibility of making anyone see reason was driving him to a murderous rage. He was tired of talking to people intent on stonewalling him. Politics wasn't his strong suit. Never had been. Now he was trying to wade through a political minefield to find out what happened to his men. They weren't going to end up being "collateral damage", no matter what people more used to the conference table than the battlefield had to say. That wasn't the way he was made.

At least he'd taken care of Joey Latrobe. No one would be able to get near him now. Or even find him, if things went according to plan. And that, at the moment, was his only hope. Joey's new medical caregiver would call Gregorio the minute the young soldier regained consciousness and could give them any information at all. He prayed hourly for Latrobe's recovery.

He was so focused on his anger he didn't notice the tall man who quietly entered his office.

"Answers? I wish I had them for you, John."

Gregorio looked up at the sound of the familiar voice. Frank Ryan stood in the doorway to the office of the Delta Force commander carrying his flight bag, fatigue and worry etched deeply on his face.

"God, you're a sight for sore eyes." Gregorio stood and saluted.

Ryan waved him off and held out his hand. "I think for the moment we can dispense with military formalities."

"I didn't know you were coming or I'd have met

you at the flight line."

Ryan dropped his bag on the floor and took a seat. "I hitched a ride on a flight with a friend. I thought it best to keep a low profile for this visit."

Gregorio frowned. "Oh, oh. Bad news?"

Ryan shook his head. "I didn't like what I heard in your voice last time we talked. You're not given to uncontrolled anger or rash actions and that's what came through to me. You're the Special Ops Forces commander here, with a lot of units on your plate. All these men—and women—of the Seventh Special Forces need your full attention. I'm here to see if I can move some mountains for you, so you can give them what they need."

"I'm sure not about to turn down any help. You can bet on that." Gregorio rubbed his hand over his face. "But Jesus, Frank. This is an impossible situation. And don't forget, we have to protect our source at all costs."

Ryan nodded toward the telephone. "I gather you've been doing some head-pounding trying to get the orders changed." He gave the other man a tired smile. "Been there, done that."

"I'm not trying to go around you, just keep you from getting your shoes dirty with my mud."

Ryan let his eyes wander to the tiny window. The afternoon sun was slanting into the small room, bringing the heat of the day with it. Outside, on the largest and busiest base in the country, boots pounded on macadam, voices called to each other and engines roared as people went about their business. A peaceful scene for a far from peaceful business. He sighed and turned back to Gregorio.

"You called Latrobe's brother? Told him of our concerns?"

Gregorio nodded his head. "He got on it right away. I'll guarantee you that by now they've gotten someone sitting on the kid to keep unwanted visitors away and they're getting ready to snatch him."

"You know, neither Halloran nor his men are novices at this." Ryan stood with his hands in his pockets, still staring out the window. "They've gone through the hard training and successfully executed some very difficult and sensitive missions. They were critical to our success in the drug battles along the Andean Ridge. How sure are you they aren't just holed up somewhere until they can make contact?"

"Positive. Joey Latrobe would never have been left alone like that, as wounded as he was. If there was danger they'd have figured out a way to hide with him and set up a different rendezvous point. Losing a team like that means someone deliberately leaked the mission. It's the only way they could have been ambushed."

"I'll ask you one more time. You're sure that's what happened?"

Gregorio pounded his fist on the desk. "Yes, damn it. I've been doing this a long time. You know that. Would Joey Latrobe, one of the best snipers in the world, be lying almost dead at Walter Reed if the mission had been successful? Wouldn't his unit have made the rendezvous point and been extracted with him?"

Ryan held up a hand, palm outward. "All right. I'm going to see what I can do. Off the cuff," he added. "And I didn't want to do it from HQ. You never know whose ears are listening around corners."

Gregorio shook his head. "I appreciate it but I'm not sure it's such a good idea for you to stick your neck out this way."

Ryan smiled again. "I guess it's my neck to stick out."

"I'm just glad I made arrangements to secure Latrobe. He's the only one who made it out and he's still unconscious. You can bet, if what I suspect is true, there are people out there who'd like to get their hands on him, try to w ring information out of him then dispose of the body. So I had to get ahead of the game here." He proceeded to outline the steps he'd taken. "At least I got that done, before the buzzards could get hold of him.

The major nodded his head, reached into his breast pocket and pulled out a cell phone. "Then I guess it's time for me to take my turn at bat."

* * * * *

The four men sat in the main room of the small cabin off the coast of Maine, the environment a complete opposite of their well-equipped offices in one of Baltimore's newest office buildings. But from the moment Rick Latrobe had received John Gregorio's call, they knew that whatever needed doing, they had to do it away from the public eye, away from any chance for someone to spy on them. They were used to being evasive and this cabin had served the purpose more than once.

The log structure was more than a hundred years old. Crude and rustic, electricity and running water had been added just twenty years ago. It sat perched on the edge of a cliff overlooking a desolate stretch of beach and the pounding surf of the water below. It was only accessible by a narrow rutted road that wound in a very long ribbon from the highway, or by climbing the almost invisible steps carved into the rock face of the cliff. It was perfect for their needs.

The men had grown up together in Michigan, each enlisting in a different branch of the service but always in contact with each other, always connected. The idea for their cover company had come up on a weekend they were together just before each of them was about to complete his service obligations. They'd chosen Baltimore for their home office because of its proximity to DC but the cabin was their bolt-hole, their secure hiding place.

Dan Romeo, six five, olive-skinned with dark hair and darker eyes, a former Force Recon Marine, was the nominal leader of the group, although they all had equal decision-making powers. Next to him sat ex-SEAL Troy Arsenault, as big as Romeo and as light as the other was dark. Next came Mike D'Antoni, as dark as Romeo. A flyboy, who'd trained with England's crack SAS. And finally Eric "Rick" Latrobe, former Special Ops and a sniper like his brother, his tall, muscular body well-tanned, electric blue eyes blazing from beneath dirty blond hair. Each brought highly specialized skills to the company known simply as Phoenix. A good name for a group that rose from the ashes of war and one that now contracted to both private citizens and the United States government for jobs that had to be conducted "off the book".

The cabin belonged to D'Antoni, inherited from his grandfather and a perfect place for them to retreat after particularly difficult missions. Or plan and implement those missions away from any prying eyes. The one on the table today was personal and therefore far more important than any contract could ever be.

Dan had done some heavy digging when Rick first got the call about Joey, looking for anything he could find about Joey's situation and his unit. The trouble sign in his brain flashed full strength when there wasn't a smell or a hint of what happened to anyone else, especially the leader, Mark Halloran. A man they'd all spent time with when the unit was between missions.

From the moment they'd met him there'd been an instant connection. He was a man like them— focused, determined, dedicated. And no bullshit. The four of them often discussed the possibility of offering him a place in Phoenix when his current term was up.

All of them were aware the mission had to have been leaked for the unit to be ambushed. They thanked God that Joey had survived. If anyone else was still alive, they didn't know about it. That they'd have to find out when the kid woke up. And whoever had set them up, for whatever reason, would not want Joey in a position to reveal any information about what happened. The fact that no one officially notified Rick, Joey's only family, that the young man had been extracted, was wounded and in a critical condition was a good indication someone wanted to put a lid on this as quickly and quietly as possible.

"Those bastards didn't give me the time of day," Rick had barely been able to conceal his anger when he returned from DC. "They were shocked when I showed up. Everyone ran around like scared chickens trying to figure out what to do, because someone's got Top Secret stamped on his hospital file. Joey could have lain there until Christmas as far as they were concerned. Or until someone got hold of him that shouldn't. If his CO, Major Gregorio, hadn't called and shared his concerns with me I still wouldn't know."

"What about the rest of the unit?" Dan had asked. "Any hint about what happened to them?"

Rick shook his head. "Not about everyone, but Halloran's not dead." He'd been unmovable on that.

"I can't tell you how I know. I just do."

None of them discounted gut instinct. It had kept them alive more times than they cared to remember, so they took Rick's feelings very seriously.

"If he's alive...and that's a big if...it's because they want information," Mike pointed out.

"Mark will never give away the source. You know that. He *would* be dead first."

"I damn sure hope so. It's your source and I'd hate to see him given up."

"Then we'd better get Joey and keep him out of harm's way. And hope when he wakes up he can give us some answers," Romeo pointed out. "And we'd better do it quickly."

"Rick, who's sitting with Joey while you're here?" Troy asked. "I know you didn't leave him alone."

"A buddy who owes me a lifetime of favors. They won't be able to budge him unless they blow up the chair he's in."

"And we're pretty sure our inside source is still safe?"

Rick nodded.

"Then let's get our act together."

Now they were in final countdown mode, reviewing the details one last time. They'd planned and discussed and memorized but Romeo always wanted that one last run-through.

"Okay." Romeo had diagrams laid out on the rough wooden table they used for eating. "Let's get to it, Rick."

They'd obtained diagrams of Walter Reed and sucked every detail of the layout and scheduling from Rick when he came back from seeing Joey.

"Here's what we've got." He pointed to a segment on the diagram outlined in red. "Here's where Joey's being kept, with twenty-four hour monitoring. Anything that has to do with him must go through the charge nurse. Her desk is in the central part of the area."

"How often do they move him? Say, for x-rays or tests," Troy asked again.

"Not too often. I was there almost all day and any testing they did was in the room, with portable equipment." His finger traced another red line. "Here are the elevators. They're just off to the side of the nurses' desk. Joey's room is right here. If we do this properly we can have him out before we get asked too many questions."

Dan looked around him. "I've got the fake doctor's orders. They'll pass muster if no one looks too closely."

Rick had taken photos of the chart with his cell phone and sent them to Dan from the room.

"Good, good." Dan consulted a list on the pad in front of him. "Troy, Rick's given us a good list of the equipment in his brother's room. How are we coming on that?"

Arsenault had been a medic in the Navy and responsible for medical support on his SEAL team. He made notes on his own pad of paper.

"Got almost all of it. Mike and I will be fitting out the van as soon as we land in DC."

"And the medicines listed on the chart?"

"All set. I called our usual source and they'll arrive here when the chopper comes to pick us up."

Romeo turned to D'Antoni. "Mike, you'll waylay the doc right here." His finger stabbed a spot on the diagram. "And neutralize him. Expect any problems?"

Mike snorted. "No sweat. But you guys better be set to go the minute I show up in the room."

Arsenault glared at him. "We'll be ready. Aren't

we always?"

"All right, then." Dan shifted the papers to slide another on top. "As usual, my brother's flying the copter. He'll take us to DC where the vehicles are and we can get the van ready. Then he'll be waiting at the Discount Records Warehouse."

They all smiled grimly at the use of the name. Phoenix had purchased the abandoned warehouse with its surrounding acreage to give them a place separate from their main operation. They'd left the faded Discount Records sign up but a twelve-foot-high chain link fence topped with razor wire surrounded the property and big signs ordered "Keep out, this means you." They'd modified the inside of the building to contain four different vehicles and the helicopter and the entire place was booby-trapped, the sensors and codes known only to the four men.

"Rick, you'll be up in the room with Joey," Dan continued. "As soon as Mike gets the doc out of the way, he and Troy will show up in scrubs with orders for an MRI. That's one test they can't do in the room."

"Are you sure it's safe to unhook him from all that stuff to move him?" Rick asked.

"No problem," Troy answered. "We'll leave the IVs in place and it won't be more than a few minutes before we get him hooked up to everything else in the van."

"I'll be waiting at the ambulance exit with the van," Dan said. "We'll only have seconds once the elevator hits the ground floor, so don't dawdle."

They all looked at each other, thinking the same thing. They'd done operations like this one thousands of time, always with precise planning and timing. But those had all been for people none of them had emotional ties to. This one was for

Joey. The four men had been friends since college and Joey had been the little brother to all of them. The reality that he was now a highly trained sniper didn't change the fact that to them he'd always be the kid with the freckles, and feet and hands he needed to grow into. It made them all the more determined to pull this off.

"All right. When we get him back here we'll work out the shifts. Tonight we'll do one last check of the electronics and the perimeter security." Dan picked up the papers from the table and held his hands out for the notes everyone had made. "Got it in your heads? Good."

He dumped all the papers in the fireplace and set a match to them. Mike went to the kitchen cupboard and took down a bottle of bourbon and four shot glasses. They all raised their filled glasses in the signal of a toast. This would be the last drink any of them would take for a very long time.

* * * * *

Mr. Green and Mr. Brown sat in a Ford Expedition with blacked-out windows, in an isolated corner of Rock Creek Park.

"I feel like a criminal," Mr. Green said in a bitter tone.

"You are a criminal," Mr. Brown pointed out. "Or will be if we can't put a lid on this whole thing."

Mr. Green reached for a cigarette, then remembered he wasn't supposed to smoke any more. What a hell of a time to quit.

"This thing has been fucked from day one. We just should have figured out how to get the Wolf out of there and scatter Escobedo's group. Halloran and his men would have found nothing, the mission would have been aborted and we'd be dining at

94

Club 1776 instead of sitting in this stupid car like fugitives."

Mr. Brown cut him a derisive look. "Oh, yes, that would have been great. The Wolf does what he wants and Escobedo is...Escobedo."

"The serpent." Mr. Green snorted. "He's a snake, all right. Getting into bed with him makes me feel slimy."

"The money doesn't seem to bother you," his companion pointed out.

"Whoever said money is the root of all evil certainly knew the man calling the shots on this."

Mr. Brown barked a laugh. "It's from the Bible, a book that I'm sure you barely have nodding acquaintance with."

Mr. Green shifted in his seat. "We have to get Latrobe out of that hospital before he regains consciousness. I've got a place all picked out and the paperwork ready to transfer him. We should have moved him when I said to."

"Who knew the damned brother would show up out of the blue? He's usually so far under the radar he's invisible, so who in the hell called him?"

"Someone else who's worried about our boy for a different reason."

"That's what I'm afraid of." Mr. Brown stared through the windshield. "Either leaks are sprung in two directions, or someone's got a damned good nose at sniffing things out. There's absolutely no way anyone could get a smell of what's going on."

"Well, either someone did or there are people out there smarter than we'd like to think."

"We'll have to do it tomorrow." Mr. Brown looked at his watch. "It's noon. We'll meet at this time tomorrow at the hospital. At lunchtime there's a lot of confusion and people don't check things as carefully as they should. Or take time to make objections."

"What's the big deal?" Mr. Green asked. "We've got the paperwork. We're making an official transfer."

"I just don't want to have too many people asking us questions."

"You've got the doc on standby?"

Mr. Brown nodded. "And a list of what we'll need. He'll get the stuff tonight."

Mr. Green drummed his fingers on the dashboard. "Maybe we'd be a lot better just to get rid of the kid the way we planned."

Mr. Brown shook his head. "We have to find out if he knows who Halloran might be sending these crazy messages to. We can't afford to have someone running around like a loose cannon digging into our business. There's too much at stake."

Mr. Green sighed. "All right. Noon tomorrow. The ambulance will be waiting outside and doc will bring a gurney up with him."

"Fine. Now let's get the hell out of here."

* * * * *

Faith was consumed with frustration. Her body was still sore from the pain that had battered it, her mind was in turmoil and no matter in which direction she looked she couldn't find a thing. Not a clue. Nothing. Apparently you couldn't just find a website called SpecialOpsRUs and type in someone's name.

She'd found the scrap of paper on which she'd scribbled the name of Mark's commanding office and she knew he was based out of Fort Bragg. That was it. She should have been smart enough to figure out a click of the mouse wouldn't just call up the names of the men in his unit. Secrecy meant exactly that—no exposure to public scrutiny.

It took five tries for her to get through the switchboard at Fort Bragg and reach Major John Gregorio's office, only to be told he was in a meeting and couldn't be disturbed. She left her name and number with a pleading message that he call her. Four hours and several additional tries later she still hadn't been able to speak with him.

She did manage to cull a lot of general information from both the Special Ops and Fort Bragg websites. The members of SpecOps were considered the elite of the military—Army Rangers now members of Delta Force, SEALs, Force Recon Marines and a very few elite flyboys, all of them with a minimum of four to seven years experience in the service before their applications were even accepted.

After a second period of selection and assessment, they entered the training that would include their own version of Hell Week, designed to prepare them to survive in any situation. They were then assigned to teams, each with a leader and began building the trust and relationships they would need to take into the dangerous, highly specialized missions that were the hallmark of SpecOps. This was the first time she actually understood what Mark did in the military and how hazardous his assignments were. No wonder he didn't want to promise her anything in a situation where he felt he only contributed uncertainty and loneliness.

Oh, Mark. I wish I'd known. I could have told you that any relationship with you was better than none.

She learned one other fact from the Fort Bragg site—the Delta Force units based there were responsible for military actions in Central and South America. Swell. That was a whole hell of a lot of countries and no hint of where to start.

Mark. Can you hear me? I'm trying. I swear to God. Can you just give me a little more of a hint? Please? I swear I won't let you down. Somehow I'll find you

By eight o'clock that night she was convinced she wouldn't be hearing from Major Gregorio any time soon. That meant she'd need help getting in to see him. And help discovering who else was in Mark's unit. Sighing she picked up the phone again. Time to reach out to people.

* * * * *

"I can't believe I let you drag me away from my favorite television program to hack into government computers."

Andy Moreil sat hunched at Faith's computer, fingers flying over the keys, a cold can of soda at his elbow. Four years ago when computer hacking had been at the core of one of her books, Faith had been referred to him as a resource and he'd given her more information that she'd ever use. Under the condition, of course, she never use his name. Andy did work for corporations and sometimes the government in the field of computer security.

"If the people who pay me mucho bucks knew I was doing this, not only would they cut off my jobs they'd probably put me in jail."

"I swear on a pile of chocolate they'll never hear it from me."

Faith replaced the empty can with a full one. Andy lived on caffeine, in any form, at any time.

"Oh, right. That gives me a lot of comfort. You'd eat the chocolate before you ever got to take

98

an oath on it?" He snorted.

"Never mind the bad jokes. Just see what you can find. Okay?"

"Yeah. All right. Jeez." He ran his hands through his spiky hair.

Faith perched on the arm of the leather chair beside her desk and glued her eyes to the screen, watching as numbers and letters flew by with dizzying speed. Every so often a screen with a message would pop up. Andy would click some keys and he'd be off with the numbers and letters again.

"How's it coming?" she asked finally, unable to contain herself.

"Holy cow, Faith. Don't rush me. The government doesn't make it easy for you to steal their information."

"I know, I know. I'm just..."

"Impatient." He grinned. "A terminal disease with you."

She jumped up and began pacing. "But this time it's..."

"It's what?" he prompted when she didn't go on.

Personal, she wanted to say but she couldn't. "It's critical to my deadline," she improvised.

"Hah." Andy swigged from the soda can. "When isn't it? Quit marching around me like the infantry and I might get done sooner."

Faith dropped down into the big armchair but she couldn't make herself relax into its soft leather embrace. She was as rigid as a guy wire and tense enough to nibble on her thumb.

Mark. Can you hear me?

Need you...can't...bad.

Faith nearly bolted out of the chair, shocked that he'd actually answered her.

I'm here, I'm here. No one will tell me

anything.

Silence, while she twisted her fingers until they ached and tried to focus her mind to a narrow channel, blocking out all interference.

Betrayed...can't trust...

Can't trust who, Mark? Someone in your group? Your CO? Who?

Don't give up...

Never. She pounded her small fist on the chair. *Never, never, never.*

"Hey, Faith, banging on the chair isn't helping," Andy commented.

"What?" The connection was broken as cleanly as if a thread snapped. Damn Andy, anyway.

"I said, don't beat up the furniture. Anyway, I've got something for you. Come take a look."

Faith went to peer over his shoulder, staring at the information on the screen. "Holy shit."

"Yup. I couldn't get everyone in the Seventh Special Forces assigned there but I did manage to dig around and get the names of the men in Mark's unit." He glanced up at her. "That's all you want anyway, right?"

"Yes," She exhaled a breath she didn't even know she'd been holding. "Can you print this list out for me?"

Andy hit a key and the printer began to make noises. "Anything else?"

"Yes. I want you to do a check on each of these men and see if there's any clue as to where they might be right now."

"Jesus, Faith, you don't want much, do you?" He handed her the empty soda can. "I should charge you more than a night's worth of caffeine for this."

"Just...can you do it?"

He rolled his neck and cracked his knuckles.

"Can I do it? Hah. Andrew the Magnificent can do anything." He accepted the fresh drinks she handed him. "But remember. I've got a time limit here. I stay in their system too long and their electronic patrols will catch me."

"Damn. Well, just get as much as you can before you have to log off."

She went back to pacing while Andy started clicking the keys again.

"Oh, by the way," he interjected. "The Seventh Special Forces are responsible for action in Central and South America. Did you know that?"

"Yes, I did. Thanks but keep going."

An hour later Andy pressed the printer button again and sheets of paper began to roll out into the chair. At the same time he went through the process of backing out of the system, wiping away his electronic footprint. When the papers were finished he handed them to Faith.

"All the men in his unit. Background, families, what have you."

Faith's eyes widened. "You got all of this? How?"

Andy grinned. "If I told you, I'd have to kill you."

Faith scanned each of the sheets of paper. "There's nothing recent on any of them," she said slowly. "Except this Joey Latrobe. It says he's at Walter Reed but it doesn't say what for or how long he's been there."

"You might be able to find out with a phone call. Maybe not." Andy shrugged. "Depends why he's there." Andy stood up and finished the last of his soda. "I gotta call it a night." He stared out the window. "Or morning, depending on your point of view. Got to meet with a new client at nine and I think at least a shower is in order."

"Yeah, yeah, knock 'em dead Andy." Faith was already engrossed in studying the sheets, her mind spinning in a dozen different directions. "Thanks for everything."

"Talk at you soon," he called as he let himself.

Faith checked the time.

Midnight.

No one she could call at this hour. Even a call to the hospital right now might raise someone's suspicions. And the man she needed to speak to would still be lying in bed next to his wife, hoping today the alarm would let him sleep in.

Finally deciding she ought to get some sleep herself. She dragged herself to her bedroom, lugging her pile of papers. Not even bothering to undress, she climbed into bed in her jeans and t-shirt, pulled the covers over her head and prayed for a dreamless night. But even as she tugged the covers tightly under her chin, the threads of a memorable weekend reached out to her.

Chapter Eight

Four Years Earlier

The book signing at Barnes & Noble had gone exceedingly well. Faith always experienced warm satisfaction when readers flocked to her with great enthusiasm, discussing her characters as if they were personal friends. The journey from thought process to paper to the reader's mind was often a convoluted one and she took great pleasure in knowing the end product produced pleasure and satisfaction for people.

Today people had stood in line for three hours just to have her sign one of her books and maybe exchange a few words with her. The Customer Relations Manager had hustled to set up coffee and cookies to feed the inner person of the people waiting, comfort food to take the edge off the long wait. By the time the last person had left, Faith was sure her face would crack from smiling. In addition to the people who came in person, there were more than one hundred pre-solds she signed before the event actually began. Tonight she'd be soaking her hand in a large bowl of ice.

But she was pleased. Very pleased. The people at the store were beyond gracious and made everything as smooth as possible. But she'd be glad to get back to her hotel just the same. Abigail had found a sumptuous boutique hotel in Chapel Hill, about twenty minutes away. Built and decorated like a Tuscan villa, it offered every amenity a guest could wish for, including total privacy. Tonight she could order from room service and just veg out before she caught the plane home tomorrow.

She'd wondered vaguely if Mark might show up. She'd sent him one of their by now usual mental messages and backed it up with an email. Usually they stayed away from electronic communications owing to the nature and secrecy of his position. No traces that way, he always said, even as innocuous as their messages might be.

So she'd opened her mind and focused, hoping he'd get what she was saying. Of course, he could be anywhere in the world on assignment, concentrating on his job rather than nonsense from an old friend. But she could still hope.

At last she was finished, all her thank yous said, along with a promise to return with her next release. Gratefully she headed to the parking lot in back, digging in her purse for her keys. When she looked up she almost dropped keys, purse and tote bag. Leaning against her rented car was Captain Mark Halloran, out of uniform, wearing slacks, a soft collared shirt and a huge shit-eating grin.

Faith finally managed to close her mouth. "I was afraid you didn't get my messages."

He uncrossed his arms, moved forward and took her tote bag and other gear from her. "You think I'd miss a chance to see my favorite author in my own back yard? Come on, let's get you out of here. You must be exhausted."

Without objection she let him pluck the keys from her hand. Before she could blink she was buckled into the passenger seat and Mark was backing out of the parking lot.

When she got her mouth to work at last, she asked, "How did you even know which car was mine?"

He winked at her. "Abigail Loudon is susceptible to my charms. She even had her secretary call the rental agency and get the plate number."

Faith couldn't help the laugh that bubbled from

her mouth. "So I guess this means you really wanted to see me."

The smile wiped itself from Mark's face. "You have no idea, Tidbit. You just have no idea."

She frowned. "Why so serious?"

"Later. First I think a drink is in order to celebrate the success of the famous author, Faith Wilding. I have some places in mind but where are you staying?"

"The Siena in Chapel Hill. It's not too far away and it gives me exactly what I want, besides every amenity in the world. Complete privacy."

"I've heard of it. Small and elegant." He honked the horn at a truck that cut too close to their front bumper. "How's their restaurant?"

"I only had breakfast there but I think the chef is directly from heaven."

"Sold." He clicked on the signal light and turned at the next corner. "Privacy is just what the doctor ordered."

At the Siena he handed her vehicle over to valet parking, then held the door to the lobby open for her.

"I'd like to take these things up to my room first, if that's okay. Want to come up with me?"

He looked down at her, his eyes the dark-blue of a storm-tossed ocean. Heat danced in them. "More than anything but if I do we'll never get dinner."

She stared at him, suddenly off balance.

"Don't over think, Faith. Go put your stuff away and meet me in the bar. I'll get us a table in the corner."

He was as good as his word, lounging easily in one of the Italianate chairs pulled up to a wood and marble table. A sudden attack of nerves swept over her, a partner to the unexpected pulses throbbing everywhere in her body and the unfamiliar heat of desire. The memory of her prom came back to her, tantalizing her. Did Mark intend to pick up the ball he'd dropped that night? One part of her shied away from it, the other reached for it eagerly.

When she sat down she folded her hands in her lap until she could control their shaking.

"Don't look so anxious," he grinned. "I'm not going to eat you." Then his voice dropped. "At least not out here in public."

Faith felt a blush creep up her face to her hairline. How embarrassing. At her age she should be way past blushing. "I, um..." She fumbled for words. Just being in his presence already made her want the things she remembered. His touch. His mouth. His cock inside her.

Mark waved at a waiter. "Let's have a drink and talk about nothing and just relax. You're wound up tighter than a drum and I'm not far behind you. That sound good?"

She nodded. "I'd like a White Russian, please."

Mark cocked an eyebrow. "Well past the single glass of wine stage, I see."

Faith chuckled and felt the knots inside her unraveling. "I've grown up, in case you hadn't noticed."

His eyes darkened again. "Oh, Tidbit, I've noticed. Believe me."

The conversation over drinks was light and insubstantial. Her books, her career. His career in the Army, although she knew there was very little he could tell her. An Army Ranger, after enough missions under his belt he'd volunteered for the vaunted Delta Force, responsible for conducting Special Operations around the globe. She knew his parents worried all the time about the dangerous path he'd chosen but looking at him now, Faith

hadn't a doubt in the world that in any situation
Mark Halloran could take care of himself.

"Another drink?"

Faith's mind had wandered back to her prom
night and Mark's words startled her. "Oh, well,
maybe after we eat. I'm not sure I remember the
last time I put food in my stomach today."

He leaned across the table and took one of her
small hands in his larger, warm one. "Tell me if I'm
out of line here, Faith. Or if I misread the signals
I've been living on all this time. But would you
scream and run off if I suggested we order dinner
from room service?"

Her eyes widened and those pulses kicked up a
notch. "Room service?"

"Mm-hmm. After."

She met his eyes directly. "After what?"

"After what we've both been thinking about all
these years. Right?" His fingertip caressed her
knuckles. "I was wrong to stay away from you,
Tidbit. I thought I had nothing to give you, that I'd
be unfair asking you to wait. But Faith, I swear it's
been pure hell without you." He gave her a lopsided
grin. "There's not much fun in being noble."

Faith raised her eyes and saw the intense look
on his face, the desire heating his eyes, felt her
breasts tighten and the throbbing between her legs
intensify. She remembered that time—the only
time—and she wanted it again. No other man had
ever come close to making her feel what Mark had.

"I don't think the restaurant's where I want to
be right now," she told him.

Mark lifted her hand to his lips and brushed a
light kiss on it, then signaled for the waiter. "Are
you concerned about people seeing us go up to your
room? I don't want to compromise your situation.
We could go somewhere else."

Faith smiled. "I'm fine, Mark. No one's spying on me here and no one can really find me. That's why Abigail picks places like this. Besides, wait until you see the room."

His smile melted her insides. "Then lead the way."

The waiter had brought the check and Mark dumped some cash on the table, then followed Faith out to the elevators.

She hadn't been kidding about the room. Sumptuous was the only word Faith could think of to describe it when she checked in. The bedroom, decorated in shades of gold and burnt orange, was centered around an oversized king bed. Wall sconces provided soft lighting and the nightstand and dresser held every conceivable type of convenience.

She blushed as she opened the nightstand drawer to reveal a box of condoms discreetly tucked away.

Mark laughed. "I like a place that thinks of everything."

"We can have music too," she told him and showed him the concealed sound system.

"I think music would be great." He reached around her to turn it on, then fiddled around until he found what he was looking for. Soft instrumental music flooded the room, a slow melody that reminded Faith of the prom.

Mark pulled her into his arms. "We haven't danced in a long time, Faith. Remember how good we were together?"

She fitted easily into his embrace, her hand resting in his, her head nestled against his shoulder. She could feel his heart beating against hers and realized he was as nervous about this as she was. Their one and only time had been so long ago.

Would they still want each other as much? Would it still be as good?

"You feel so soft in my arms," he murdered, as they swayed to the music. "I love holding you."

Faith could feel just how much he loved it by the thickness of his erection pressing into her soft abdomen. Her nerves tingled in response.

Mark feathered kisses across her forehead and her cheeks and along the column of her neck. She was barely aware of it when his hands moved between them and he began unbuttoning her blouse.

"So soft," he repeated, his hands touching her, his mouth never still.

She barely realized she was naked from the waist up when he mouth captured hers in a drugging kiss that swept away the sense of anything but here and now. When his lips moved from her mouth to her shoulder and down to her breasts she arched up into him, eyes closed, swept by such a feeling of desire she could hardly stand.

She felt his body move and realized he was kneeling before her, his hands making quick work of her silk skirt and sliding her panty hose and thong down to her ankles. One by one he lifted each foot and removed her shoes and the delicate lingerie.

And then she was totally naked before him. She heard the hiss of his breath as he touched her thighs, her knees, even her ankles. When he pressed his mouth to the heated flesh between her thighs and gave her a hot kiss there she shook with sensation, clutching at his shoulders for support.

"I've waited so long for this I could do it forever." His voice was husky. "I could make a meal of you, Tidbit and I don't think one meal would be enough."

He picked her up, reached down with one hand to pull back the bed covers and placed her with infinite care on the clean cotton sheets. She felt his body shake with the effort to hold back and go slowly. She wanted to shout, *You don't have to wait* but she knew he wanted to make this special for her. For both of them.

She opened her eyes and saw his burning into hers, holding her gaze while he stripped off his clothing. She gasped at the sight of his magnificent body, his erection jutting proudly in the pale golden light from the bedside lamp. His body could have been the work of a sculptor, shoulders broad and hips narrow, thick muscles well-defined.

They stared at each other for a long moment and then he was beside her, his strong body pressing against hers. His hands did a slow minuet on her skin, dancing from breasts to thighs and everything in-between. Every pulse in her body began to throb, moisture pooled between her thighs and her breathing hitched and stuttered.

His mouth was seductive, tasting her lips, invading her with his tongue, darting and retreating until she wanted to open her own mouth and swallow him whole. And it was everywhere, following the patterns left by his hands, savoring every inch of her as if it were the finest ambrosia.

Her fingers moved through the matted curls covering his hard, muscular chest, touching his nipples, grazing the points with her fingernails. Loving the feel of him hardening against her when she did. The sensation of him pressing down on her, consuming her with his touch. Their bodies danced as one, until she could hardly tell where his body ended and hers began. Nothing she had ever dreamed could compare to the reality of this, a sensual mating that took her beyond every peak, dropped her through every valley and lifted her again.

She moaned beneath him, reveling in the feel of his hair-roughened skin against the smoothness of hers. His nips and licks drove her wild, speeding up the tempo of the dance, a wildness invading her. He drank of her as if she were a fine wine, his tongue lapping each drop like a liquid treasure, while his clever fingers stroked and plucked and teased at the quivering walls of her cunt.

Beneath him her body arched upwards, urging him. Heat raced through her like wildfire, the pleasure burning her alive. When he moved to kneel between her thighs she almost climaxed from the sheer anticipation of what he was about to do. He bent his head and that first lash of the tongue shot such pleasure through her she could hardly breath.

Again and again he licked her, his thumbs opening her moist pussy to his eyes. The heat she saw in them nearly scorched her. His breath on her labia was a warm, moist breeze that sent shivers racing through her.

He ate at her, just as he'd promised, exploring the inner walls of her sex with his tongue, scraping it along the sweet spot and rimming the opening. She bucked beneath him but he held her firmly in place, his tongue dancing over every sensitive surface. When her orgasm erupted he let her ride his tongue, her inner muscles clenching it, until the last aftershock died away.

But when he reached out to open the drawer with the condoms in it, she batted his arm away and shoved him to his back. Only the element of surprise gave her the ability to move his hard, muscular body that way.

"What?" he asked.

"I've been waiting to do this for a very long

time," she whispered.

Wrapping her slim fingers around his swollen cock, she placed her mouth over the broad, flat head and drew it into her mouth. It tasted just as she's imagined, hot and hard, but the skin covering it was like velvet. Such a bolt of heat flooded her that she almost couldn't breathe.

"Careful." His voice was tight. "I'm so close to ready, darlin'."

But she wanted this pleasure, even if just for a few moments. Sliding one hand between his concrete thighs she cupped the soft sac of his balls and rubbed her fingers over the pleated skin. Every muscle in Mark's body tightened as he reached for control but he was obviously determined to let her do this.

Pulling her mouth back she licked delicately at the surface of the head, dipping the tip of her tongue into the slit.

"Enough." His voice was a low growl.

Grabbing her arms he rolled her to her back. Now he did yank out a condom, ripping the foil with his teeth and rolling it on with a dexterity she chose to ignore.

"No more time for foreplay," he rasped.

He thrust into her with one hard stroke, then held himself still to give her time to adjust to him. But not too much time. In seconds he was rocking into her, a gentle motion that pulled at the walls of her sex and sizzled her nerves. He manacled her wrists with his fingers and held her hands flat on the pillow on either side of her head.

"I love you," he said in a hoarse voice. "Jesus, but I love you, Faith."

And then he fucked her in earnest, his strokes harder and faster, his eyes watching her for signs of her rising need. She wrapped her legs around him to hold him in tighter, thrusting her hips up to him. He moved one hand to take her clit between his thumb and forefinger. When he pinched it she exploded and he was right there with her.

The spasms went on and on, turning her bones to liquid, and she spun and shattered.

His hard cock flexed inside her again and again until she didn't know where her own body ended and his began. At some point the shudders subsided to aftershocks and then even those dies away and she lay limply on the bed, his big body caged around hers.

He touched his lips to hers. "I love you, Faith. No matter what, never forget that."

"I won't," she whispered, barely able to speak. "I love you, too."

They lay twined together for a long moment, hearts hammering, lungs gasping for breath, The whisper of air from the air conditioning cooled their sweat-slicked skin. He was heavy but she wouldn't have moved him for the world. She knew sex with Mark would be unbelievable but nothing in her fantasies even came close to the almost mystical experience. Every other man in her life faded into oblivion, permanently tucked away in the shadow of an overwhelming presence.

Letting out a long breath, Mark rolled to his side, taking her with him, cradling her against his body.

"You are amazing," he told her, his voice still thick with desire. "Better than I remembered. None of my dreams come close to matching this."

She drifted her fingers through the fine hair on his chest. "You dreamt about us?"

His laugh was warm and sexy. "More times than I want to admit. Every night since the prom." One hand came up to caress her cheek. "That night together has kept me sane through a lot of tough missions. Why have I been so stupid as to waste all the time since then?"

"Because you have a job to do." She stated the simple fact.

He rose over her, his palm cupping her cheek, his eyes like the night sky. "Faith." He stopped, closed his eyes as if dredging up words.

A tiny stab of pain pierced her heart. "It's all right, Mark. You don't have to say anything."

He shook his head. "No. You don't understand." He smoothed the hair away from her forehead. "I have the weekend off because my unit's being deployed again in three days. I have no idea how long I'll be gone, or what's coming after that. I don't have the kind of life that makes room in it for the kind of commitment I want to make with you. Not right now."

She swallowed hard, three times, before she could get any words out. "It doesn't matter. I'll never stop loving you. And one day it will be our turn. In the meantime, no matter what happens, I'll always be here for you. If you ever need me, all you have to do is call."

"I wish I could offer you more. Offer you what you deserve. There'll never be anyone else for me after this, Tidbit. How could there? But I just re-upped last year, so I've got three more years to go before I can make any decisions about my future. What I do is dangerous. I could be dead tomorrow. There's no way I can ask you to put your life on hold for me."

She pushed herself up and stared at him. "My life won't be on hold, Mark. My writing is doing very well. My books are selling, for some unbelievable reason. And I have goals I want to accomplish. But three years isn't that long. I'll wait.

And that's a promise."

He brushed his lips against hers. "So now we just need to get past these next three years. Meanwhile..."he rolled on top of her again..."we have the whole weekend. Right? You can stay here with me?"

She nodded. "I'll change my reservation. Think we can figure out how to occupy our time?"

His rich, full laugh was like an aphrodisiac to her and she pulled him down to her, arms wrapped tightly around his neck.

They never left the room for three days, opening the door only for room service and clean towels. They made love in ways that Faith hadn't even dreamed possible. Their bodies, as if aware that time was short, never seemed to tire. They bathed each other in the huge marble tub and made slow love in the warm, fragrant water. They learned every nook and crevice of each other's bodies. Ecstasy was the constant peak against which they hurled themselves.

It wasn't all sex. They talked. About the past. The present. But they carefully avoided any mention of the future. For these three days that was a forbidden topic.

When Mark drove her to the airport Monday morning and put her on her plane, her heart squeezed so painfully she was sure it would stop beating. But she managed a bright smile for him, even if her kiss was filled with desperation.

Her comfort was knowing that no matter what separated them, their minds would always communicate. She'd just have to pray that three years passed quickly.

* * * * *

Tidbit!

The scream woke her sharply, dragging her from the warmth of the dream wrapped around her. Pain knifed her heart at the tortured sound.

I'm right here.

She waited through an interminable silence before his voiced broke through again.

Holding on but...much longer...

No, no. Don't give up. I'm working on this.

Love you...

Her heart turned over. The word they'd never dared speaking, knowing time was their enemy.

I love you too, Mark. And I'll get you out of there. Hold on. Just a little longer.

She waited for his voice again but instead sensed a heavy, evil presence. Whoever was intercepting and blocking was doing it again. Could he tell who Mark was telepathing to? The thought sent shivers of terror along her spine.

Don't say my name, Mark.

She prayed the message would carry without the other man realizing it.

She looked at the clock. Almost seven in the morning. Still early times to call Walter Reed but she'd hardly slept and she was too edgy to wait. She shoved her feet into her disreputable fuzzy slippers and not even bothering to pull on a robe, hurried downstairs, started the coffee and found the sheets Andy had printed out the night before.

One hour later she slammed the telephone down in frustration. All her pleading and cajoling in the world hadn't gotten her past the frosty switchboard operator at Walter Reed. If she wasn't a relative, she got nothing. Not even an acknowledgement Joey Latrobe was there. She'd tried lying through her teeth, pretending to be his sister but apparently they could check his records and knew he didn't have one. She asked for his doctor and got nowhere with that. After trying every trick she could think of, she finally called Andy and rousted him out of bed.

"Jesus, Faith, have a heart," he griped. "You kept me up half the night and I've got a big meeting this morning. What now?"

"Can you please just jump on the super duper computer of yours one more time for me and look something up?"

"Can't this wait?" he complained.

"No, it can't," she snapped. Taking a deep breath, she lowered her voice. "I just need one thing, okay?"

"All right, all right," he grumbled. "What is it?"

"I need to know if Joey Latrobe has any family. I know he doesn't have a sister but—"

"Tried that already, did you?"

She could almost see his grin, despite his irritation. "Just shut up and click those keys."

She heard the snicking sound of the keyboard as he did his thing. Then, "Okay. Got it. I'm emailing it to you right now but delete it ASAP. Okay?"

"Of course. Send it on over."

The email arrived in less than a minute and Faith printed it out. No sister, just as they'd said. And both parents dead, killed in a plane crash when Joey was twenty-one. But he had an older brother, Eric, a Special Ops sniper like his brother but out of the service now for two years. He was a partner in a company in Maryland called Phoenix. No description of what the company did or anything else about it. Just a telephone number.

She was pouring her coffee when the phone rang, the sound making her jump.

"No, I don't have time to research Phoenix for

you right now," Andy said, reading her mind. "I'll call you this afternoon when I'm finished. If you haven't gotten any further by then I'll get to work on it. But it may be tough."

Faith wrinkled her forehead. "Why? What's wrong with it?"

"I have no idea but I couldn't get into it with my usually programs. They've got firewalls around firewalls. All right. Gotta go. Stay out of trouble, please?"

"I'll try."

So. Joey's older brother was still doing something off the radar. Okay, she'd try her usual line first and see if that worked. She dialed the number but after four rings it clicked over to an answering machine.

"You've reached Phoenix. Leave a message and we'll get back to you."

"This is Faith Wilding. I'm looking for Eric Latrobe. I'm a writer and he was referred to me as a possible resource for a book I'm working on. Please call me back as soon as you can."

She left her number and hung up. She needed to call Senator Trey Winslow, who'd been a great resource for her in two of her books. He'd also introduced her to a number of other people who had opened doors for her when she needed them. Now she'd ask for his help once more but as carefully as she could. She didn't want to give away her real purpose until she had to. And she'd have to do it in person. Strangely enough, for a senator, Trey didn't do well with phone calls.

But it was too early to reach him so she booted up her computer and checked to see if she could get on the early flight to Washington. Which left, she realized looking at the screen, in two hours. She snagged one of the few remaining seats, printed out

her boarding pass and called a cab. She'd call for
hotel reservations on the way.

She called the number for Phoenix again and
added her cell phone number to the previous
message, indicating that she planned to be in
Washington and on the move. She wasn't sure what
to do after that if no one called her back.

When the cab arrived she was showered,
dressed and waiting with her suitcase and her
laptop, the printouts from Andy stuffed in the
laptop bag along with her cell phone. Halfway to
San Antonio International Airport she called up the
number for Senator Trey Winslow.

"Faith!" His voice boomed over the long
distance connection. "Good to hear from you. How's
the new book coming?"

"Well, actually, that's what I wanted to talk to
you about."

"Oh?" His voce carried a mixture of caution
and enthusiasm.

"I'm actually doing something a little different
this time." She cleared her throat. "I'm planning to
be in Washington this afternoon and wondered if
you could spare me a few minutes."

"You know I always have time for you. But how
about drinks? At five? I have meetings on the Hill
until four thirty today and I can't sneak out." He
chuckled. "Too many reporters, you know."

"Five will be fine. Some place where we can talk
without a lot of interruptions."

"Like that, huh?" He was silent for a moment.
"How about coming out to the house? Georgia is
good about making herself scarce. I can send the
driver for you."

She'd meet him in the middle of the Potomac if
it meant he could help her. "That sounds great. I'll
call your office as soon as I get in and let you know

where I'm staying."

"See you this evening."

Next, hotel reservations. For special appearances she always splurged and stayed at the famed Willard but this time she wanted to blend in with tourists. Luckily the Grand Hyatt had rooms available. Once that was confirmed, she sat back in her seat and tried to collect herself. She'd get nothing done if she couldn't get her mind to function in a disciplined manner.

Faith's plane landed on time and she hurried through the terminal to where the cabs waited. She checked her messages again. Nothing from Phoenix. Damn! She tried the number again, leaving yet another message for them. She made a mental note to call Aunt Vivi and see what she could do to counteract the energy of whoever in the terrorist group was a telepath.

That was all she could do right now. She'd left a message for Tess and would call her when she got to the hotel.

Meanwhile she could only pray she'd be able to do what was necessary before it was too late.

* * * * *

Dan Romeo listened to the message on the Phoenix answering machine, hung up and stared at Rick. "Who the hell is Faith Wilding?"

Rick shrugged. "Haven't got a clue."

"What does she mean, someone told her you might be a good resource. Resource for what? If she's calling you Eric she can't be too connected to you."

Rick threw up his hands. "I'm telling you, I don't know. The only people whoever called me Eric were my parents, my teacher and sometimes my

CO, when he wasn't referring to me as 'you arrogant asshole'.

Mike poured himself a glass of juice. They were almost ready to leave the cabin. Dan's brother was waiting outside with the helicopter, ready to lift off as soon as they were all on board. They were running a tight schedule and didn't have time for distractions and possible monkey wrenches.

"Maybe she's someone from the people who are behind this whole thing. Could be she's trying to scope us out and find out if we're involved, especially after Rick showed up at the hospital."

"Maybe, although this number isn't exactly well-known." Dan locked his briefcase. "We'll have to keep a sharp lookout. Otherwise, put her on the back burner until we get Joey out of harm's way. Then we can check her out."

"I don't like this," Troy said. "We've got Joey to handle and our source to protect. We don't need some strange woman popping up out of the woodwork to screw everything up.

"No, we don't." Mike swallowed the rest of the juice and rinsed his glass. "But we have no choice at this point. Too late to make major changes. Or postpone this little adventure. And we can't leave her hanging out there as unfinished business. She's too much of an unexpected wild card."

"All right, gentlemen." Dan headed for the door. "Lock and load."

Chapter Nine

They'd outfitted the van in record time. Ed Romeo had barely set the copter down before the men were out and at work. They drove quickly but carefully to Bethesda, knowing they were racing the clock but not wanting any traffic stop to screw up the operation.

Troy and Mike continued to work on the equipment in the back of the van as they drove. By the time they pulled into the parking lot at Walter Reed Hospital, Troy gave them the okay and told them they were ready.

Dan pulled the van to the side of the ambulance doors, parked it and left the engine running. "Time check, everyone. I have eleven forty-five."

"Got it."

"Set."

"We're good."

"All right, then." Dan looked at each of the men. "Get to it."

Rick was the first out, walking around to the front entrance and into the hospital. They gave him time to get up to Joey's room and send his buddy on his way.

Troy and Mike exited the van next, as unassumingly as possible. Dressed in scrubs, with Troy carrying a clipboard, they slipped into the stream of people entering the emergency room doors, careful to pick a large enough group to blend in.

The ER was in its usual chaotic state. The waiting area was jammed, the overflow standing or sitting on the floor. Hospital personnel and visitors moved in every direction, gurneys rolled past them, voices called back and forth with questions and instructions. The confusion made it easy for the two men to ease their way through, appropriate an empty gurney without being stopped and move down the hallway. Troy punched the button for the elevator and indicated Mike should move ahead with his task.

D'Antoni headed for the stairs. Rick had relayed a comment he'd overheard Joey's doctor make about never taking the elevator down to the cafeteria because he ate at noon, the busiest time of the day and he couldn't waste the time waiting. D'Antoni stationed himself at the landing between the first and second floors and waited. The doctor would be along any minute.

When Troy walked into Joey's room, pushing the gurney, Rick was sitting in the chair beside his brother's bed. He nodded at Troy, eyes asking a question with his eyes. Troy blinked once. All set.

A nurse was just taking Joey's vitals. She looked at Troy with raised eyebrows.

"Orders for an MRI," he said, showing her the clipboard with the papers Dan had prepared.

"I'll have to check with his doctor," she told him.

Rick stood up, an imposing presence in the room. "If the doctor ordered the test, why do you have to check with him?"

"This is a special case—"

"And I'm telling you my orders say the doc wants this done ASAP," Troy interrupted. "And I want to eat my lunch. Just let me get him out of here."

The nurse frowned. "He has to be unhooked from the monitors. I just don't know..."

"Mary?" Another nurse bustled into the room. "I need you stat. We have a problem with the patient in 247."

Mary looked at Troy, who did his best to look both irritated and bored, then back at the other nurse. "All right. I'm coming." To Troy she said, "Just wait right here. Don't do anything until I get back."

She had barely hurried out of the room when Mike hustled in.

"Doc's out of commission. How are we coming?"

"That damn nurse is giving me a hard time," Rick told him. "We need to move Joey before she gets back."

"Done."

Troy made quick work of disconnecting the machines. He and Mike moved Joey to the gurney, clamped his IV bag into the holder.

"I'll go get the elevator," Rick said. "We don't want to have to wait out there in the open."

Troy watched from the door and at Rick's signal checked to make sure the nurse was still out of sight. Then he and Mike moved the gurney out of the room. Rick was right. The noon hour was the best time for something like this. In addition to nurses everywhere dispensing medications and attending to patients' needs, lunch was being served and people were moving in all directions. No one gave them a second glance. They rolled the gurney past the nurses' station and into the waiting elevator. Mike punched the button, the doors closed and the elevator began its descent.

"On our way," he said into the tiny mike clipped to his scrubs top.

The minute they hit the ground floor they headed for the ambulance bay as quickly as possible, without attracting attention. The van was waiting for them, Dan tense in the driver's seat.

"Move it." His voice was clipped. "Someone will

be looking for him any minute now."

"You don't have to tell us," Mike answered.

In less than a minute they had Joey inside and strapped down. Troy was already in place connecting Joey to the equipment, Rick on the opposite side of him.

Mike climbed into the passenger seat and slammed the door. "Go, go, go. Get the hell out of here."

Dan drove out of the parking lot and onto the street, eyes moving back and forth to the rear view mirror, ready to spot any trouble.

Nothing.

They merged into traffic, breathing a collective sigh of relief.

* * * * *

The ambulance rolled up to the bay on the heels of the van, although neither man exiting the vehicle gave it a second glance. Mr. Green and Mr. Brown, intent on their mission, paid little attention to what was happening around them. They arrived at the nurses' station on Joey's floor with two men in the uniforms of orderlies and their own gurney. At the desk they presented their papers and announced they were moving the patient, Joey Latrobe, to a more secure medical facility.

While the woman behind the desk was examining their papers, a nurse flew out of Joey's room.

"He's gone." She looked rapidly around her. "Who saw them take him?"

"Who's gone?" Mr. Green asked.

"The...special...patient. Latrobe."

Mr. Green and Mr. Brown looked at each other, each wearing an expression of dread.

"What do you mean he's gone?" Mr. Brown asked. "How the hell could he be gone? Don't you people watch your patients?"

The nurse gripped her hands together to still their trembling. "I was just in his room. Two men came with orders to take him for an MRI. I had an emergency situation and I told them to wait until I came back. But they're gone and so is the patient."

Mr. Brown turned to the woman behind the desk. "Maybe there's a simple explanation, although I can't imagine why a test would be ordered today. But call down and see if he's in fact having an MRI. Do it. Right now."

The woman paled at the menace in the voice and her hands shook as she dialed the extension. She was even more nervous when she hung up the phone.

"They don't know anything about it."

"Where's the doctor?" Mr. Green demanded, looking around as if he expected the man to materialize before him.

The nurse was trembling visibly as she punched numbers on the phone, calling one extension after another. "No one's seen him." Her voice was unsteady.

"God damn it." Mr. Green slammed his fist on the raised counter. "How the fuck did this happen."

"Sir!" The nurse, in spite of her distress, looked at him with shocked eyes.

"Cool it," Mr. Brown warned in a low voice. "Now is not the time to lose it."

Mr. Green dragged in a deep breath and let it out slowly. "All right. Who's the nurse who was taking care of him?"

"I am." Joey's nurse stepped forward. "Anna Rice. Latrobe is...was...my patient."

"Then maybe you can tell me how he got away

from you."

Mr. Green's face set in grim lines as he listened to her recitation of what happened in the hospital room. Mr. Brown gestured to the two orderlies behind him to move back with the gurney, then pulled his companion to the side.

"We've got a big problem here and I'm not looking forward to calling this in."

"It's the damned brother. You can bet on it. Him and his renegade friends."

"We'd better get back downstairs and call this in, then figure out how we're going to find Latrobe. Hang on. We're about to get our asses handed to us." He turned back to the nurse. "You'd better figure out how they got in and out under everyone's nose. Someone's going to pay for this."

The two men stomped to the elevator, the orderlies dragging behind them.

* * * * *

"You just up and flew to DC?" Tess's voice was unbelieving and tinged with hurt. "Without even calling me?"

"No biggie. I wanted to talk to Senator Winslow and I just decided to go ahead and do it. I'll only be here until tomorrow."

"Faith, this is so not like you." Silence. "You want to tell me what's really going on here? This isn't just about a book, is it?"

Faith nibbled on her lower lip, wondering exactly how much she could tell Tess. The woman could keep a secret, that was for sure. But this involved someone's life. Mark's. In any event, it wasn't a subject to discuss on the telephone.

"It's...a bigger project than I expected." And what a lame excuse that is. "I'll call you in the morning and give you my fight arrival time. How about if you meet me, we'll pick up Chinese, go back to my house and I'll tell you what I can."

"I'm getting funny vibes about this, Faith. Are you in some kind of trouble?"

"No, not at all." At least, not yet. Meanwhile, everything in the media seems to point to trouble spots in Peru more than anywhere else in South America. Can you dig up more stuff about terrorist groups there and anything that links Special Ops missions to them, anything that might have made it into the media or onto the Internet blogs? Whatever you can find."

She could hear Tess's sigh over the long distance connection. "All right. I'll get to work on it. Call me in the morning." She paused. "And be careful, okay?"

"I will."

She disconnected and immediately dialed Andy Moreil's number.

"Are you haunting me from around the country?" he asked.

"Don't be such a wiseass. I need another favor."

"Jesus, Faith. Can't I have a day to breathe?" But his voice was warm rather than irritated. Andy had been a good friend for a long time. Teasing her was one of his great pleasures.

"Okay, if you do this one thing for me I won't bother you for the rest of the week."

He laughed. "Yeah, yeah, yeah. I've heard that before. Okay, what is it?"

"Have you had a chance to check on Phoenix yet?"

"You do realize I actually do a job I get paid for." But she heard the teasing note in his voice and could already hear the computer keys clicking. Where's it located?"

"And what am I, chopped liver? My checks are good."

"Just kidding."

"Sorry. My sense of humor is a little out of whack right now. Dig as deep as you can and call me back on my cell the minute you have anything."

"Later." And he was gone.

She tried Vivi next but got the answering machine and decided to try again later. She ordered a light lunch from room service and tried to eat something but her stomach was too knotted to accept food. The television provided no distraction and she couldn't concentrate enough to work at her laptop. She was about to take two aspirin and try to lie down when her cell rang.

"Holy shit, Faith." Andy's voice had a note of awe.

"What?" Her hand tightened on her phone. "What did you find?"

"Do you actually know these guys?" He sounded like a small child asking about The Lone Ranger.

"Andy, cut the garbage. What did you find?"

"Not as much as you like but as much as I'm going to." She heard the clicking of the keys. "I'd rather hack the government any day than these guys."

Who in God's name were they and what did they have to do with Mark? "Just tell me what you've got."

"Basically they're all former military—SEALs, Rangers, like that. Now they're mercs. Mercenaries, contracting to the highest bidder. Including good old Uncle Sam."

"I don't understand." She sat down on the bed, trembling slightly. Did they have something to do with Mark's capture? No, that was impossible. One of them was the brother of a young man in his unit. "Why can't you find out more about them?"

"Because they have so many firewalls I'd need a sledgehammer to break through. And they have every warning in the world on their site. Unless you have all the secret passwords all you get it a home page with a brief bio of the four partners and a place to leave a message. You know that old saying, if I tell you I'll have to kill you? I think these guys are in that business."

Faith's mouth went dry. What did it all mean? She glanced at her watch and realized it was later than she thought. "Listen Andy, thanks for doing this. I won't bother you again for a while. I promise."

"I'll hold you to that." He paused for a moment. "Faith, whatever you're into, please be careful."

"I will."

She clicked off and stared at the wall. Nothing was making sense right now. Well, it was time to get ready to see Trey Winslow. Maybe he'd have some answers for her. Or at least get her in to see this Major Gregorio.

* * * * *

Ed Romeo was pacing in the warehouse when Dan drove through the gate at Discount Records and pressed the button to open the big bay door.

"Everything okay?" His voice was tense.

"As good as can be expected," his brother told him. "Let's get loaded up."

The sleek Bell 429 stood ready, its doors open, rotors waiting for that first crank of the turbine. They'd chosen this one over others because its cabin could be reconfigured in many ways—for seats, for litters, for equipment. An all-purpose, all-mission rigged bird. And it flew faster and further than any other helicopter they'd looked at. Its graceful black presence dominated the hangar area with an air so lethal it was almost as if the inanimate object knew it was entering a high stakes game.

Troy climbed in the open door to the copter, checked the setup he'd put in place that morning and nodded to Mike and Rick. With infinite care they lifted Joey from the van to the helicopter, taking care not to dislodge any vital equipment. Rich let out a long sigh when his brother was finally in place and securely strapped in, wiping the sweat from his face with his forearm.

"Preflight's done," Ed told them. "Let's get it in gear."

In seconds everyone was in the helo, strapped in place, headphones on. Ed cranked the rotors, abnormally loud in the cavernous building, then side-slipped out through the open door. Dan opened his door slightly, pressed the button to close the big metal door and they were rolling. The helicopter was registered under a different company name, so even if someone tracked down Rick, there was no way to make a connection.

In seconds they were airborne, heading out over the Potomac. After ten minutes everyone relaxed a tiny bit, happy to have the worst of it over with.

"Don't."

The hoarse cry startled all of them. Dan turned in his seat. "What the..."

"It's Joey," Rick told him. "Jesus, of all times for him to wake up."

"He's not really awake," Troy corrected. "But he will be before long."

"Don't." The same tortured cry again. "Get away...Mark..." He started to thrash against his restraints.

"Joey." Rick bent over him. "It's okay, kid. Take it easy." He looked at Troy. "Can't you give him something? I'm afraid he'll pull out all these needles and stuff."

"Right with you, buddy." He was already filling a syringe, injecting the solution into Joey's arm. "Rick, hold him down until this stuff takes effect. We just need to keep him calm until we reach the cabin."

It seemed like an hour but in actuality less than five minutes passed before Joey relaxed back into unconsciousness.

"Well," Dan said, "maybe he's got some information after all. That makes it even more important that no one knows where he is."

No one in the copter disagreed.

* * * * *

"It's always a pleasure to see you, Faith. Come in, come in."

Trey Winslow was his usual political affable self. Faith couldn't remember ever seeing him without the practiced smile on his face and the carefully cultivated tone of welcome in his voice.

When her first book startled everyone by rocketing to the top of every bestseller list, she'd become the darling of her publisher. So when she wanted first hand information about politics for book number two, he'd arranged a meeting with his good friend, the junior senator from Rhode Island. Although at fifty-one, junior was somewhat of an erroneous description.

Now, six years later, aware of his new appointment to the Senate Armed Services committee, she was about to presume on his good graces again.

This was the first time she'd been to his home. Usually they met at his office and once for drinks at The Willard when he was in-between meetings. The house was a graceful two-storey brick with slender white columns soaring to the roof and a wide open verandah across the front.

The foyer was a miniature rotunda, with a slate floor and coffered ceiling. An elegant spiral stairway curved up to the second floor and wide doors opened to a dining room on the right and a living room on the left. The whole thing had the feeling of a movie set specifically ordered up. Cue one mansion for a well-heeled, well-connected politician. Dust with an air of old line respectability.

Tucked behind the stairway was a very masculine wood-paneled study to which he led her. Barbara Winslow was just setting a coffee tray on a low table. She held out her hand to Faith.

"I've wanted to meet you ever since Trey first mentioned you. I find your books absolutely fascinating and so true to life."

"Thank you." Faith shook her hand. "I have to thank your husband for that. He's been a wellspring of information."

"I'll leave you two to get on with it. Please come visit us again." She smiled and closed the door behind her.

Trey gestured for Faith to join him on the wide leather couch and poured coffee for them. "Black, right?" he handed her a cup.

"Yes. How nice of you to remember."

They got the obligatory "how are you" chatter out of the way, both of them aware she'd come there with an agenda.

"You've had really great success with your books, Faith." The grin appeared again. "You must feel very good about it."

She nodded. "I do. And thank you again for all the help you've given me."

"No problem. So. I gather there's another one on the horizon and that's why you're here."

"Yes, it is." She set her cup down. "I'm actually here to ask you to use your influence a little, if you wouldn't mind."

"Oh?" One eyebrow lifted.

"I'm deviating a little this time, taking a lot of the action out of Washington." She composed her words carefully. "I have a very good friend who's in the Delta Force, Mark Halloran, and I thought in this book I'd like to make that the central theme. You know, kind of dedicate it to him."

Trey cocked his head. "Delta Force? Isn't that quite a departure for you?"

"Yes, it is." She set her cup precisely in its saucer. "But as I say, Mark's a good friend of mine and I'd like to know more about Special Ops. I guess I'd like to do this as a tribute to him and the men in his unit. There's so much going on in the world now, so much danger these men are sent into. I thought it would be a good idea to give people a glimpse into what they actually do. Maybe even find out what their current mission is, if possible."

Trey was silent for a moment but a tic had developed in his left eye. He rubbed at it absently. "Getting information isn't going to be easy, even for me. Most of those missions are highly classified."

"I know but I'm hoping you can at least open some doors for me." She gave him her best smile, surprised by the sudden tension in his body "Especially with your new appointment."

He laughed, his polished political chuckle. "I'm still the new kid on the block there but why don't you tell me what it is you want?"

Casual, Faith. Don't make it seem unduly important.

"I'd really like to interview Mark's commanding officer, a Major John Gregorio, at Fort Bragg. But I can't even seem to get him to return my phone calls."

"I'm not surprised." Trey frowned. "This is a busy time for Special Ops. And exposure of any kind isn't something they encourage."

"I know. But you've had experience with me. You know I'm discreet and will accept whatever he chooses to give me." She wet her lips. "I think there's a good story to be told here." Careful, Faith. "They must be aware that every mission has a great chance of failure. I'd like to show people how carefully planned everything is, the risks analyzed and so forth."

He was silent for so long she wasn't sure he'd even answer her. Finally he leaned forward, refilled his cup and stirred sweetener into it. "All right," he said at last. "How long will you be in town?"

"Only until tomorrow. But it doesn't matter. You can always reach me on my cell. And wherever I am, if he'll see me I'll hop on the next plane."

"Fine." He rose, indicating the meeting was over. "Let me see what I can do. It will probably be tomorrow before I can get back to you."

"Whenever," she told him and held out her hand. "Thanks once again for coming to my rescue."

"Any time. I'll have the driver take you back to your hotel."

As she climbed into the limo, Faith had the distinct feeling that Trey Winslow had been very anxious to hustle her out the door.

* * * * *

136

Trey Winslow watched the limo move slowly down his driveway, eyes narrowed, muscle jumping in one cheek. Was Faith's visit mere coincidence, or did she have a deeper motive?

No, impossible. Faith was too open too easily read. Besides, how could she have gotten involved in any of this? Still, it didn't hurt to be on the alert. He'd get her entry to Fort Bragg. No harm there. Gregorio wouldn't give her anything. He knew better. But it wouldn't hurt to give everyone else a heads up.

Back in his study, he opened the bar in the cabinet and poured an inch of Crown Royal into a shot glass and tossed it back. Then he picked up the phone and punched speed dial for a number he was growing more and more reluctant to call.

"Faith Wilding was just here. You should know she's suddenly decided to write about Special Operations. Something completely different from all her other books."

There was a pause on the other end of the line. "Do you think she knows anything?"

"I don't see how she could. But it seems Halloran's a friend of hers, which makes me a little nervous. She says she wants to talk to his CO, maybe find out what his current mission is."

"Well, shit. Isn't that just dandy. Just how close is she to Halloran?"

Winslow shrugged, even though no one could see him. "It can't be much of a relationship if we don't have it on our list."

"Just the same, we need to check it out. You know how that stuff can sometimes slip through if it's way under the radar. This is an anomaly and you know how I hate that. What did she want with you, anyway?"

"An appointment with John Gregorio."

The voice on the other end barked a sharp laugh. "I don't like the sound of that. Why Halloran's CO? Why not just any Delta Force officer?"

"That's why I called you. I got the same reaction."

"She'll get nothing out of Gregorio. Even we can't get him to open his mouth."

"But we certainly can't have her running around asking questions willy-nilly. That wouldn't be good for either side of the fence we're sitting on. That's the only reason I'm doing it. Maybe if she hits a wall she'll give it up."

"Just the same, have someone look into it. You have better resources than I do. Check her out thoroughly."

"Fine. Let me know what you find out."

* * * * *

Mr. Green didn't enjoy the telephone call he got, either.

"Not one trace," he repeated. "We questioned everyone in the area. A few people vaguely remembered a black panel van but no one paid attention to the license plates, or even which direction the van went."

"Damn." The voice on the other end was harsh. "There'll be hell to pay over this. Don't think you won't come in for your share."

Mr. Green knew an apology was useless. He was not expected to make mistakes. When he did the focus of his world shifted in a bad direction.

"I'll keep looking."

"No." Sharp. Cutting. "Any more questions and you'll call too much attention to the situation. Go home and wait for my call. I'll have someone do a more thorough check on Latrobe and see if we turn anything up there."

"What about the brother?" Mr. Green asked.

"bHe supposedly works for a consulting firm called Phoenix. I think that's where we'll start."

"You'll call me?"

"When I have something."

Mr. Green disconnected the call.

"What did he say?" Mr. Brown stood nervously to the side.

"Nothing good."

Chapter Ten

She hadn't eaten much of her lunch and although her appetite lagged her stomach was grumbling. Tossing her purse on the table and kicking off her shoes, Faith ordered a light supper from room service. Then she headed for the shower, pulling her clothes off as she went.

She had just reached to turn on the water when the pain hit her, doubling her over. Just like the other day, searing and sharp, like a thousand fire ants burrowing into her skin. She gasped, trying to suck air into her lungs and ride it out. Consumed b it, she sank to the tiled floor, leaning against the tub.

Help me.

Mark! *I'm here.*

Don't...name...

What? She could barely focus her mind over the wracking pain.

Name...who you are...

Sweat covered her body as she tried for deep breaths, willing the pain to subside. Whatever hell Mark was in must be worse than anything she could imagine. She gritted her teeth and at last the intense agony eased, allowing her to concentrate on the messages.

Names. What did he mean? Whose name? Hers?

Of course. She couldn't believe she was so dense. Whoever the telepath was in the group, he was trying to intercept their messages and discover her identity.

I get it.

A long silence. Then *Good.*

She was awed at the inner strength he had that

Jungle Inferno

allowed him to hang on through whatever torture he was being subjected to. God, she had to move faster. But how?

Hang on, Mark. I promise I'll get you out of there.

And then, just like before, the presence of a dark evil rolled over her, almost choking her. She closed her eyes and huddled against the tub until at last the feeling dissipated. Then she hauled herself into the shower and stood under the water for a long time. By the time she'd dried off, pulled on her robe and admitted the room service waiter she was feeling halfway to normal again.

Except, of course, for the sickening feeling of dread lodged in her stomach. Before she sat down to eat, she pulled out her cell phone and punched in the number for Phoenix again.

"I'm still trying to reach Eric Latrobe. Please call me at any time. It's urgent."

And tomorrow, with or without Trey Winslow, she'd make John Gregorio talk to her.

* * * * *

If I get out of here, I'm going to take each of these bastards and skin them alive.

Mark kept himself together by repeating this to himself over and over. Nothing he'd been through in all his years in the Army could even come close to this and he'd been helpless at the hands of some real badass people during that time.

He was sure the multiple cuts on his body were infected. It was impossible for them not to be, as dirty as he was. It was a miracle the cut on his leg wasn't worse than it was.

Tidbit!

He had to keep himself from thinking her name

but at least he could call up her face. And the memories of that unbelievable weekend. Why had he been such an egotistical ass, thinking his career came before anything else? Thinking he had all the time in the world to tell Faith how he felt about her? To think about a life together? If he got out of this hellhole in one piece, the first thing he planned to do was put a ring on her finger.

He closed his eyes and at once her image came to him. The lushness of her naked body. The dusky nipples tipping the firm, round breasts. And the scent of her arousal. He was inside her, the walls of her cunt clutching at him, her liquid heat bathing his cock. As always he had to grit his teeth to keep from coming immediately.

He bent a head to take first one swollen nipple and then the other into his mouth, swirling his tongue around them, then nipping lightly with his teeth. His balls tightened as desire slashed through him, hot and molten.

He lifted his head to trace the edges of her mouth with his tongue before taking her in a kiss that was hungry and devouring. God, she always tasted so good. Like fresh peaches or fine wine. Her scent and her taste were everywhere inside him. He—

"I cannot help but admire you, *capitan*." Escobedo pushed aside the flap and walked into the tent and immediately the image dissipated. "I don't know another man who could have held out as long as you have with our, shall we say, inventive treatment."

Anger fueled him and gave a boost to his waning strength. "Go fuck yourself."

Escobedo's mouth turned up in an evil caricature of a smile. "Still full of spirit. I think we haven't shown you the full extent of our hospitality yet."

Mark said nothing, just waiting. The man wanted something. What now?

"Imagine our surprise to learn that one of your men actually eluded us." He shook his head. "Unbelievable. I was sure we'd gotten every one of you. My men will pay for their failure."

Joey. Still alive? And where?

"I see by the look in your eyes you know exactly who I mean." He pulled out one of his ever-present cigarillos and lit it. "Apparently your extraction team found him when we could not and brought him home, alive but unconscious."

Mark watched and waited again. Did Escobedo's contacts in the States have Joey? Was that it?

"Ah, yes. You're wondering if we've been able to retrieve him. Perhaps he might be more forthcoming about the sources of your information. Unfortunately, just as our people were about to move him to another facility, it seems he was snatched literally from under their noses."

Phoenix. That's who it had to be. Damn it, Mark, wipe that name from your brain.

But he hadn't been quick enough. Escobedo's eyes narrowed.

"I see in your eyes you know who took him. People who move like ghosts with honed precision. Well, then. We'll have to have a little discussion about who they can be. We'll have our little conversation shortly. My...guest...would like to observe and he's occupied at the moment. Enjoy the respite, *capitan*. It won't last long."

As he walked past Mark he leaned down and pressed the lighted end of the cigar against Mark's tortured chest. It was all Mark could do to swallow the scream.

Desiree Holt

* * * * *

"Aunt Vivi, I'm losing him."

Faith sat at the little table, finishing her coffee. She'd had a restless night, her dreams filled with images of Mark, flashes from their unforgettable weekend interrupted by scenes of him bloody and beaten. Twice she woke up covered with sweat and choking. When morning arrived she was more tired than when she'd gone to bed and increasingly depressed.

"Sweetheart." Vivi's voice across the distance was calming and comforting. "You have to try to separate your empathetic reactions from the telepathic messages. The pain is acting as a roadblock."

"But—"

"I know that's easier said than done. Especially because you are so receptive. But if you want to keep the thought connection viable and fight the one who's trying to interfere, you have to call on that strength I know you have."

"You're right. It's just so hard."

"Of course it is, my darling. Here's what you do. When he contacts you, close your eyes and visualize a narrow stream running between high banks. Focus on keeping the water inside those barriers. And I'll call Sarah and Emily and tell them we need to form a circle of energy. Reach out to us, Faith. Receive our strength."

"I'll try, Aunt Vivi. I'll do exactly what you say."

"When will you be home?"

"Maybe tonight. Tomorrow for sure."

"Call me as soon as you get in and I'll come over."

Faith let out a sigh of relief. "Thank you so much. For everything."

145

Her next call was to Tess.

"What time does your plane get in today?" her assistant demanded.

"I don't know yet. I may have to change my plans a little. Why?"

"Listen, Faith." Tess's voice dropped. "I don't know what you're looking for but I've dug up a bunch of stuff you need to see."

Faith's heartbeat speeded up. "Can you give me some idea of what you've got?"

"I'd rather wait until you're here. I tried—"

"Hold on a sec. My call waiting just beeped." Faith pressed the Talk button to connect to the incoming call.

"Okay, Faith." Trey Winslow was his unctuous self. "You've got your appointment with Major Gregorio. Tomorrow." He gave her the time. "Can you get there by then?"

A tiny shiver of excitement rippled through her. "He agreed to meet with me?"

"Not very happily. I had to go over his head to get it done. But I don't think you'll get much out of him."

That's what you think.

"I'll be grateful for anything he gives me. Thank you so much. I really appreciate it."

"Let me know how it goes. And of course, I want one of the first copies of the book." The artificial laugh drifted over the airwaves.

"Of course. I'll deliver it myself." She disconnected and was back with Tess. "Listen, I have to find a flight to North Carolina."

"What? Faith, I—"

"I promise to call you later. And to get home as quick as I can. Gotta run."

Dodging Tess would take some broken field running. Was it time to let her in on things? No.

Tess had no idea of Faith's psychic abilities. Faith didn't know how open the woman was to them and if the revelation would damage her credibility. No time to think about that now. She could worry about it when she was finally headed home.

She managed to snag a seat on a flight to Raleigh-Durham leaving in two hours. Once she got to the airport she cold do a search for a place to stay near Fort Bragg. Hustling, she packed her few things, checked out and was in a cab headed to the airport in thirty minutes, planning a full frontal assault on Major John Gregorio.

* * * * *

The cabin had two bedrooms. They set Joey up in the larger one. They'd take turns in the other one, since only one or two of them at a time would be sleeping. Rick helped Troy get his brother settled, then pulled up a chair next to the bed and dropped into it.

"He's still knocked out from the shot I gave him," Troy pointed out.

"I don't care. I'll just be here when he wakes up again." His jaw was set in a stubborn line.

Troy was in and out throughout the night checking on Joey's vitals, careful not to disturb Rick who dozed restlessly in the chair. When he saw the sleep the younger man had fallen into was a natural one and his vitals were stable, he disconnected all the monitors, leaving only the IV that pumped vital antibiotics and narcotics into his system.

He examined the incisions where the doctors had removed the bullets from his leg and shoulder. Neither wound had done serious damage, fortunately. The coma had been due mostly to shock and loss of blood and the trauma of the surgery.

Troy made sure to give him plenty of pain meds, then assured Rick they'd see steady improvement.

Rick grunted. "Getting him out of that hospital ought to help."

In the morning Troy brought him a steaming mug of coffee. "He's slept off the shot I gave him and his breathing's a lot more normal than when we fetched him. I think he'll wake up soon."

Rick raked his fingers through his hair. "God, I hope so."

"Something else for you to think about." Dan came into the room carrying a satellite phone. "I checked in to make sure our paying clients were being taken care of."

"And?" Rick raised his eyebrow. "We pick our staff carefully. I can't believe anything's falling through the cracks."

"That's not it. All that's going well. It's that woman."

Rick raised an eyebrow. "Woman?"

"Faith Wilding. She's left three more messages for you." One corner of his mouth lifted in a grin. "Are you sure this isn't one of the many women you've blazed your path of destruction through?"

"Damn it. No. You think I'm such a shithead I wouldn't remember?" He made a sound of disgust. "Anyway, no one I ever slept with would call me Eric. I can't think of a single person who uses that name any more."

"Well, she's damned anxious to talk to you." He held out the sat phone. "Find out what she wants."

"Not until Joey's awake and I can get a handle on things. Right now that's all that's important."

At that moment his brother groaned, a raw sound that made the hair on Rick's neck stand up. He leaned over the bed.

"Joey? It's me, kid."

Joey's hand flailed and Troy locked his fingers around the younger man's wrists to keep him from knocking himself loose from the equipment.

"Give him a second," he told the others. "He's coming around but he's fighting it."

Troy was right. In a moment Joey settled back and his eyelids opened slowly. When he caught sight of Rick bending over him a look of shock spread over his face.

"Rick?" His voice sounded as if it was scraped from the bottom of a barrel. "God. That really you?"

"It's me, kid."

Joey struggled to sit up and they had to restrain him again.

"Take it easy," Rick told him. "Wherever you were, you're safe now."

The younger man's head fell back on the pillow, pain slashing across his face. His breath rasped from his lungs. "Safe. A joke."

"Joey?" Dan moved to the bedside. "Are you up to talking at all?"

"What he needs is rest," Rick told them.

"No." The word rasped from his throat. "Have to tell you. Need...to talk."

Troy filled a glass with water, stuck a straw in it and helped Joey to sit up so he could take a few sips "Just go easy, okay?"

"Rick," he began again. "Please. Listen."

Rich looked up at Troy, who nodded his head.

"Okay, kid. Let's have it."

"They're all...Oh God." Tears filled his eyes. "They're all dead. Everyone except Mark."

The men looked at each other. Finally Dan asked, "The whole unit?"

Joey nodded. "They were...waiting for us. Someone told them we were coming."

The tangos had been ready for them, guns

chattering even before the unit was fully in place. All hit. Except for Joey, who was already settled high in a tree.

The young man's eyes were haunted as he told about the dead men dragged to the campsite in the bowels of the Peruvian jungle and burned. And Mark, beaten and bleeding, dragged away.

"Shit." Rick ground out the word. "Fuck all anyway."

"Are you sure Halloran's still alive?" Dan asked.

"Yes." Joey's breathing was labored but he was obviously determined to get his story out. "They wanted to find out who told us about this meeting and where it would be. He'll...hold out...but..."

"According to your CO, you were almost dead when the team found you," Rick told him. "I'll be lighting candles over this for a long time."

Joey drew in a painful breath, forcing himself to speak again. "Do you know... Is anyone getting the captain out?"

The men all looked at each other. "We didn't even know he was still alive until just now. And the government isn't real good about sharing information."

"If we get a map can you show us where you were?" Dan asked.

"Yeah. Only... I know they moved Mark." He nodded toward the water again and Troy lifted the straw to his lips. "The place where they met wasn't their permanent camp."

"That's enough for now." Troy gave Joey another sip of water, then waved everyone out of the room. "You too, Rick. This little bit has drained him."

They could see that, despite his fierce need to tell them everything, Joey's strength had waned. The meds kicked in and his eyes slammed shut.

Troy eased him back down to the pillow.

"Let's talk." Dan led them out of the room and they settled around the table. He took the lead, a grim look on his face. "We've got to get details," he said, giving voice to what was in everyone's mind.

"When Joey wakes up again I'll get some nourishment into him," Troy told them. "Then we'll let Rick handle the rest of the questions. Everyone okay with that?"

They all nodded.

"Let's figure out what we need to do and divvy it up." Dan reached behind him to the counter and snagged a pad of paper. "Rick and I will work with Joey on the map of Peru. We'll have to try to figure out where the tangos moved Mark to. Where their permanent base might be. That will be the hardest."

"It won't be that far from the meet," Mike pointed out. "They were walking, remember?"

Dan shook his head. "We don't know that. They could have had their vehicles concealed."

"And we need to keep in mind," Mike pointed out, "that by now Mark could really be dead."

Heavy silence dropped like a thick fog.

"Someone needs to talk to John Gregorio," Dan said at last. "Find out what the fuck is really happening."

"I'll do it." Rick's voice was harsh. "I served under him and he's the one who called me about Joey. He'll open up to me. If he can."

"Rick, you need to call that Wilding woman back too," Dan told him. "Just on the wild-ass chance she's somehow connected to all this."

Rick lifted an eyebrow. "How would that even be possible?"

"Don't know. It's just a strange coincidence that she pops up out of nowhere while this is all going on. Meanwhile I want to check the security setup again. Mike, take a walk outside and make sure everything smells all right."

"Okay."

Rick pulled the scrap of paper from his pocket where he'd written down the number and punched it in. He listened, frowned and disconnected. "This time I got her voice mail. She said to leave a message."

"Then do it," Arsenault told him. "Get her to call again."

Rick made the call and left the message before setting the phone back on the table. "I'm going to check on my brother again. If she calls back, come get me."

* * * * *

At the moment, however, Faith was focused on other things. She'd rented a car at the airport, debated calling Major Gregorio to let him know she was on the way then decided against it. Why give him a chance to shut her down? She found a hotel to stay at and did her best to get some lseep. Unfortunately her nerves were in nhigh gear, plsu she kept waiting for Mark to contact her again. She'd had two cups of tea, which unfortunately did not settle her nerves. Now she was at one of the gates, drumming her fingers on the steering wheel impatiently while the sentry called to verify her appointment.

Through the windshield she saw men and women in camouflage and others in uniform hurrying from place to place. Cars sped along the roadways, joined by occasional motorcycle. Overhead she heard the roar of engines as planes took off and landed. She knew Fort Bragg was a large, busy place—Mark's Delta Force unit wasn't the only one based here—but the sheer size of the place was overwhelming.

"All right, Miss Wilding." The sentry handed her identification back to her. "You're cleared to Major Gregorio's office." With concise words he gave her directions. "Oh and thirty miles an hour, okay?"

"Thank you. I'll try to keep my lead foot off the accelerator." She stashed her ID, waited until he lifted the gate and rolled slowly onto the base.

She considered herself lucky that she found a parking place right next to the building and a Ranger who looked too young to be in the Army who could direct her to the office itself. Too young to go out and die, she thought. Then she realized he wasn't much younger than Mark when he'd enlisted.

John Gregorio was polite but far from welcoming when she entered his office. He extended his hand but she could tell it was ingrained courtesy and not from any real pleasure at seeing her. He was immaculate in his uniform but his face was lined with worry and fatigue. His eyes were cold as they assessed her and there wasn't a hint of a smile on his face.

"Thank you for seeing me, Major." She tried to make her voice as conciliatory as possible. "I know you're a busy man."

"When a member of the committee overseeing the Armed Services makes a request it isn't good form not to grant it." He gestured toward the wall behind her and she was startled to see another man standing there."

"I'm sorry." She was confused. "If I'm interrupting something..."

"Colonel Frank Ryan." The man held out his hand but like Gregorio, there was n o welcome in the gesture. "Major Gregorio reports to me."

Faith's pulse sped up and she had a sinking feeling in her stomach. This wasn't really going to be quite as easy as she'd hoped. Did they already know what she wanted? No. That was impossible. So. Something was up.

"Thanks to you too," she said, hoping her sudden attack of nerves didn't show. "I know you must have better things to do than spend your time with me. Especially when I'm just looking for background information for a new book I'm writing."

"Why don't you have a seat, Miss Wilding." Ryan moved forward and held out a chair for her.

Faith dropped into it and busied herself pulling out her notepad and pen. "I'll try not to take too much of your time," she began. "I believe Senator Winslow explained I'm working on my latest book and wanted information about Delta Force and Special Ops." She tried out a smile. "I like to make sure what I write is as authentic as possible."

"Let's just cut to the chase," Gregorio said, his eyes like ice. "We know who you are and I'm not just referring to Faith Wilding the author. You've called a dozen times and left messages for me in the past two days. As soon as the senator called to wave his privilege in front of my nose I checked you out."

Ryan pulled up another chair and sat next to you. "What we want to know is why at this particular moment you're asking questions about Delta Force, the branch of the Army that your friend Mark Halloran's in. What's your role in all of this?"

Faith just stared at him. Now what did she say?

Chapter Eleven

Faith wet her lips. "I don't understand what you mean. I just—"

"Cut the crap. You can forget about this story you've dreamed up. I know you and Halloran have been friends since childhood. What is it that has your tail in such a crack you're pestering me with calls and using influence to force me to see you?"

She didn't know what to say. There was no way she could tell them the truth. These hard-eyed men would never believe her. But she had to tell them something. They didn't look at all as if they'd let her just get up and walk out.

"I..." She stopped, swallowed and began again. "I'm just trying to get some information about Mark. I haven't heard from him for a long time."

"You could have called his parents," Gregorio pointed out. "I understand you're very close to them."

Well. They had done their homework after all, it seemed. "Mark doesn't tell his family very much." No. That was the wrong thing to say.

Ryan lifted an eyebrow. "And he'd tell you things he'd keep from them?"

This wasn't going well at all. She drew in a breath and let it out slowly. "All right. Please don't think I'm an idiot when I say this but I think Mark's in great danger."

Both men did their best to control their expressions but she'd hit a nerve. Something flickered in both pairs of eyes, although it was quickly blanked. Neither spoke for a moment. Gregorio broke the silence first.

"Exactly what makes you think that? Has

someone told you something?"

"Not... No, no one."

"Not what?" Ryan asked. "There's something you're holding back and I think you need to tell us."

"But I... That is..."

"Miss Wilding." Gregorio leaned forward. "We're in a somewhat delicate situation here. If you're as close to Mark as you say you are, then you know his missions are as covert as they come. So how in the hell would you have any idea what's going on with him at this particular moment?"

Faith twisted her hands together. The situation was rapidly deteriorating.

"I'd hate to have to detain you," Ryan told her. "But if you have information not available to civilians, I want to know what it is and how you got it."

Her shoulders slumped and she leaned back in then straight chair. "All right. You'll probably think I'm crazy but I'll tell you." She screwed up her courage and sat up straighter. "Are you aware that Mark is a telepath?"

The two men stared at each other. "How the hell do you know about that?" Gregorio finally asked. "Who have you been talking to?"

"No one." She spread her hands before her. "Are you telling me you know about this? That you don't think this is some kind of insanity?"

Ryan looked as if he was choosing his words carefully. "I can only tell you that the military has been aware for years that some people have...special abilities. That there are ongoing projects to determine how to refine them and best use them. We've been able to tap into Mark's...talents on a few occasions when it saved our bacon."

Faith just looked at them. "So you believe me."

"Let's say we don't doubt you," Gregorio answered. "How exactly do you know about it? And are you trying to tell us you have the same ability?"

"Mark and I discovered when we were in high school that we could communicate with each other this way. We've done it ever since then." Her lips twisted in a tiny smile. "It beats the telephone, especially when you aren't close to one."

"Go on," Ryan encouraged. Obviously from his attitude he knew about Mark's special talent but his voice was still far from friendly.

"I have an aunt who has the same abilities. She introduced me to The Lotus Circle and its members have helped me hone my skills."

She went on to explain about TLC, about all the conversations she and Mark had telepathed during the years. About their relationship, which she still was at a loss to define. And about the messages he'd been sending for the past few days.

"He said someone betrayed him," she told them. "I think all of his men were killed except for him. He's in terrible pain. I think they're torturing him to find out how you knew about whoever these people are." She turned and looked Ryan square in the eye. "I came here to see if you knew this and what you were doing to find him." Her throat tightened. "I don't think he can hold on much longer."

For the next hour both men questioned her so intently she began to feel like a bug when it had been skewered.

At last Gregorio sat back in his chair and looked at Ryan. "What do we do with her? We can't let her run around loose."

"I don't think you want to try detaining me." She jutted out her chin. "If you believe in telepathic communications, you know I don't need a

157

telephone or computer to send messages no matter where you hide me." She glared at Gregorio. "And you wouldn't be happy with the people I'd contact."

If looks could kill, she'd have been dead right then.

"You're playing with high security here," Gregorio continued. "What guarantees do we have that you won't make this public the minute you walk out that door?"

"I don't think Miss Wilding will be running to any newspapers," Ryan said. He gave her his hard stare. "Am I right?"

"I'm only concerned about Mark," she cried, anger and desperation in her voice. "Why do you think I went to so much trouble to get here? I just want to make sure someone goes after him. That you aren't hanging him out to dry."

Ryan's lips thinned. "I take the welfare of my men very seriously."

"Do you even know where he is now? He said they moved him. Are you already planning a way to rescue him?"

"Miss Wilding," Gregorio began in his frigid voice.

"Don't patronize me." She was spitting fire. "Why haven't you gone after him already? What's holding you back?"

The men exchanged glances but said nothing. A light went on in her brain. "You've been told not to. Right?" She slammed her hand on the desk. "God damn it. I don't believe this."

"Listen." Frustration was written all over Gregorio's face.

"Let me," Ryan interjected. "We have, let's say some challenges with this situation. That's the reason I'm here instead of sitting behind my desk at MacDill in Tampa. But whatever we do, we have to do it right."

"Right? Right?" She stood up, eyes flashing. "There's only one right way. Go in and do it and politics be damned." She started toward the door.

"Stop." Gregorio's voice was like a whiplash.

Faith halted in mid-stride.

"I will not let Captain Halloran down. Colonel Ryan and I are looking at some alternatives at this very moment."

"The best thing you can do for Mark now," Ryan told her, "is to go home and let us take care of things."

She fought to get her temper under control. "Fine. Thank you for your time, gentlemen."

But as she started her car and headed toward the gate, her mind was already churning with options, convinced that Mark's only real opportunity for rescue lay with her.

* * * * *

"You won't like what I found."

Trey Winslow didn't like getting the call, never mind what he was about to hear. It could only be news of the worst kind. "What is it?"

"First of all, you know for some time the military has been investigating the value of psychic abilities, especially with reference to covert ops. And other...specialized missions."

Winslow grunted. "Yeah, but I don't believe in all that junk."

"You'd better believe in it." The voice was hard and sharp. "It's been proven too many times."

"So what does that have to do with us?"

"Halloran was one of the men tested for a special program. A psi program, they're calling it, dealing with paranormal abilities."

159

"So? Get to the point."

"It means, you idiot, he can send messages through mental telepathy. He and the Wilding woman have been friends for years. Telepathy is direct transference of thought from one person, called a sender or agent, to another, called a receiver or percipient, without using the usual sensory channels of communication. Do you get that?"

"I don't know if—"

"You don't know anything, you ass. How big a leap is it to believe she has the same abilities? That they can send messages back and forth to each other?"

"Jesus Christ." Winslow sat up abruptly. "Let's say I even believe a little of it. Do you mean he could be contacting her from...from where he is?"

"That's just what I mean."

Winslow felt sweat begin to gather on his face and neck. "So what do we do about it?"

"I'm already taking care of things from this end." The tone of disgust was unmistakable. "Which I wouldn't have to do if you'd been a little more thorough yourself."

"Listen—"

"No, you listen. I'll clean up your mess. Just try not to make another one."

* * * * *

"We'll all go to hell for this." Mr. Green was hunched into a corner of the diner, drinking a cup of dreadful coffee, praying that his indigestion was the worst thing that would happen to him.

They'd chosen this particular place, a blip on the highway from DC to Annapolis, because no one they knew ever came here. Mr. Brown had once had a flat tire almost in the parking lot and waited there for road service.

"I think we're already in hell," Mr. Brown said. "One taste of the coffee and he'd switched to a soft drink.

"Funny how things look and feel different when you aren't talking about people. Just money. Everything's in the abstract. You know?"

Mr. Green took a swallow of coffee, made a face and pushed the cup away. "I guess I've gotten used to the killing as long as its thousands of miles away, I don't have to see who's being shot and I'm not pulling the trigger."

"Like I said. The abstract."

Mr. Green waved away the waitress with her coffee pot of sludge. "I can't see how this woman can possibly be a threat. She knows nothing and there's no way for her to find out anything."

Mr. Brown shrugged. "The top dog's afraid she'll start digging in the name of research for one of her damn books. And our resident geek discovered she knows Halloran. Too much coincidence for everyone's taste." He looked out the grimy window. "I warned him to wait until we were sure she was a danger. You don't make a famous author disappear without repercussions."

"You know how he is when he gets the bit between his teeth."

"He's protecting his own precious ass," Mr. Brown spat out. "Whatever we do, it had better be done with great care. I don't plan to be any sacrificial lamb."

"What we really should be doing is finding those guys who took Latrobe out of Walter Reed right under our noses." Mr. Green frowned. "That operation was too slick to be carried out by just a bunch of amateurs."

"Well, if we don't take care of both problems we won't be around to spend any of that money we've sold our souls for."

"I think we need to try some alternatives first. It's not like she's banging on every door in Washington. And we need to be sure what her real agenda is."

"So?" Mr. Brown frowned. "What do you have in mind?"

"Let's see if we can put a little fear into Miss Wilding and get her out of our hair."

"Fear? How? What are you thinking of?"

"I've got some ideas." He drained the water glass in front of him. Anything to get rid of the battery acid taste of the coffee.

"And then there's Latrobe. We've got the geek digging for everything he can find on him. Someone planned the little hospital episode slick as a whistle. He's got a brother nobody knows much about that we need more information on. Who the hell else would even be interested in him?"

Mr. Brown lifted a shoulder. "Beats me. But we won't get anything done hiding out in greasy spoons." He rose and dropped some dollar bills on the table. "Come on. We'll go back to my place, check on the geek's progress and you can tell me all about your big ideas."

* * * * *

Faith thanked all the good luck charms in the world that she was able to snag a seat on a plane for San Antonio leaving within the hour. She had to change planes in Dallas but she'd get into SAT about a quarter to six. She went through security and headed for the gate, stopping to pick up a cold drink on the way.

Seated in the waiting area, she pulled out her cell phone and called Tess.

"My plane gets in just before six," she told her assistant. "Can you still pick me up?"

Tess's chuckle sounded strained. "Only you would ask me to drive through the rush hour logjam on I10. Sure, I'll fetch you. I'll call in the order for our food and we can pick it up on the way to the house." She paused. "Are you okay? You don't sound too chipper."

"I'm fine." Liar. "I'm anxious to see what you dug up for me."

"Listen, Faith." Tess began and stopped.

"Yes?" Faith prodded.

"Nothing. I need to wait until you get here and show this to you. Be careful, okay?"

Faith disconnected the call, wondering if Tess was just giving her usual travel warning or if she'd actually found something disturbing. The indicator on her phone showed messages, so she clicked to access them. Two from Abigail. She'd have to call her back. One from her mother asking if she'd be around to come for dinner Sunday. A call from Trey Winslow asking if she'd kept her appointment at Fort Bragg and did she get what she needed.

And one from a voice so devoid of emotion it sent shivers along her spine.

"This is Eric Latrobe. I can't imagine what we'd have to discuss or who suggested you call me. However, if you leave another message at Phoenix I'll get back to you."

No hello or goodbye. Well, a pleasure talking to you too, Mr. Latrobe.

She dialed the now familiar number to the Phoenix answering machine, told him where she was and gave him both numbers again. Her luck he'd call back while she was on the plane and her phone was off.

She was still fuming over her meeting at Fort Bragg. She wished she'd carried a better feeling out of that office with her but all she had was a mixture of anger and dread. She wasn't a neophyte, oblivious to what went on in the world. She'd heard and read enough about failed missions where no cleanup crew went in because it was deemed to admit the details would be politically embarrassing. How many men had been left behind because of politics?

She wanted to throw up. Yet she sensed that Ryan and Gregorio were as frustrated as she was. The difference was, she wasn't hampered by rules and restrictions. Unfortunately she had no idea how to go about a rescue mission. If only she at least had some idea where in Peru Mark was. It was a big country.

Maybe Tess had something in whatever she'd dug up.

Tidbit!

She startled. Mark.

Watch yourself...danger...

Danger. Well, that certainly wasn't news.

I will.

A long silence, while she strained to receive anything at all. Then...

I love you. Don't ever...forget

I expect you to tell me in person.

She waited, shutting out everything around her but nothing else came through. Finally she slumped back in her chair, nauseated and shaking, with a distinct feeling she was running out of time.

* * * * *

"Joey's awake again." Troy Arsenault walked

out of the bedroom. "I'm going to heat up some soup for him. As soon as I get it into him, Rick, you can talk to him again."

"I'll feed him." Rick rose from the chair where he was sitting, poring over the map of Peru.

"Okay. Just small sips, though. We need to make sure he can eat without barfing it back up."

It was a long process, made more so by Joey's anxious need to talk and Rick's insistence that he eat first. Finally the soup was all gone, Troy had checked Joey's vitals again and given him a lighter dose of the pain medication, just enough to keep him comfortable but still lucid. They propped him up with pillows, taking care not to jostle his wounds and finally they gathered around, Rick sitting beside him.

"Okay, kid." His voice was gentle. "Think you're up to this?"

"I have to be," he croaked. "You gotta get Mark outta there."

"Start at the beginning," Rick told him.

"No one knew the details of the mission but us," he began, his voice stronger than before. "You know how it goes, Rick. Once the order comes down, the unit's in isolation."

"Which means," Mike interjected, "the leak had to come from the top, from someone near whoever gave the order."

Joey nodded. "There's no one at Fort Bragg who knew enough about it to tell anyone anything."

"So what happened?" Rick asked.

"We were told the terrorists headquartered near Iquito, because it isn't easy to get to them." He spoke haltingly, choosing his words. "Only by air and water, so they can pretty much set up a wide defense perimeter. They headquarter in the jungle and that's where the meet was set. Whoever gave us the info also had the coordinates."

"Who knew the location?" This from Mike.

"Whoever set the mission. Major Gregorio, Colonel Ryan and us."

"And the people at the top," Mike reminded him.

"Yeah." Joey frowned, "You don't think..."

"Anything is possible, kid. But we're not jumping to conclusions here."

"Go on," Rick urged him. Joey's agitation was obvious. Getting him back on track would help him pull himself together.

"The insertion was smooth as glass. We went all the way by helicopter. Took a little longer but we didn't have to expose ourselves changing vehicles. The helo took us to the insertion point, about two miles from the target area." He looked around at the faces watching him. "I think we weren't too far from the Amazon, either. The jungle comes right down to the river."

He went on to tell them how they'd stealthily made their way to the spot, sure they were undetected. Joey had climbed up and positioned himself in the tree and as the others crept forward, the tangos had opened fire, cutting them down. He was sure they didn't kill Mark because they wanted to get information from him.

"It was a massacre. And then, when those animals burned up the bodies..." He couldn't help the tears in his eyes.

"It's okay, kid." Rick squeezed his arm. "We'll do what we have to."

"I think whoever is calling the shots wanted to get rid of all of us," Joey told him.

Rick's face tightened. "What do you mean?"

"I kind of drifted in and out the last couple of days at the hospital. I had a funny feeling I'd be better off if no one knew I was awake." He reached for the water glass. "Anyway, these two guys came into my room the day before you got me out. They talked about moving me someplace and finding out what I knew."

"Gregorio anticipated as much," Rick said, his fists clenching. "That's why he called me."

"I think it's time for you to pay the major a visit," Dan told him. "See if they're going to do anything about getting Mark out."

"If they can't move because they're handcuffed politically, we'll have to do it ourselves, you know."

"A done deal," Dan agreed. "Go make your arrangements."

They all looked at each other as Rick walked out of the room, each of them mentally gearing up for what they knew was ahead of them.

* * * * *

Mark wasn't sure if he'd dozed or simply fallen into unconsciousness. The sun had been broiling overhead when he closed his eyes, the heat settling in the tent like a suffocating blanket. Not even a whisper of a breeze stirred the jungle trees. The heat still enveloped him but through the tent flap he could see darkness outside and hear the now familiar songs of the night birds.

His skin felt hot to the touch and he wasn't sure if it was from the tropical sun or a fever raging through his body. Sweat had mingled with the dirt on his skin forming a layer of mud. He tried to clean his wounds with a little of the water they brought him each day but he didn't put much faith in his efforts. He wasn't even sure how safe the water was but letting more dust pile up in the open cuts or his body becoming totally dehydrated was a more unpleasant prospect. Maybe the easiest thing to do was just give in to it and die.

No! Get it together, Halloran. You've never given up before. Don't start now. You finally got your head out of your butt enough to realize you love Tidbit and even sent her a message. Are you going to wimp out now and let these bastards kill you before you can tell her in person?

Memories of their unbelievable weekend washed over him. The feel of her lush body, the silken smoothness of her skin. Her muscles clenching around him like a hot, wet glove, pulling him deeper into her. Pulling him home.

Home. Shit, he'd certainly taken long enough to understand that's where it was. With her. Talk about having a thick skull. Maybe the whacks he'd taken on the head here had knocked some sense into him.

Right at the moment he'd give everything he owned to be with her, the love of his life. In a bedroom with soft light spilling over them and clean sheets beneath them. To taste her mouth that was sweet as honey and inhale her fragrance.

He closed his eyes again and she was there, her body close to his. This time she was on her knees beside him, her back delicately curved as she bent over him. Slim fingers wrapped themselves around his throbbing cock.

"Mmmm," she hummed, as her tongue darting out to lick the drop of pre-cum from the slit at the top of the ultra-sensitive head.

She did it again. And again, her tongue like a wet flame brushing over him, igniting nerves he didn't even know he had. When she dipped the tip of her tongue into the slit his cock jerked in her hand.

"Suck me," he growled in a low voice.

Obediently she opened her mouth and slowly took his shaft inside. The thick, ropy vein pulsed against her tongue, every drop of blood in his body shooting straight to that spot.

She set up the familiar motion, the one that took him to heaven and back. Except that when she did this, heaven was a raging inferno, consuming him. The silken wash of her liquid bathed him, the sensation making his hips jerk upward, his cock riding deeper into her mouth.

She slid her mouth from the head to the root, pausing before moving upward again, the movement so slow and deliberate it was exquisite torture. She did it again, this time slipping one small hand between his thighs to roll his balls with her fingers.

"Harder," he urged. "Faster."

She hummed again, this time a purr of satisfaction, and increased the tempo of hand and mouth. Down, up. In, out. Pressure on his balls. Fire in his groin. More, more, more.

He exploded, erupting into her mouth like a dormant geyser, spurting over and over. She swallowed every bit, squeezing his cock and his balls to draw the very last drop from him. When he was spent she slid her lips down the length of him one last time before releasing him. When she pressed her mouth to his he could taste himself on her lips, a flavor carried deep inside him when she thrust her tongue into him, seeking a mating with his own. A dance they'd done many times.

Only when she'd explored every inch of his mouth and carried every drop of his cum still resting on her tongue through that wet cavern did she finally sit back on her heels. And smile, that wonderful, secret smile.

"I love you, Mark."

He lifted a hand weakly and stroked her arm.

"I love you, too, darlin'. More than you can possibly know."

But even as he continued to reach for her the feel of her dissipated and she faded away. He opened his eyes to nothing but the empty tent, filth and pain. Somehow he'd find a way out of this mess. Back to Faith. Back to the woman who held his heart

And tell her he wanted to spend the rest of his life with her.

If he survived this hellhole, that is.

Stop thinking about it.

Okay, try to figure out who pulled the trigger on you and got you into this mess.

One more time. The source had gotten information to Rick Latrobe, former SpecOps. He'd given it to his brother who'd passed it along to Mark, the unit commander. Mark had shared it only with Major Gregorio. He'd taken it to his CO, Major Ryan who'd gone straight to the top at JSOC. From there it went to the Pentagon. And the order finally came back from the top. Take out the Wolf and the burgeoning Al Qaeda cell working to pick up the slack left by Shining Path. Erase them as if they never existed. Get rid of one of the most notorious arms dealers and a group of men bent on wreaking nine kinds of havoc from Peru all the way to the States. They could ignore Tupac Amaru; they had become too small and insignificant to matter.

No one else on base knew the details and the unit was isolated during the planning session. And they were never out of each other's sight from that moment until wheels up from Fort Bragg. He trusted John Gregorio with his life—frequently did, as a matter of fact—and Frank Ryan was on that list too.

So how many people along the way knew about it and who was the wink link? Someone at SpecOps headquarters at MacDill? At JSOC? The Pentagon? Any of the possibilities made him sick, He hated to think that anyone who held the fate of the country in his hands would sell out to death merchants, although he knew it had happened before.

He was still dissecting the possibilities when the tent flap opened and the Wolf entered. Even after a week in the Peruvian jungle in accommodations far more rudimentary than anything he was used to, he still looked immaculate and self-possessed. The same arrogant look was still stamped on his face.

"Well, Captain Halloran. I have to say you're disrupting my life far more than I like. Not to mention forcing me to stay in this pigsty much longer than I planned."

"Isn't that just too damn bad." Mark's throat felt raw. Speaking had become an effort and he knew he shouldn't keep pissing this people off but he just couldn't help it. If they were going to kill him—and he was sure they'd get to it sooner or later—at least he'd have the satisfaction that he never gave in to them. They'd remember that Captain Mark Halloran cursed them until his last breath.

"My patience is running out." He took out one of his cigarillos, lit it and blew out a stream of smoke. "I know my reputation. Part of it is built on the fact that as long as I have been in business no one has ever been able to pinpoint any of my meetings. It makes my customers feel secure in their dealings with me. You seem to have found a way to change that. So there it is. I want to know how someone found out about this one."

I can't give up Alex. We have to protect him at

all costs. He risked his life to help us do this. I may have to let them kill me after all.

No, not yet. Not until he knew who pulled the plug on his mission. Somehow he had to stay alive and avoid giving up information until he knew that and could somehow pass that on. Despite the pain that racked his body, he managed to return the Wolf's stare.

"And of course there is the even more urgent matter of the recipient of your so-called mind messages." He shook his head. "I hardly believe in such hocus pocus but both Escobedo and Felix assure me it's true. You've put someone out there in danger, Captain. We will learn who it is and dispose of them."

Mark never broke eye contact, putting as much hatred into his eyes as possible.

"No comment?" The smile on the man's face was a grotesque mockery of humor. "I must say, your stamina and endurance amaze me. Most men would have broken long before this. Well." He looked at the tip of the cigarillo. "Well. Enjoy your rest, Captain. In a very short while we'll be inviting you to answer questions again. I hope this time you show a little more willingness to cooperate. We will find out who your contact is. Make no mistake about it."

Mark watched the man leave, trying to still his racing heart. He had to protect Faith at all costs. He only hoped that whatever she was doing to help him, she being extremely careful about it. He had to trust her good judgment and common sense. And pray that she'd been able to find the right people.

Tidbit. Are you there?
Please be there. Please, please, please.
I'm here.
*Watch yourself...danger...*And finally, finally,

getting the words out. *I love you.*
Tell me in person, soldier.
Oh God, Tidbit. I pray I'll be able to.

* * * * *

Ed Romeo flew Rick in the smaller of Phoenix's
Bell helicopters to a private air strip outside
Raleigh, where the owner had a black SUV waiting
for him. The man was an old friend of the Romeos
and while his shrewd eyes scanned Rick's face, he
asked no questions. He knew what the brothers did
and was glad to help in any way he could.

In less than an hour Rick was driving through
the gate at Fort Bragg, thanking his old Army
credentials and blessing the sentry who got a
telephone call at that exact moment and so didn't
look as closely at them as he should. It hadn't been
that long since he'd been based here himself and he
knew the way to John Gregorio's office without
directions.

No one gave him a second look as he parked
and made his way into the building and down the
corridor to the scarred door. He opened it without
knocking, startled to see Colonel Frank Ryan
standing beside Major Gregorio's desk.

Gregorio looked up at the interruption. His
eyes said he knew why Rick was there.

"Did you get Joey?" were the first words out of
his mouth.

"Yes. We've got him stashed."

Gregorio blew out a breath of relief. "Thank
God. I was afraid the people who leaked the mission
might have, shall we say, plans for him."

"They did." Rick's lips thinned. "The kid
actually had two visitors who discussed it in his
room, thinking he was unconscious. That was

before I got my buddy up there to sit with him until I got back. But yeah, we got him out in time."

"Good. Where is he?"

Rick shook his head. "Sorry, Major. Even you don't get that information."

Gregorio started to say something, then just sat back in his chair.

"We're on your side, Rick," Ryan told him. "Don't forget that."

"Oh, yeah? Then tell me what you're doing to find Halloran."

"You know it's not that easy," Gregorio told him. "I don't have the luxury of mounting an operation without official sanction. If I did, I'd lead it myself."

"John's not in this alone," the colonel added. "That's why I'm here. I've been calling in every chit I have, trying to fight my way up the ladder past the roadblocks."

"And not having any luck," Rick guessed.

Ryan lifted a shoulder. "Face it. We don't even know if anyone's still alive."

"Halloran's still alive. Joey told us and I know he told you. Are you planning to leave one of your best team leaders to the sophisticated torture of those terrorists?"

The major banged his fist on the desk. "You think I don't feel the same thing you do? Right now I'm about ready to resign my commission and get down there myself."

"But you won't do that." Ryan's voice was firm. "You won't because you have a big responsibility here and a lot of other men who depend on you.

Gregorio made a rude noise. "How much do you think they'll depend on me if they find out I let this get away from me?"

"The thing is, Rick," Ryan added, "it appears

there's a determined effort to slam the door shut on this. No one wants to listen, no one wants to know. Something funny's going on and I can't figure out what."

"I'd say whoever leaked the word is covering his ass." Gregorio's lips thinned. "And it's obviously someone high up enough to do this." He slammed his fist on the desktop. "Damn it to hell. I'd like to find him and squeeze the life out of him myself."

"All right. Enough." Rick's voice cut into the back and forth. "I came here to ask you face-to-face what you were doing. I get the answer. Nothing." He opened and closed his fists. "Fine. And I understand what you're facing. But there is one thing you can do. Don't get in my way."

"Listen," Gregorio began.

"No, you listen, Major. That could be me stuck in the bowels of the Peruvian jungle. I've been on enough missions like this that had every chance of going south. And this one's a little different for me. Mark Halloran had my brother's six all the way. Now I need to have his."

Gregorio's face was twisted in frustration. "You don't need to remind me of that."

"And one more thing. We have to protect the source at all costs. He came to me. I won't sell him out."

"Understood."

"Rick." Ryan moved toward him. The expression on his face was hard and unyielding. "Will this be a Phoenix operation?"

"Don't say it, Colonel." Rick felt the anger building inside him at the question. Not everyone approved of the company's existence and what it did. "Whatever it is."

Ryan's face relaxed and he held out his hand. "I just wanted to wish you good luck. And please.

Don't tell us anything until afterwards."

Rick took the man's hand and shook it. The grasp was firm. "I'll pass that along." One corner of his mouth turned up. "Afterwards."

Five minutes later he was speeding away from Fort Bragg, cell phone to his ear as he filled Dan in on the conversation.

Chapter Twelve

By the time her flight landed in San Antonio, Faith felt as if every nerve in her body had been unwrapped and sandpapered. There was no message on her cell phone from Eric Latrobe and the more she thought about her meeting at Fort Bragg, the madder she got. Time was spinning out of control and she was powerless to stop it. Maybe if she could at least figure out where in Peru Mark was... No. Who the hell was she kidding? She had no way to mount a rescue operation. She had no contacts, no resources.

And she didn't think Trey Winslow would stick his neck out for her. It wasn't just that he put his image and position before anything else. She'd learned that during her first interview with him. No, it was something else. Trey wasn't one ever to get his hands dirty with something that might spray blowback on that carefully constructed political career.

But who the hell else was there? All through the plane ride she'd racked her brain for a name, a contact. Anything at all. A place to start.

"I know this isn't what you want to hear," Tess said when she pulled up outside baggage claim, "but you look like shit."

"And thank you so very much." Faith fastened her seat belt, then leaned back and closed her eyes. "Could I please wake up and find out it's last week instead of today?"

Tess was silent while she negotiated the exit traffic. "You know," she said once they were on the Interstate, "we've known each other a long time. I'd like to think by this time you felt you could trust me with whatever it is that's dragging you down."

"Oh Tess." Faith pressed her fingers to her temples. "I'm not sure I'd even know where to begin."

"Why don't you just lean back and relax for the moment. We'll pick up the food and get to your house. I'll show you what I've found digging around on the Internet. And maybe that will shake a few things loose from you."

Faith had seldom been so glad to arrive home. She put her laptop on the floor next to her overnighter and tossed her purse onto the little hall table.

"I need to check my email and answering machine, before I do anything. Abby's probably going crazy. I haven't answered any of her cell phone messages so there have to be a ton of them here."

"No. Go shower, we'll eat, then you can play catch-up. Give yourself a break."

Faith showered and pulled on shorts and a t-shirt, while Tess set out the food. She called Abby and soothed her anxieties, then allowed herself to be distracted from any messages that night be waiting for her. However, she resisted Tess's efforts to get her to eat before looking at what the latest research had uncovered. She was too edgy and too anxious to see what the Internet had turned up. They sat at the kitchen table, sharing sweet and sour shrimp and cashew chicken while Tess dug the printed sheets out of her briefcase.

"Okay. You said to focus on Peru, so I googled anything with Special Ops related to it." She chewed on a crisp noodle. "Of course, as you can imagine, all I found was whatever they approved for release after a mission. These guys have been active against the drug cartels in the countries all along the Andean Ridge. Here." She pulled out a printed map.

"How recently?" Faith asked. "How new are the news items you found?"

"The last story was about two months ago. And you can figure that's well after the fact."

Tess nodded. "So then I tried to figure what other kinds of things go on down there that would merit covert operations, something that would be the basis for a good plot for you." She slid another sheet to the top of the pile. "This wasn't connected to Special Ops, at least in specific stories. But there's growing concern about the rise of Al Qaeda in Peru. Experts—whoever they are—claim they're stepping in to fill the terrorist void left by the decline of Shining Path and one other group, a smaller one. Faith, this stuff scares the shit out of me. Surely you aren't thinking of getting involved in this."

Faith pulled the paper over closer to her, ignoring Tess's words. "This says they've been responsible for small terrorist actions but their activities are escalating. The assumption is they'll use this is a launching pad to move north through the rest of South and Central America and up to the states." She sat back in her chair. "Jesus."

"Jesus is right." Tess quirked an eyebrow at her. "Is this what you were looking for?"

"Maybe more. We need to find out if Delta Force, the Army's Special Ops division, would be sent down there to handle anything like this."

But I know they would. That's why Mark and his team were there. And these people are known for horrific torture. Oh God, Mark. I need help here.

"Faith." Tess put her hand on Faith's arm. "I know how you immerse yourself in your stories. Do not go off to Peru where you are very likely to get yourself killed."

But Mark is there. If I don't do something, he's the one who'll be killed.

"All right. I can see you aren't paying one bit of attention to my warning. Why did I think you would?" Tess refilled their cups with hot tea from the ceramic pot. "But I've done my part. Now I think it's time for you to come clean with me. Why the sudden change of plot? Abigail has to be having a fit."

Faith laughed, the first taste of humor she'd had in two days. "Abigail's fits are legendary but she gets over them."

"But you have a reason for this, Faith," Tess insisted. "I know you too well."

Faith stared at the woman who'd worked with her for ten years now. Tess was more than an assistant. She was a friend, a confidant, a one-person support group. But in all this time Faith had never revealed anything to her about her special abilities. Or The Lotus Circle. Or how Aunt Vivi had helped her all these years. Somehow she'd always had the feeling Tess would look at her as too weird and it would fracture a wonderful friendship.

But now, maybe she was left with no choices. She'd gotten nowhere at Fort Bragg and no one else would believe one word of what she had to say. She pushed the remains of her food around on her plate, trying to find a starting point.

"Just let it out, Faith." Tai leaned toward her. "Whatever it is, it can't be worse than keeping it inside. And maybe I can help."

Refilling her tea cup, Faith took a calming breath and began her story.

* * * * *

"We won't get shit out of Fort Bragg."

Rick stomped into the cabin seconds after the helicopter set down and tossed his sport coat on a chair. He wanted to wring someone's neck with his bare hands. At the same time, he understood the frustrating position Colonel Ryan and Major Gregorio were in but that didn't solve the problem. No, that would be left to Phoenix to do. And damned soon.

"I take it the visit didn't go the way you expected?" Dan asked.

"Actually, it did. That's the problem. I wish I could blame those guys but someone on top is sitting on this whole thing."

Rick related his conversation with the two officers almost verbatim, doing his best to control his own irritation with the political red tape that hamstrung them. He wanted to blame someone but logically that would be the traitor who'd leaked the mission. So he simply passed along what had been said and waited for a response.

Dan handed him a cold drink. "Joey was awake for a while, a bit more lucid and able to give us some more information. Let me show you." He bent over the map on the table, his finger tracing a line to a spot marked with a pen. "The team landed at Iquito. It's well known in Peru the terrorists base themselves there. They chose a place accessible only by air or water, easily protected and just as easily defended. No surprise attacks for them to worry about. Except the one from SpecOps."

"Did they do a helo drop? And wasn't that a little dangerous? The noise of the bird alone would have warned these people someone was coming."

Mike, who had been standing to the side, shook his head. "Iquito's a port on the Amazon. That means there are a lot of places for water landings. The helo dropped them and a Zodiac at night far enough downriver from the target spot. They moved up while it was still dark, ditched the boat and set up the comm gear at the extraction point."

Dan picked up the thread again. "By the time the helo would return it wouldn't matter who heard them. Except the tangos were ready for them. Joey got into position, the others moved forward and all holy hell broke loose."

"Okay." Rick's finger moved over the surface of the map. "Next question. If this was a temporary spot, where's their permanent encampment? Someplace they could train, also."

"That's the rub," Mike answered. "There's about five different spots an hour or two away from there. We have to figure out which is the one. And do it quickly."

"Yeah." Troy walked in from the bedroom. "Joey's very uptight about what kind of hell they'll be putting Halloran through. They'll want to know who told about this meeting so they can do their own cleanup."

"One more thing." Dan's jaw was set and a muscle jumped in his cheek. "There was someone meeting with the tangos, I think the real target of this little exercise." He looked around the table. "The meet was to conduct business with the Wolf."

The tension in the room ratcheted up several notches. The men knew the Wolf too well by reputation. The most prolific arms dealer in the world and supplier to every terrorist group with the bucks to pay him. In Central and South America, drug money provided an endless bank account to purchase an inexhaustible supply of weapons. He alone had been proven to be the supplier for the firepower in the worst of the Al Qaeda attacks as well as arming the rebels in several third world countries. In South America he sold to both the drug cartels and the guerillas, creating circumstances that put the government troops at risk on two fronts.

Whoever talked about him did so in whispers. Disloyalty was, in his mind, the worst crime of all. It was rumored he'd personally shot his own wife because he thought she'd betrayed him to one of his enemies. He would go to any lengths to learn who had told the United States government about his meeting with El Serpiente. If he thought Mark Halloran could tell him, hell would be a more pleasant place for the captured soldier.

Mike broke the tense silence. "We have to get this going ASAP."

"But not until we have every bit of information," Dan told them, "and know exactly what we're doing. It won't do Halloran any good if we get shot too."

"I'll boot up the Dragon and get everything I can," Troy said.

The Phoenix and the Dragon were Chinese good luck symbols and seemed appropriate for their organization. Dragon was their very sophisticated computer system with the ability to tap into anything anywhere. Phoenix had seemed appropriate since it rose from the ashes of too much war and too many disappointments.

"Remember, guys," Dan went on. "This is why Phoenix was formed in the first place. To do things the government couldn't even consider. Off the books missions that needed doing. And to service corporations that couldn't approach normal organizations. That's never been truer for us than right now."

"Rick." Mike looked at the tall man staring through the bedroom door at his brother. "Did you get hold of that woman yet?"

"Negative. We've been exchanging voice mail messages."

"Do it," Dan told him. "I have an itch at the back of my neck that tells me she's more involved in this than just someone looking for an interview."

"You think this is someone who knows Mark? Why wouldn't she use his name?"

Dan shrugged. "Could be he never discussed us with her. Why would he?"

"I guess for the same reason all he told us about the woman he's lost his mind over is her nickname. The less anyone knows about his life, the harder it is for anyone to get at him. He's all about keeping people safe."

"Well, now it's time to take the lid off the pot. Find out who she is. She could be someone trying to get information on us and if we're going to do exactly what we're planning."

"That would mean someone's actually admitting they pulled the switch on this." Mike's voice was heavy with anger.

"We could sit here and speculate all day," Dan commented, "and get nothing done. Troy, set up the Dragon and ride its tail. Rick, talk to this woman. Mike, you and I will go over this map again with Joey and expand what we know as soon as Troy gets something for us." He rapped his knuckles on the table. "Let's do it."

* * * * *

The day had not gone well for Mr. Brown and Mr. Green. They'd done a few things they thought would give Faith Wilding at least second thoughts about whatever she was doing but they all depended on her being home, which hadn't happened yet. They needed her to check her email and answering machine. And their boss didn't think too much of their plan. Too many holes, he said.

Now his voice was pounding in Green's ear.

"What you want to do takes far too much time. We can't wait to see if you frighten her. And from what I've learned about her, she's one determined bitch, anyway. Get it done."

Green laughed, an unpleasant sound. "We can't exactly walk up to her house and shoot her."

"Be inventive." The voice was nasty. "That's what I pay you for. And while you're sitting on your asses there and making empty gestures," the voice snapped, "I promise you she's stirring the waters any place she can. Get her out of it before someone takes her seriously."

"How do you know they haven't already?" Mr. Green asked.

"So far we've only got kicking and screaming from one source and I've gotten it squashed. All the way down the line. We're keeping as tight a lid on this as possible but there's always some rogue out there who wants to be a Boy Scout. And I certainly don't want her connecting with Latrobe's brother."

"You're sure that's who made the snatch?"

"I feel it in my bones. Right now I just see it as a former military person who's overreacting to those negative reports about Walter Reed. Wants to keep his brother close and doesn't trust anyone. We need to make sure that's all it is. That somehow this woman hasn't gotten to him." The voice was like a sharp icicle.

"I thought you could find out anything about anyone," Green said resentfully.

There was a long, empty silence. Green thought maybe the other man had hung up when the hard voice spoke again. "There are some people who know the government so well they can protect themselves from it. Unfortunately."

Well, well. The great man has found a pie he can't stick his fingers in.

"So what would you have us do?"

"We know she flew back to San Antonio today. Go there. Dispose of her and I mean dispose. Forget your stupid plan. Let people think she's still traveling. Figure out how to accomplish that. Call me when it's done."

"But—"

"Don't give me any more of your crap. Quit stalling and do it. And I don't want it coming back to me, you hear me?"

"Yes, sir." Green snapped his phone shut and stared at it. He felt a major case of indigestion coming on. He was about to do something for which he was long out of practice and mistakes would not be tolerated.

"Well?" he partner asked, impatient with the whole thing.

"We're out of time. His Highness wants this taken care of right now and all evidence swept under the rug."

Brown snorted. "Easier said than done. Doesn't he know that?"

"He doesn't care."

"So what do we do?"

Green popped a Tums in his mouth. "We get on a plane and go to Texas."

* * * * *

"That's quite a story." Tess finished the last of her tea and wiped her mouth very carefully with a paper napkin.

"But not one you believe," Faith commented, a sinking feeling in her stomach.

Was this where she and Tess would part company? Where her friend would say she couldn't work for someone this crazy? On the other hand, she hadn't leaped up from the table, a look of total disbelief on her face.

"On the contrary. I know a lot about psychic powers. My grandmother had them."

Faith's eyes popped open. "She did?"

"Yes. She could sense things before they happened." She balled her napkin and threw it on the table. "The family blamed her for a lot of things that weren't her fault because of that. I wish she'd had something like The Lotus Circle to help her. She could have used the support."

"Aunt Vivi and her friends have been lifesavers," Faith sighed. "I don't know what I'd do without them. And they've really helped me with this situation."

"So all those attacks you've had, or whatever you want to call them, have been you empathizing Mark's pain?"

"Yes. God, Tess, I know he's in agony. I can't even begin to imagine the kind of torture he's going through. What I feel is just empathetic pain. His is the real thing. I don't understand how he's even holding on."

"He's strong, kiddo. Men like Mark outdo us all."

"Yes but where do I go from here? I have to get help from someone."

Tess began clearing away the debris of their food. "Your friend, Senator Winslow, couldn't help you?"

Faith made a sound of disgust. "Trey Winslow won't do anything that would compromise his image or his position."

Whatever Tess was going to say next was

interrupted by the ringing of the cell phone, which Faith had placed on the counter.

"I'll check your emails," Tess mouthed and headed for the den.

"Miss Wilding?"

Faith frowned. The voice was unfamiliar. "Yes. Who is this?"

"Rick Latrobe."

"Rick?"

"You seem to know me as Eric but I haven't used that name since I enlisted."

"Oh, I'm sorry. Thank you for calling me back."

"What can I do for you?" There wasn't a note of friendliness in his voice. Ice would have been warmer.

Faith clutched the phone. "I-I'm a writer. You may have seen some of my books." She rattled off some of the titles. "I'm working on a new one, about Special Ops and I was told you might be able to provide me with some information about how the missions are run. I strive for accuracy as much as possible."

She could feel the chill racing through the connection.

"Can I ask you exactly who gave you my name?" His voice sounded like an executioner's might—cold, sharp. Emotionless.

No, because my friend found you by hacking into secret databases.

"I'm not sure I remember at this moment," she waffled. "I've been talking to so many people."

"I see." Pause. "What is it exactly you're looking for?"

"I actually have a lot of questions. About how things are run, how the—I believe they're called units—are put together. What happens if a mission goes bad. Perhaps if you tell me where you are I can fly there and we can meet. Lunch or dinner on me."

"I see." The chill escalated but something more had been added in just those two words. Suspicion.

Faith waited through the silence on the line.

"Sorry. I'll have to think about that. I'm a little busy at the moment. Perhaps if you could be a little more specific, I could suggest someone else."

No, no, no. It has to be you.

She was losing him. "Actually, you came so highly recommended I'd prefer to work something out with you. Where are you right now?" she persisted.

"I sense something behind this that's a little more than just research for a book." His voice still had that frosty edge. "Otherwise anyone might do, right?"

"I—"

"Miss Wilding. Or whoever the hell you are. Can we just cut to the chase?" If the voice was cold before, it was lethal-sounding now. "What is it in fact you want from me? What's really going on here? You haven't made this many calls to me just for some interview. There are resources all over the place you could contact."

"Mr. Latrobe. Rick. I—"

"Faith?" Tess's voice from the den. Panicky. "Faith, you need to come here right now."

"Could you hold on for just a moment?" she told the disembodied voice on the other end of the connection. "Just one second. Please."

She hurried into the den where Tess had booted up her computer and was checking her emails. A message in large type filled the screen.

"Drop your story. Don't talk to anyone else. This is your last warning. Next time you'll be dead."

"Oh my God." The words fell out of her mouth on a gasp. She dropped into the chair in front of the desk, hands shaking.

"Hello?"

She'd actually forgotten the man on the phone. "Oh! I'm sorry. I...Mr. Latrobe. Rick. I can't talk to you right now. Is there a number where I could call you back in a few minutes?"

"Something's wrong," he guessed. "What is it?"

"Nothing." Her voice sounded false even to herself. "I just have to hang up right now."

"Miss Wilding? Listen."

"I told you. I have to go. I have...my email...I just..." She couldn't stop stammering.

"Email?" The tone of his voice had changed. "What kind of email?"

"I can't..." She let out a shaky breath. "I have to check this out."

"Don't hang up." He snapped the words as a command. "I'm going to assume you know who I really am so we can cut through all the bullshit. Has someone sent you a threatening email?"

"Y-Yes."

"Leave it. Don't touch it. I'll be in San Antonio first thing in the morning. Whatever's going on, will you be all right until then?"

"I don't... I guess..." Would she? What did this email mean? Was someone even now watching her house?

"I can have someone there in ten minutes if you're in immediate danger."

Was she? No, the email was just a warning. She had a little while before the threats become physical, didn't she? Didn't people like whoever this was always give warnings first?

"No. Thank you but I don't need anyone right now." She hoped that was true.

"Lock your doors. Set your alarm."

"I-I don't have an alarm system." *But I sure*

wish I did now.

The silence that followed was so heavy Faith could almost feel it reach through the connection and wrap itself around her.

Then Rick said in a measured tone, "You don't have an alarm system. Well isn't that just great. All right. Then definitely check all the locks. Windows too. Don't answer the landline. I'll call your cell when I get in."

"What is it you know that I don't?" She tried to stifle the fear overtaking her. "What's going on and why is someone after me?"

"I'll explain when I see you. But first you can answer some questions for me and we'll see where we go from there."

The line went dead. Faith stared at it before hitting the End button. Then she leaned forward toward the computer.

"Can you tell where this came from, Tess?"

She shook her head. "It says Admin but that could be anything. It's got to be a false IP address. Call Andy. He can find out for you."

"No. Not yet." She couldn't pull her eyes away from the screen.

"Well, you can believe you're rattling someone's cage. And badly, if they're resorting to stuff like this." Tess snapped her fingers. "You haven't checked your answering machine."

She pushed the button next to the blinking red light that showed fifteen messages waiting. As predicted, several were from Abigail Loudon. Two were from her publicist about a book tour. There were some from her parents wondering when she'd be home. Even one from Andy that made her sit up and take notice.

"Curiosity got the better of me, Faith," his nasal voice droned on. "Most of the stuff I found I can tell

you when you call but you should know that Mark
Halloran spent a lot of down time with Joey
Latrobe, his brother and their friends. Someone
who should know—and who'll deny they ever told
me—said there was even an offer on the table to join
Phoenix when Mark's current hitch was up."

"What?"

"Uh-huh. Play this one close to the vest,
please."

Mark surely had mentioned her to them, so
why hadn't they recognized her name in connection
with his? Because he only referred to her by her
nickname? More than likely. Mark was very
closemouthed about things like this. Part of his
"keep things separated" philosophy.

The last message made the blood drain from
Faith's face.

"Consider this warning number two, Miss
Wilding. Stay out of things that don't concern you,
or you could be out of them permanently."

"Faith, you have got to call the police," Tess
insisted.

"No. No, no, no. How will I explain this?" She
ran her fingers through her hair, pushing off her
face. "I just need to get through until morning. Rick
Latrobe will be here in the morning. Then we'll
discuss it."

Tess threw up her hands. "Fine but I'm staying
here tonight. No way am I leaving you alone."

"Okay, okay."

She gathered up all the papers from the kitchen
and locked them with her other notes in the wall
safe in her den. Upstairs she found an oversized T-
shirt for Tess to sleep in and clean towels for her.
Then she climbed into bed but her mind was too
restless for sleep to come.

Tidbit.

Mark? She sat bolt upright in bed. *Oh, Mark. God, are you all right?*

Hanging...on...love you...

Me too, soldier. I'll get you out of this, I promise.

Careful...messages...intercept...

The other telepath. He was right. Especially if Rick Latrobe turned out to be an answer to her prayers. She couldn't inadvertently give anything away.

Okay.

She waited for a response but all that surrounded her was black silence. Then the pain hit her again, so sharp and swift it took her breath away. Sweat broke out on her skin as she tried to ride it out. Eventually it eased enough for her to stumble to the bathroom and find some aspirin.

When she lay down in bed again she was shaking from head to tow.

I'll get you out, Mark. I swear it.

She finally fell asleep with her cell phone in her hand, 9-1-1 already punched in and a sharp carving knife on the nightstand next to her bed. But her night might have been even more anxious if she'd known about the black sedan that cruised by her house every hour or so, the faces of both the driver and the passenger set in grim determination.

Chapter Thirteen

"All right, smartass, what now?"

Mr. Brown stared through the windshield of the big Lincoln, eyes narrowed, as they made their first pass of the morning down Faith Wilding's street.

"We're lucky someone hasn't reported us as peeping toms," he pointed out.

"Shut up," Green snapped. "Let me think."

"At least we know she didn't leave after she got home yesterday."

"Big deal." Green slid the car around the corner. "She's got that woman staying with her."

"So what?"

"So what, you ask? Are you dense?" His indigestion had returned with a vengeance. "We don't want witnesses to whatever we end up doing. And we don't want two bodies to dispose of."

"I don't know why we didn't outsource this," Brown grumbled. "This isn't our normal line of work."

"Tell me about it." He chewed on the Tums. "I'd rather not try to get into the house. That's not our usual line, either. We'll watch for the right opportunity."

Brown pulled a piece of gum from his pocket, unwrapped it and stuck it in his mouth. "Like I said, if we don't get arrested first."

* * * * *

Avoiding the inconvenience of commercial flights, Rick had Ed take him in the chopper to where the two Phoenix Gulfstreams were hangared. One phone call to roust the co-pilot and have him get the plane ready, half an hour when they got there to make final arrangements. Then Ed climbed into the pilot's seat and cranked the engines. By five a.m. they were wheels up.

Rick was not a man given to fidgeting but he couldn't keep his leg still as he sat strapped into the comfortable chair, or his fingers from drumming on the leather arm. He hadn't bothered dragging the steward out of bed so he brewed coffee for himself and the pilots, sucking far more caffeine into his system than he needed.

He had a bad feeling about the whole situation. Whoever Faith Wilding turned out to be, she was apparently someone who'd stepped in a whole pile of shit. He just wished he knew whose pile it was. And where she fit into the picture.

Was she somehow connected to Mark? He'd never heard him discuss any women in his life, with the exception of some idiot female he insisted on calling Tidbit. He could just imagine what she was like—a buck-toothed tomboy, barely five feet, lugging around a king-sized crush on her hero.

He didn't like flying blind but he had to talk to her, whoever she was. Last night she'd sounded scared to death, even if she hadn't wanted to admit it. Something had spooked her and badly. And the tension riding his spine told him it was all part and parcel of this goatfuck.

At the private hangar where they landed, the black SUV he'd called ahead for was waiting. He shook hands with the man who'd delivered it, told the pilot to be on standby and tore out of the exit. He had an uncomfortable feeling that speed was definitely called for.

* * * * *

Faith was awake at five o'clock too restless to sleep. She dressed hastily in slacks and a silk shirt, pulling her hair back into a clip at the nape of her neck but didn't bother with makeup. She'd been too nervous to bother with it. Anyway, it wasn't as if she was going on a date.

She made coffee, a rarity for her, then paced while she drank most of the pot, giving herself a caffeine high that she didn't need. She tried reading through Tess's notes again but her mind refused to settle down. She couldn't seem to find enough to occupy herself. Time seemed to have weights on its feet, dragging so slowly it felt as if days passed rather than minutes.

Tess finally dumped the dregs in the coffee pot and brewed some Chai tea for both of them, forcing Faith to sit at the table and drink it.

"You're driving me nuts," she told her boss. "I think you've already worn a groove in the floor. What time do you think he'll get here?"

"I don't know. He said early. What's early?"

"Well, it's eight o'clock right now. To some people that's early. To others it's late."

Faith shuffled the papers in front of her, pretending to study them again. "I just hope he gets here soon."

Tess moved to the living room window, watching the street through the slatted blinds. "Do any of your neighbors own a black Lincoln?" she called out.

"A couple of them." Faith came in from the kitchen where she was getting coffee ready to brew. "Why?"

"I swear this is the second time I've seen this one roll past the house."

Faith shrugged. "I've got at least two neighbors who parade them around like icons of affluence.

You probably saw both of them leave."

"Maybe. I guess after last night everything's making me nervous."

Faith flipped the switch to the coffeemaker. "I'll check it out. I'm going to get the newspaper."

"Are you crazy?" Tess grabbed her arm. "People threaten your life and you go around like everything's normal?"

Faith gave a nervous laugh. "Not exactly. But what's going to happen to me on my own street? The paper's just at the edge of the driveway."

She shrugged off Tess's hand, unlocked the front door and hurried down the pavement. A black town car sitting in front of the house four doors down, engine idling, registered peripherally in her vision. The Thompsons. Obviously. Harry Thompson was probably cursing as he waited impatiently for his wife, the habitually tardy Gail.

As she reached the end of the driveway the car began moving down the street. She shaded her eyes, waiting, planning to wave at them. And then it all happened before she could blink. The town car picked up speed and seemed to be heading right for her. At that exact moment a black SUV pulled up to the curb and a man leaped from it as it rocked from the fast stop. The car was scant feet away from her coming faster and she didn't seem to be able to make her feet move.

Then strong arms wrapped around her and carried her to the lawn as the car whizzed by, so close it almost brushed her legs. Her face hit the turf and the breath was squeezed from her lungs by the heavy body on top of her. Seconds ticked by while she struggled to breathe, unable to make her body, her mouth or her brain work.

Finally the pressure was gone and big hands reached down to help her to her feet.

"What the hell are you doing out of the house?"

She looked up. And up. And up even more. Mark was well over six feet but this man topped even him. At the moment he wore an expression of mingled anger and disgust on his face. His blue eyes looked like twin torches.

"I-I was getting the newspaper." She was shaking so badly she wasn't sure she could stand upright.

"Get the hell into the house before they decide to come back."

Gripping her arm with fingers like steel, he frog-marched her into the house and practically threw her inside, where Tess stood waiting in the hallway.

"Don't move." He jogged to the SUV and dragged the keys from the ignition.

Tess was standing with her arms around Faith when Rick strode back inside seconds later, slamming the door and locking it.

"Faith, my God." She brushed Faith's hair back from her forehead. "Did that car almost run over you?"

Rick glared at Faith, who was trying to gather some semblance of dignity. "Damn straight it did, thanks to your friend's stupidity."

Faith couldn't stop shaking, nor could she get the image of the black car closer than a whisper of breath out of her mind. She had to fight the urge to race to the bathroom and throw up.

"She was just getting the newspaper, for heaven's sake," Tess snapped at him.

"After I told her last night to stay in the house with the doors locked." He glared at Faith. "Did I not? Was I talking to myself?"

"Y-Yes." Faith moved away from Tess, her hands gripped tightly together to still their trembling. "But I just—"

"Someone is obviously trying to kill you and you have to go out for the newspaper? You got a threat last night, didn't you? It came up while you were talking to me."

She nodded. Her brain wouldn't come unstuck. She was shaking so badly she wasn't sure if she could stand upright.

"How?" he demanded.

"Ph-Phone. And email."

Tess moved closer to Faith and put an arm around her again. "Can't you stop shouting at her? She's obviously in shock."

"She's lucky she's not dead."

"I assume you're the mysterious Eric Latrobe?" She looked up at the mountain of a man looming over them. "At least I hope that's who you are."

"So you don't let just any stranger in the house?" His voice was edged with sarcasm. "Good for you."

"O-Only men who save my life," Faith told him. She was getting some control back, her pulse settling down to a manageable beat.

"Smart mouth too." He inhaled a deep breath and let it out slowly, working to get his temper under control. "All right, Miss Wilding. You've been trying your best to get hold of me so let's cut out the crap here. What do you want and why does someone want to kill you? Besides claiming to be an author, just who the hell are you?"

She wet her lips and struggled to keep her voice even. "I'm Tidbit. And I'm trying to get help for Mark."

Rick stared at her as if she'd just descended from Mars.

* * * * *

"Well, that was a huge success." Brown banged his fist against the armrest.

"Shut up." Green wheeled the car around the corner and sped through the residential streets, nearly clipping a convertible backing out of a driveway. "A perfect opportunity and some asshole ruins it."

"Who was that guy, anyway?"

"Who the hell knows? I don't suppose you got a good look at him."

Brown gave an unpleasant laugh. "You're kidding, right?"

"Damn, damn, damn." He took out his cell phone. "We need to ditch this car. Give the rental agency some excuse and get something completely different. Then we need to check into a hotel."

"No kidding."

"But first we need someone to sit on the Wilding woman and make sure she doesn't fall off our radar." He punched in a number and when the person at the other end answered, barked out terse instructions. "Let's hope he gets his ass here ASAP. We can't afford another fuckup."

They had reached the Frontage Road and took the closest on-ramp to the Interstate.

"So what now?" Brown asked.

"What now? Did you ask what now?" he snorted. "So you think that maybe just once you could come up with an idea yourself, instead of waiting to see what I decide?"

"You jackass." Brown's voice was tight with anger. "Maybe that's what I should be doing since none of yours seemed to have worked out so far."

"What's that supposed to mean?" Green was changing lanes, speeding ahead of cars, trying to get...where? Where did they go now?

"Only that we lost the Latrobe kid, we aren't any closer to finding out who knows what and who might still be on our ass and now we not only didn't take out the target, we served notice in a very big way that she's in danger. And whose brain masterminded it all?"

"Just shut up," Green said again. "We have to figure out what to do. And no, calling our boss is not an option. Yet. I want to have some options first."

* * * * *

Rick stared at the woman in front of him. "You're kidding, right?"

This slender female with the flashing green eyes and tawny hair was a far cry from what his overactive imagination had conjured up. If they got Mark Halloran back, he'd better hang onto this one before someone snatched her away from under his nose.

"Why would I be kidding?" She gripped her hands together and willed herself to stop trembling. She could still barely process what happened.

"But then..." His voice trailed off. His eyes raked her from head to toe, assessing her.

"Mark Halloran and I have been...friends all our lives. He always teased me about my height. That's where the name came from. I've been Tidbit since I was twelve."

"I think the coffee is ready," Tess broke in. "I could sure use a cup. Why don't we all go into the kitchen?"

"Good idea," Rick said.

Tess poured coffee for herself and Rick, but Faith was careful to brew tea for herself. She was still hyper from the caffeine she'd absorbed earlier. Big mistake, she told herself. Now she could hardly stop her hands from shaking. Or was it the near miss that had her trembling so badly?

When they were seated at the table, each with a steaming mug of liquid, Rick nailed Faith with a cold glare.

"Okay. Truth or consequences time. You say you want to get help for Mark, but why? As far as we know, Mark's dead." Bitterness crept into his voice. "Killed by the same people who nearly did in my brother. And I'm not a person whose name people toss around lightly, or who can easily be contacted. So give."

She sipped at her coffee, trying to collect her scattered thoughts. "You're right. I had to dig very deep to find you."

"Here's another question. How the hell did you even know who I was? I have no idea of what your relationship with Mark is...was...but I'm damn sure he didn't discuss me with you."

"To tell you the truth," she sighed, an ache in her heart, "I think we almost waited too long to find out what that relationship is. And no, he never told me about you. Mark...compartmentalized his life. He had this outrageous idea he had to protect me from everything beyond the two square feet around me. That we would just be status quo until he was through playing solider..." She broke off and swiped at the tears trickling down her cheeks.

I will not cry. I will not fall apart in front of this man. Mark needs me. I'm his only hope.

"Here." Tess grabbed napkins from the counter and shoved them at her.

Faith blotted her eyes and balled up the napkin. "Sorry. I'm not usually such a running faucet."

Rick's face softened a little. "That's okay. Take your time." His mouth twisted in a rueful grin. "You were talking about Mark playing soldier."

"Oh, God, I'm so sorry. I didn't mean...That's not..."

"That's all right. Don't worry. I understand."

"Do you?" She leaned toward him. "Do you really? Like I told you, Mark and I have been friends... I mean really friends, before anything else...for a very long time." She paused to weigh her words. She didn't want to give intimate information away to this man unless she had to.

"Go ahead," he urged.

"But despite how we felt...feel...Mark didn't think we could move forward as long as he was in the service. Too risky, he said. We needed to do what we needed to and then see where we were when he was finished." She twisted her hands together. "Can you understand how I admired what he was doing but resented it at the same time?"

"Yeah, I can."

"When I learned that he spent time with you and your...friends and might join Phoenix when his current tour was up, it was a shock but that's why he kept that to himself."

Rick narrowed his eyes at her. "And just how did you learn all this?"

She gave him a watery smile. "What's that old line? I could tell you but then I'd have to kill you."

All the muscles in his body tightened. "Miss Wilding. I need to know some things here. Like exactly why you contacted me and how the hell you even knew to call me. How did you find out about Phoenix?"

"I found out about your brother because he's in Mark's unit. You're listed as his only close relative."

"Yeah? Just where did you find this

information? We've gone to great length to be impenetrable to random searches. Yet someone got you information. I want to know who and how."

"I'll tell you what, Mr. Latrobe. You help me with my problem and I'll even introduce you to that person."

"Rick," he corrected. "Call me Rick. I think we're way past being formal here. And what kind of problem are we talking about?"

"I'm talking about someone sending me threatening messages and trying to kill me." She had her mug in a death grip. "Who's cage have I rattled that would take such drastic steps to shut me up?"

Rick rubbed his hand against his cheek. "I'd say you pushed someone's button. We'll need to go over everything you've done for the past few days. I want to check both those messages out, too. What else?"

"How do you think they got to me? To go after me?"

"I think if you tell me why you ferreted me out, we might find the answer to that. And what you mean about Mark sending you messages." His eyes were like bolts of lightning staring at her. "Tell me, Miss Wilding. Messages from a dead man? What kind of crazy story is that?"

"Faith," she corrected. "As long as we're dropping formalities."

"Fine. Faith. Let's not be coy here, okay? What did you mean you have a message from Mark?"

She got up to refill her coffee mug. "I get the impression you know Mark pretty well.

She sat down in her chair again, aware that Tess was watching both of them with avid interest. *Waiting to see if I'm going to let Mark's secret out. Well, I don't have much choice any more.* "How much do you know about Mark's special ability?"

Rick's eyebrows lifted a fraction. "Special ability?"

Faith pursed her lips. He knew. She could tell by the involuntary flicker in his eyes. "Mr. Latrobe. Rick. I think we need to be honest with each other. We each have an agenda here. We have to put them both on the table and we can't play games with each other. So I'll ask you once more, do you know about Mark's special ability?"

Rick stared into his coffee cup, then looked up as if he'd come to a decision. "If you're referring to his telepathic ability, then yes, I know about it. We discussed it because Major Gregorio wanted him to be tested for a special unit Delta Force is working on. I wasn't aware anyone else knew about it."

"As I said before, Mark and I have been friends forever. We discovered that we could communicate this way years ago. It's been a...special bond between us." She brushed a stray hair away from her face and visibly pulled herself together. "All right, then. Before I go on, I assume your interest in this whole thing is because of your brother. I understand he's still unconscious at Walter Reed Hospital."

Again the same, emotionless eyes reading her face. "Actually he's no longer there. And that's all you need to know about that. But I think what you have to tell me may coincide with Joey's situation."

Faith just sat for a moment, gathering herself to plunge into her story.

Tess patted her arm and got up to make fresh coffee. "Go on," she said in a soft voice. "You're out of options and this guy seems like someone you can trust. It's obvious Mark did."

"You're right. I don't have any more time to waste."

Staring into her mug, she told Rick about

communication between Mark and herself, the details of the messages, trying to remember as much of each one as she could. She also told him about her empathic abilities and her belief that Mark was undergoing terrible torture. In return, he reluctantly told her about Joey, about John Gregorio's phone call and about snatching his brother out of the hospital.

"Joey's conscious now and giving us some information."

Faith grabbed his wrist. "About Mark? What happened to him? Then you know he's alive, right? Do you know where he is?"

"In a minute. Let's get to what's happening to you. People don't just run around trying to kill innocuous authors. Who have you talked to about this so-called project of yours?"

"No one. I was trying to take the roundabout way, get to Major Gregorio and see if I could pry anything loose from him and if he'd listen to what I had to say without thinking I was crazy. The only people I've talked to in the last couple of days, besides my aunt who I can swear to you isn't involved in this, are the major, his CO Colonel Ryan, who was in his office when I got there and Trey, er, Senator Winslow."

Rick lifted one eyebrow. "You and the senator on first name terms?"

"He's been a good resource for me for my books. I couldn't get Major Gregorio to return my calls, so..."

"So you used a little political muscle." Rick's mouth twisted. "I don't suppose it occurred to you he could be involved in whatever's going?"

"Trey?" She was shocked. "Oh, no. I don't think so."

"I promise you the major didn't call out a hit on

you. That doesn't leave a lot of other people."

"I can't believe the senator would be involved in anything like this. Whatever this is."

Rick looked at her for a long time, as if making up his mind about something. Finally he drained his mug and set it down with great care. "What I'm going to tell you goes no further than here." He slid a glance at Tess.

"You can trust her," Faith assured him. "Believe me."

He shrugged. "It's your life and Mark's we're playing with here, so it's your call. Okay. Here's what Joey gave us."

Using the information from his brother and the messages from Mark, at the end of an hour they had a very unpleasant and frightening picture of what had happened and what the situation was with Mark.

"But we have to find him," Faith insisted. "I don't know how much longer he can hold out."

"We will. We have to do this quickly but carefully."

"How will you find his exact location? You said Joey told you they moved him."

"We'll find him. But the question is what to do with you."

"Me?" She looked at him, puzzled.

"You can't stay here. They'll make another run at you."

"He's right," Tess agreed. "They won't just say so sad, too bad and walk away."

Rick nodded. "If someone wants to kill you badly enough to do that in broad daylight, they won't stop until they get the job done."

Panic suddenly clawed at her. "But what can I do? Where can I go?"

Rick stood up and pulled his cell phone from

his pocket. "Give me a minute."

He headed for the front hall, punching in numbers as he walked. Faith strained to hear what he was saying but he was turned away from her and spoke in a tone of voice too soft to distinguish the words.

"What do you think he's planning?" Tess's forehead was creased with worry.

"I don't know." Faith was trying to conceal her own anxiety. "But he's right. We can't stay here. Oh God, Tess. I'm so sorry I dragged you into this."

"Hey." Tess rose from her chair and hugged Faith. "You didn't drag me into anything. When I found that stuff on the 'net about Al Qaeda I could have told you to bag the plot and go back to the original book. Or said I didn't want to work on this. I'm a big girl. I make my own decision."

"All right." Rick was back in the kitchen. "Here's the plan. Faith, do you have something like a gym bag you can just throw some things into?"

"Yes but for how long? Where are we going?"

"Later. Right now we need to get out of here. While I was on the telephone I spotted a plumbing company truck across the street. Now, your neighbors may actually have sprung a leak but it showed up just a little too coincidentally."

Faith swallowed hard, willing herself not to panic. She had to trust this man. Her life, Tess's and most of all Mark's depended on it.

"All right. I'll go get ready. What about Tess?"

"She'll have to come too. Sorry," he told her. "It's too risky to leave you here. Even if you go home they could follow you, grab you to use as bait for Faith."

Tess paled. "But I can't just pick up and leave like this." She twisted her hands together. "People will ask questions. I mean..."

Rich ground his teeth. "They'll ask a lot more questions if they have to identify your body."

"God, Tess." Faith felt as if they were falling through Alice's Looking Glass. "This is all my fault. I am so very, very sorry."

Tess visibly pulled herself together. "Quit saying that."

"It's nobody's fault." Rick's voice was sharp with impatience. "Except for the person who dropped the dime on the mission. But we don't have any time to waste here. Faith. Is there another way out of here except through the front?"

She nodded. "On Halloween the kids cut through the hedge at the back of my yard to my neighbors."

"Okay. Go get ready."

"You can wear some of my stuff," Faith told the other woman. "We're about the same size. Come on."

"Warm clothes," Rick told her. "And tell me how to access your email while you're doing this. I want to look at the message and also play the one on the recorder."

Faith gave him the information as she and Tess headed upstairs.

"Don't bring anything fancy," Rick called after them.

Faith just snorted.

The two women were back downstairs in under ten minutes, Faith lugging an oversized duffle bag filled to bulging. They'd both changed into jeans and t-shirts and carried jackets.

"Good," Rick said. "Very good. All right. Here's the drill. Tess, you go first. Through the hedge to the next street over. Faith, as soon as she's out of sight, you go. Let Tess take the duffle."

"And then what?"

"I'm going to get in my car and leave. They won't follow me. They'll think I'm leaving you alone so they'll get a chance at you. I'll pick you up on the next block."

Faith's heart hammered the whole time they went through the routine but in less than five minutes they were in the big SUV and speeding toward the Interstate.

"Where are we going?" Faith asked.

"Right now, the airport. When we get on the plane I'll answer all your questions."

They had just pulled onto the Interstate when Faith was hit with a sharp pain that doubled her over and left her gasping.

Rick slid her a quick glance. "What's wrong?"

"It's Mark." She struggled to breathe. "They're torturing him again."

Chapter Fourteen

Trey Winslow picked up the phone in his den, sure the call waiting for him would be anything but good news.

"You were right to be suspicious of Faith Wilding's relationship with Halloran," the disembodied voice barked.

"I just had a feeling." A sense of dread settled in his stomach. "What have you found?"

"Faith Wilding and Mark Halloran have been friends for more than twenty years. I promise you she knows about his psychic abilities."

"Damn."

"Worse yet, she may even have some of her own."

"What?" The voice rose about twenty decibels.

"I suppose you also don't know she has an aunt who is a psychic? That she belongs to something called The Lotus Circle?" He spat out a brief description of the organization.

"I don't—"

"Of course not. Sometimes I wonder how you ever got elected. I'll bet my job—which I may be doing anyway—that my original suspicion is correct. The Wilding woman's got the same psychic abilities he has. She's got to be the one he's been sending the messages to."

Winslow felt a sweat break out on his forehead. "Have you talked to Escobedo about that? Has he confirmed it?"

"No, damn it. But he does have a man of his own with the same abilities. He's supposed to be able to intercept mental messages."

"And has he?

"Unfortunately that asshole Halloran's

obviously figured it out and is forcing himself not to think of her by name. That means there could be two females who need eliminating. Damn it," he repeated. "We could all be looking at spending the future in prison if this falls apart."

"Maybe it's time to cash in our chips, take what we've got and all retire."

"Oh," the man barked, "wouldn't that look sweet? A senator and a high-ranking member of the government suddenly saying bye-bye. Get serious, will you? We have to get rid of that woman. I've passed on all this information to those two idiots we hired. They'd better deliver for us."

"We also need to find Joey Latrobe," Winslow reminded him. "Your resources are far more extensive than mine."

"I'm on it."

"Well, you better hope we find him. And that your men get rid of the Wilding woman. I don't think either one of us is ready to have our lives turned upside if neither of those things happen."

Winslow slammed the phone down and poured himself a drink. He was afraid the sound echoing in his head was his world cracking around him.

* * * * *

"I don't know who the man is," Green said into the telephone, "but if he's gone here's your chance. Ring her doorbell. Tell her whatever you have to in order to get her to let you in. Then get it done."

He disconnected the call and wiped his forehead with a white linen handkerchief. He and Brown were facing each other in one of the hotel rooms they'd rented, an air of apprehension hanging over them.

"He'll screw it up," Brown said at last.

214

"No. He won't. He's one of the best."

Brown shook his head. "We need better than the best for this. We can't afford another disaster."

"There won't be one."

As he spoke the phone in his hand rang.

"Is it done yet?" the voice on the other end asked.

Green automatically reached in his pocket for a Tums. By the time they were through with this, his digestive tract would be completely shot, he figured.

"As good as."

"Unsatisfactory," the voice bit off. "We're under the hammer here and she's a loose cannon. Get rid of her now." The dead air indicated he'd killed the connection.

"Was it him?" Brown asked.

"Who else." He looked at his watch. "We should be getting a call any minute now."

* * * * *

Mark had long ago learned to let his mind take him out of his body. Otherwise he never would have been able to tolerate the abuse his body was often forced to take. This time especially it helped him to survive. He didn't think they could find any new ways to torture him but El Serpiente's mind was as twisted as the reptile he was named for. Surely hell would be a respite.

But he didn't break. They could kill him but they'd never get a thing out of him. Two people were depending on him—the source and Tidbit.

In disgust they'd finally tossed him back into the tent, sending him sprawling on the filthy ground. They no longer even bothered to chain him up. His condition had deteriorated so badly there was no chance he'd get away.

At least so they thought.

As long as I can breathe I can figure out how to escape. But I sure hope Tidbit's getting through to someone.

He felt himself drifting into semi-consciousness when he heard the Wolf and Escobedo outside his tent. He roused himself and strained to hear what they were saying.

"I have to leave." The Wolf's voice was sharp, tinged with anger. "I have business to conduct and I've spent far too much time here already."

"You don't say." Escobedo's own antagonism was evident. "For the amount of money you take home from us, a few days is the least you can give us. Especially in a situation such as this."

"Don't pressure me, Ramon. It's true you are an excellent customer but I have others I must attend to, also. And you don't seem to be getting anywhere with this man, no matter what tortures you apply to him."

Escobedo spat on the ground. "That pig. He is close to breaking. Another few hours and he'll be mine."

"Your pet mental giant, Felix, hasn't gotten anywhere, either."

At that moment Mark heard the distinctive ring of a satellite phone and the Wolf answering it.

"You found her and you lost her? What asinine nonsense is this?" A pause. "You can't get rid of one stupid woman? Is everyone there incompetent?" Another pause. "Go into her house and drag her out, if you have to. And do not let her anywhere near anyone who can give credence to whatever she might say."

"News?" Escobedo asked.

"More than you've given me. They have identified the woman Halloran is probably sending messages to. They have her in their sights. She'll soon be history."

Mark felt panic claw at him.

Oh, God. Faith, please be safe. Use that wonderful brain of yours.

"But then we have to make sure she hasn't already contacted anyone. And there is the matter of who leaked the word of our meeting to begin with. That's a hole we definitely have to plug."

"When are you leaving?"

"The helo will pick me up in fifteen minutes. I'll be back by noon tomorrow. Have my answers by then."

Mark heard the Wolf walk away. One moment later Escobedo entered the tent.

"Last chance, soldier boy. You have until noon tomorrow to tell me what I want to know. After that it's out of my hands."

He drew back his foot and kicked Mark forcefully in his chest which was criss-crossed by cuts and then on the open wound on his leg. Mark barely retrained himself from screaming.

Hurry, Tidbit.

* * * * *

"Are you feeling better?" Rick's voice held deep concern.

They were in the Phoenix plane, preparing for takeoff. Faith had barely held herself together until they reached the airport. Rick had carried her onto the plane and strapped her into one of the luxurious leather armchairs, introducing her to the pilot as Ed Romeo, brother of one of the partners. Then he poured a shot of brandy from the bar, knelt beside the chair and insisted she drink it. The fiery liquid burned on the way down but she felt the pain begin to subside almost at once and her breathing eased.

"Yes, thank you. I'm sorry."

"Don't be. I've heard about empathetic episodes like this but never witnessed one before. Does this happen often?"

"More in the last couple of days." She tightened her hands into fists. "I think the torture is getting worse. Rick, I'm really afraid for him."

"What a disaster." He stood and slammed his fist against the wall of the cabin. "God damn politics anyway. Gregorio should have been able to send in a rescue mission long before this."

Faith wiped her face with the damp towel Tess had placed on her forehead and handed it back to her friend. "Have you seen him? The major?"

"Yes. And I can tell you his hands are tied. Even with the support of his commanding officer, who made the trip to Fort Bragg to work with him, he can't get approval for anything and he's frustrated as hell."

"That would be Colonel Ryan."

"That's right." Rick made a sound of frustration. "Gregorio was my CO when I was in SpecOps and I had a lot of respect for him. I still do but I feel sorry for the poor bastard. He's between a rock and a hard place."

"What was the last thing he said to you?"

His laugh held no humor. "He wished me luck. He knows what we'll do."

"And who is we, exactly?"

At that moment the pilot poked his head into the cab in to let them know they were preparing for takeoff. Sure enough, seconds later the sound of the jet engines filled the cabin.

"I'll tell you everything once we're airborne. Oh and by the way. I sent your email to my friends. We'll see if we can track down where it came from and go from there."

He checked to make sure Faith and Tess were both properly buckled in before strapping himself into one of the armchairs across from them. And then they were taxiing down the runway.

By the time they lifted off, Faith was feeling considerably better. But she needed to see if she could contact Mark. A feeling of desperation was creeping through her, the sense that time was running out and they weren't moving fast enough. While they were still climbing, she closed her eyes, visualized a stream with high banks as Aunt Vivi told her and projected to Mark.

I'm with Rick. We're going to get you out of this. Please hold on.

There was such a long silence she was afraid he didn't hear her. Or couldn't answer. Finally she heard his voice, even fainter than before.

Rick...good...

Yes, yes. He and his friends are helping.

Hurry...running out...

We will. Mark? I love you.

She waited.

Love you too...

Then he was gone. None of her efforts elicited a response. She slumped in her chair and saw Rick eying her with curiosity.

"Were you communicating with Mark just now?" he asked.

She nodded. "Just a short message, though."

"That's amazing. I've read about this. And of course, Mark explained about telepathy once he felt comfortable enough to confide in us. But I've never actually seen it in action. You could hear him? Talk to him? For real?"

"Yes."

"Jesus. No wonder the military wants to

develop this."

Her eyes clouded. "He sounds so weak."

"All right. Let me get us all something to drink and I'll tell you what you need to know. As well as where we're going."

When they were settled with filled glasses, Rick began by giving her the capsule description of Phoenix, the background of the partners and a rough outline of how they operated.

"Joey asked one time if he could bring Mark home with him, an unusual request considering how tight our little circle is." Rick smiled. "We had to get a look at this guy that my little brother thought was better than God."

"You said something about wanting him to join the company," Faith reminded him.

"Yes. He's exactly what we need. But that's for a later time. First we have to get him home safely. Then he can decide what he wants to do with the rest of his life."

"You say you do contract work for the government. Would they have come to you for this mission, since apparently nobody wants anything official happening?"

"Probably. But there hasn't been enough time for it to make its way up the ladder. And this can't wait. Joey himself impressed us with the urgency of the situation."

"Where are you taking us now?" Faith wanted to know.

Rick explained about the cabin and the men waiting there for them. "We'll be getting ready to roll shortly after we arrive there. Dan's been pulling all the details together while I was checking you out. You both will be safe there while we're gone. We'll have someone on you and Joey all the time."

Faith didn't contradict him but she had no

intention of being left behind. But the time to tell him that was when he was left with no choice. Meanwhile she leaned back in her chair, admiring the plush cabin with its abundance of electronics equipment and letting her mind drift.

Mark, I'll get you out if I have to kill someone myself to do it.

* * * * *

Mr. Green and Mr. Brown's day continued to get steadily worse.

"What do you mean she's not there?" he shouted into the phone.

"I mean she's gone," the fake plumber, a man named Damon, told him. "The house is empty."

"Did you get inside?"

"Sure. Piece of cake. No alarm system and the locks are a joke. She's gone. Car's here but she's not. Nor is the woman who spent the night with her."

"Shit. Damn it all to hell." Green was sweating again at the thought of the call he'd have to make. "How the hell could they just disappear with you there watching them? Did you fall asleep?"

"Listen," Damon snapped, "don't blame me. I was doing my job exactly as you told me to. You should have let me go in last night and take care of them both."

"Oh, sure." Green made a sound of disgust. "Then we'd have two bodies to dispose of instead of one. And two sets of questions." He thought for a moment. "What about the man who showed up?"

"You mean the one who dragged her away from your car just in time?" Damon's tone was nasty.

"You know who I'm referring to. What happened to him?"

"He got in his car and left."

"Alone?"

"Yup. I waited about fifteen minutes to be sure he wasn't coming back, then I went up to the door. Nada."

Green thought for a moment. "Could they have left with him?"

"Not unless they snuck out the back."

The silence thickened as both men looked at each other and reached the same conclusion.

"Damn it, damn it, damn it," Green swore. "Didn't you have an eye on the back?"

"Get real. You can't see everything from the street. And who expected her to do a Houdini?"

More silence.

"All right," Green said at last. "Go home. I'll call you if I need you again."

"Don't forget my pay," Damon reminded him.

"Your pay? You let the woman get away, didn't you?" He disconnected the call and threw the cell phone on the bed.

Brown, who was sitting at a small round table drinking coffee, eyed him with a mixture of curiosity and dread. "She got away?"

"Yes. And who the hell knows where she's gotten to? Fuck all, anyway." He heaved a sigh. "Too bad that damned peacock Winslow wasn't smart enough to have her thoroughly investigated the first time he ever met with her. Now we have to do his work for him." He picked up the phone and tossed it at Brown. "Call the geek. Tell him we need him to do some digging."

"Where are you going?"

"To replenish my supply of Tums."

* * * * *

"What do mean she's gone?"

Trey Winslow sat in the paneled office to which he'd been summoned, ostensibly for a meeting regarding his work on the Armed Services committee. He had never seen the man behind the desk quite so agitated, not even in times of great crisis. What was he thinking? This was a great crisis.

"Just exactly what I said. Right out from under our noses." The man picked up a paper clip and began twisting and bending it. "Those bumbling idiots we use couldn't track a pigeon if it left droppings every two inches."

"They certainly didn't use their brains trying that trick with the car," Winslow pointed out. "What if the neighbors had been watching?"

"Morons. That's what we have working for us." The man threw the misshapen clip onto the desk blotter. "They've bungled this thing from the very beginning."

"Well, we're in a pickle now, Digger," the senator pointed out. "You'll need a pretty big shovel this time around."

The man known to his friends as Digger grimaced. "You've got that right. Did they at least find out who the man at the house was?"

"No but they got the license plate and we're tracing it now."

"We would have known about her connection to Halloran if you'd found out everything about her the first time she met with you."

Winslow snorted. "Give me a break. Her publisher's an old friend of mine. I do this pretty often for him. If I had every author who interviews me investigated I wouldn't have time for anything else." He rose and began pacing the length of the office. "At least I got the ball rolling this time."

"Hopefully not a day late and a dollar short,"

Digger pointed out. "Now we have to hustle our butts to find out where she could go to hide and who she's hooked up with."

"We still don't know where Joey Latrobe's being hidden or what he can tell people. And we have to identify the man who visited Faith Wilding."

"Working on it, working on it." A muscle twitched in Digger's cheek.

"It's probably time to get rid of Halloran, now that we know who he's sending the messages to."

Digger shook his head. "Not until we find out if he knows who gave them the info about the meeting."

Winslow frowned. "Would he even know? That order came down from—"

"Damn it," Digger bit off. "I know where it came from. Don't rub my nose in it. But there had to be a source and that may have been in the mission briefing." He slammed his hand on the desk. "All right. I'll give our friend a call, tell him he's got forty-eight hours to get that information. Then we have to cut our losses and figure out how to do damage control.

* * * * *

The rain had been pounding down since early morning, the wind whipping it against the windows of the cabin. Standing at the bedroom window, looking out over the cliff, Mike could see the water of the Atlantic Ocean churning into sharp waves. Springtime in South Central Texas where Rick was at the moment might mean soft breezes and sunshine but on the Maine coast it meant brutal storms and bone-chilling cold as winter refused to release its hold on the countryside He only hoped the wind would die down before the helicopter landed later in the day.

Joey was propped up in bed eating soup with Troy's assistance. His pallor concerned the men in the room with him and they could see the pain in his eyes but he refused to let Troy medicate to the point where he couldn't think.

"Captain Halloran doesn't have time to wait for me to get better. Those fuckers are probably ripping him to shreds right now. I'm good to go. Let's get on with this."

Dan looked at Troy with raised eyebrows.

"He's in a lot of pain," Troy answered the unspoken question, "but I'm watching him. If I see he's pushing himself too far I'll cut it off."

"No, you won't." Joey jerked his head and a soft moan of pain escaped his lips.

"That's what I was afraid of," Mike said.

"No. Please." Joey took a deep breath, as deep as he could and let it out slowly. "Let me at least get the rest of the basics out."

"All right." Dan pulled his chair closer to the bed and unfolded the map of Peru. "We've circled Iquito there." He pointed with his finger. "Can you figure how close to the city the temporary camp was?"

"I'd say no more than an hour." He moved his good arm to run his fingertip over the spidery lines that indicated crude roads. "The insertion was at night and we could still see the lights of Iquito. We calculated the distance by that."

"That still leaves a big circle to choose from," Mike said. "Anything else you remember?"

Joey frowned in concentration. "We came in over the water and did the drop not far from where the Amazon curves in here." He pointed on the map. "I remember that little cover because the river takes a sharp turn there."

"Then what?" Dan prompted.

"Okay. Let's see. We had the GPS coordinates so I'd say we found them right about...here." He touched another spot. "But they moved from there and took the captain with them." He looked up. "I get the feeling they didn't go more than five or ten miles though."

"All right." Dan folded up the map. "This gives us a starting place. And you, my young friend, need to take your meds and get some more rest."

"But—"

"No buts. I'm going to make some calls. Reach out to some people who can get us more specific information."

"Yeah." Mike turned away from the window. "We've got folks we can contact. This terror cell may have picked a temporary place for their meeting to keep it secret but their camp won't be as well hidden. Word of it can't help but filter out. Someone will know where it is, now that we've got a starting point."

Troy took the empty soup cup from Joey and picked up a syringe from the nightstand. It had been less than forty-eight hours since they snatched him from the hospital so they were still giving him antibiotics to fight off possible infection and pain meds strong enough to keep him comfortable. It would be a while yet before they could cut back on the dosages, despite his constantly stated desire to stay awake and talk to them.

"Time for your nap, tough guy," Troy told him now, as he shooed the others out of the room. "Don't worry. You'll get all the gory details."

When they were gathered around the table again with filled coffee mugs, Dan picked up the satellite phone. "I think it's time to do some reaching out. Rick will be back here with our two guests in about..." He looked at his watch. "Three hours. I'd like to have everything locked down by then and be ready to roll."

"Yeah, our guests." Mike fiddled with his mug. "What the hell are we going to do with two women up here along with our patient?"

Dan punched some numbers into the phone. "I'm getting my cousins up here to stand sentry. They're just back from that job in Guatemala so I know they're available." When a voice answered on the other end he walked away from the table and spoke in low tones.

Mike and Troy looked at each other.

"What a fucking mess," Mike said.

"Ain't that just the truth." Troy looked out the window. "I hope this weather goes away before we have to hit the air."

"I just hope these women don't give us any shit."

Troy snorted. "Yeah, right. I can hardly wait to hear Rick's story on this Wilding woman."

"He didn't give you any clue?"

Troy shook his head. "Only that he'd rather tell us in person."

"About what?" Dan asked, coming back to the table.

"About why someone's so hot to kill Faith Wilding and why he needs to stash her away here instead of some hotel."

"Well, we'll find out soon enough. Meanwhile we have things to do. Mike, get the firepower out and make sure everything's clean and in working order. Troy, you get the clothes out of the chest over there. Camo suits, wet suits just in case, grease paint. Then pull out all the comm gear and check each piece over. I'm going to give the map another shot, then see what Dragon can tell us about the layout."

"Be nice if he could pinpoint exactly where the camp is," Troy said in a wry voice.

"He may just do that. All right, everyone." He looked around the room. "Let's get to work."

Chapter Fifteen

Mark had dozed off and on after he heard the Wolf walk away. He felt fuzzy and his skin was hot. He was sure that his very meager efforts had not been able to stave off infection from his wounds. He had no idea how long it had been since anyone entered the tent. Except for the rising and setting of the sun he'd lost all concept of time.

Tidbit, he thought.

God, if there was any way at all to get him out of this unholy mess, he was never going to let her go again. Other men in his situation got married and made it work. Why had he been so dumb as to think he couldn't? And why hadn't he even given Faith a chance to make her own choice. If he had the strength he'd have hit himself on the side of the head.

At some point one of Escobedo's men brought him his ration of water and whatever passed for food. Barely enough to keep him alive but apparently they weren't ready to kill him yet. He used a torn piece of his shirt to clean his wounds as best he could, then drank the rest of the water slowly. He might not die of dehydration, he thought wryly but he'd be lucky if dysentery didn't get him.

He forced down whatever the food was, then closed his eyes and lay down on the ground, unbearably tired. He didn't know how much longer he could hold on.

"Hola, capitan."

Mark opened his eyes to see Escobedo standing in front of him. He tensed, waiting for the usual kick.

Escobedo laughed. "I think I've had my fun, capitan. I came to bring you news."

Mark just stared at him, unblinking.

"Your friend, Miss Wilding, appears to have rattled some cages. It seems we no longer need Felix to discover the recipient of your messages."

Faith. Oh, Jesus.

He'd been terrified of this since he overheard their conversation, but his mind was too fuzzy to think straight. If they'd really gotten their hands on her...He mustered all of his waning strength to keep from lashing out at El Serpiente. This was his fault. He never should have reached out to her but she was his only hope. What if they'd already gotten their hands on her?

As if he could read Halloran's mind, Escobedo gave a nasty laugh. "No, unfortunately we do not have her yet but that's a situation easily remedied. It won't be much longer before we can bring her here to join you. Then we'll see how long you protect the traitor who sold us out."

I'd like to find the one who sold out my unit, you asshole. And even if I knew who you were looking for, I'd never tell you.

"Still the silent type. Very well. Enjoy your respite. Use the time to think. I would hate to see anything happen to the beautiful Miss Wilding."

Then he was gone.

Mark lay there feeling sick. Faith! They could kill him if only he had a way to keep her safe. Somehow she'd found Rick. That was his only lifeline. Did Phoenix now have her in a safe place?

He closed his eyes again, trying once more to think who could have sold them out. And were they too, now after Faith.

* * * * *

"It took a lot of digging to get this information."

Green was once again on the cell phone, having yet another unpleasant conversation.

"Well?" The voice was sharp. Impatient. "Do I have to wait all day for you to tell me?"

"You won't like it," Green warned.

"There is absolutely nothing about this situation that I like, so one more thing won't matter. Let's have it."

Green sighed and picked up the pad he'd been making notes on. "The SUV at the Wilding woman's house was rented by a company called Arizona, LLC."

"Who the hell are they?" the voice demanded.

"Nobody." Green sighed again. "They're just a shell. We had to do a lot of tracing and a lot of hacking to get any further."

"Quit dancing around it. Get to the meat."

"Okay, okay. At the top of the pyramid we found a company called Phoenix."

There was dead silence on the other end of the line for a long moment. "Shit," the man finally said.

"My sentiments exactly."

"Well, now we know how Joey Latrobe got taken from the hospital and who did it. Well, go and find them."

Green laughed, a very unpleasant sound. "Easier said than done. They don't even have an office that we can find."

"And their homes?"

"Yeah, right. Even my hacker couldn't find out where they live. Any of them. Talk about people who know how to go to ground."

"If we can't resolve this little problem," the man said in a tight, clipped voice, "we may need to take lessons from them."

Green gripped the telephone. "We're doing our best."

"Do better. Find them and find that damned woman. Smoke her out. Get rid of her. She asks too many questions and can get to too many people."

Green slammed the phone onto the table in the hotel room and reached for the ever-present bottle of Tums.

"More bad news?" Brown asked.

"Is there another kind these days? He wants us to find the Wilding woman and locate the partners from Phoenix. He thinks where one is we'll find the other."

Brown nodded. "I'd say he's probably right."

"Then he wants us to get rid of them all."

Brown's face paled and a fine sheen of sweat broke out on his forehand. "That's a joke, right?"

"I wish." Green popped two Tums in his mouth.

"Listen." Brown squirmed uncomfortably in his chair. "We've always had other people clean things up for us. I'm not about to put my head in a noose by killing someone."

Green fixed him with a hard stare. "Yeah? Let me point something out to you. Whether we do it ourselves or hire it done, the law will see us just as guilty, so forget about being so squeamish."

"I just—"

"And if we don't take care of this, we'll be going to prison. You want to spend the rest of your life with some three hundred pound gorilla who thinks you're his girl friend?"

Brown paled at the implications

Green stared at nothing for a moment. Then a phrase from his conversation tickled his brain. Smoke her out. He picked up the phone again, searched through the contacts and found the number he wanted.

"Are you available?" he asked the man who answered. "Good. I have a little job for you. And whatever you do, it must look like an accident. Downed electrical wire. Faulty wiring. Whatever you can come up with. Fine. Here are the details. Call me when it's done."

He looked up to find Brown staring at him.

"The man said to smoke her out. This ought to do it. Literally." He rubbed his hand over his face. "Be ready to call all your media contacts. We want lots of attention on the fire at the home of a famous author."

"I thought we were supposed to keep a low profile," Brown objected. "Won't people think it's suspicious when all of a sudden her house burns down?"

"That's the least of it," Green snapped. "The people we work for and the people they do business with would take great pleasure in skinning both of us alive if this thing falls apart."

Brown got up and went to the minibar, pulled out a small bottle of bourbon and drank a large swallow straight. "How the hell did we get to this point, anyway?"

* * * * *

The flight had been a little bumpy but the landing at the private airport was smooth. Faith tried to pull herself together as Rick unbuckled his seat belt and motioned for her and Tess to do the same. Ed came forward, opened the door and pushed it down to let the stairs unfold.

A gust of wind blew through the open doorway and Faith reached for her jacket.

Rick urged her down the steps, Tess behind her and brought up the rear.

Faith pulled her jacket tight and looked around her. They seemed to be in the middle of nowhere.

233

The airport, or whatever it was, consisted of a hangar, a small building that looked like an office and a long runway. To their left stood an enormous black helicopter. Otherwise, nothing, except open space and a chilling wind.

She turned back to Rick, who was carrying her duffel. "Where are we?"

"Maine."

"Maine?" she echoed stupidly. "You're kidding, right?"

"I never kid. Come on. We have to hustle." He began leading them toward the helicopter.

Faith stopped, refusing to move. "Please don't tell me we're going up in that thing."

"Okay, I won't tell you." He took her arm and forced her to move again.

"Come on, Faith," Tess said. "It will be an adventure."

She gritted her teeth. "An adventure I could do without."

"Would you rather be dead?" Rick asked

At that the panic began to grab her again and she started to walk rapidly.

"And let's not forget the primary focus here—rescuing Mark Halloran."

She stopped, suddenly still. "You're convinced he's still alive, then?"

Rick nodded. "Not only that, according to Dan we have a pretty good idea where the terrorists have taken him. The operation is being planned even as we speak. So, do you want to stay here all day and debate the method of transportation, or do you want in on this?"

Faith literally ran for the waiting helicopter, not even concerned at the awkwardness of her ascent into the cabin. She watched while Ed Romeo took care of the Gulfstream then jogged over to the helicopter. She barely held herself together as the man did what she knew was a preflight check then climbed into the cabin and closed his door.

"You guys all set?" Ed called back to them?

"Ready to rock," Rick told him.

In seconds the air was split by the whine of the rotors, the huge bird began to vibrate slightly and then they were moving. Forward motion first, before they lifted straight up into the air.

Faith was sure she'd left her stomach on the ground. She swallowed as hard as she could, willing herself to avoid the humiliation of tossing her guts out in front of these men. She glanced at Tess in the seat next to her but the woman seemed unbothered by any of this.

Rick, seated beside the pilot, turned to check on her. "You ladies okay?"

Tess smiled and Faith nodded, afraid to open her mouth.

Rick grinned. "Good. We're heading into a little heavy weather so be prepared."

Mark. I have to keep thinking of Mark. I can stand anything if I can just get him home safely.

They'd been in the air about fifteen minutes when the bad weather hit. Rain slashed at the windshield and the wind buffeted the helicopter. The pilot didn't seem deterred by it and Rick never flinched. Faith simply closed her eyes and prayed. She felt Tess reach over and take her hand and without opening her eyes she allowed herself a tiny smile.

It felt like an eternity before she sensed a change in the angle of the bird, opened her eyes and saw they were descending.

"My God, we're at the end of nowhere," she gasped.

"Close to it," Rick agreed.

A log cabin sat perched on a bluff overlooking what she realized was the Atlantic, an angry looking ocean with swirling whitecaps. From the cabin it was a sheer drop to the rocks below. A grove of trees stood to one side of the cabin and Faith saw four black SUVs parked next to them. The rest was open space and not much of it.

"God, is this the only way up here?" Faith asked.

Rick grinned again. "I think Dan would like it that way but no. There's a road beyond those trees. Straight up the cliff."

As the helo sat with its rotors spinning, Rick helped the two women down to the ground, bending low to avoid the rotor wash. Then he grabbed the duffle, slammed the door of the helicopter, waved to Ed in the pilot's seat and the bird lifted off. They bent low under the wash of the rotors as they ran for the cabin. When Faith looked up the door was open, bright light spilling out into the rain-soaked gloom. Three men, all as big as Rick—and Mark—stood framed in the rectangle. And there was nothing welcoming about their look.

The one in the middle, dark hair, fierce eyes, came forward. "Hello, Miss Wilding. I'm Dan Romeo. Come on in. We look frightening but I assure you, we don't bite."

A fire was crackling in the fireplace, something Faith wasn't used to seeing at this time of year and it bathed the rustic cabin in a warm glow. She wasn't shy about standing in front of it and rubbing her hands. She noticed Tess, far from her usual boisterous self, doing the same thing.

"Any more trouble?" she heard one of the men ask.

"No," Rick answered. "We got away clean. But I'll bet they're rallying the troops and having fits as we speak. Any news on the origin of the email I forwarded?"

"Troy ran it through the Dragon but for the moment it's a dead end. It leads back to a laptop registered to a false name. We've got the system running comparisons on the name to see who uses it as an alias. But we may not get anything before we leave."

Faith turned to face the men. "Thank you for letting my friend and me invade your space," she said in a formal tone.

Dan dipped his head once. "We couldn't do any less for Tidbit." His face was solemn but he didn't try to hide a twinkle in his eyes.

Faith gave him a shaky smile. How nice to have a tiny bit of humor in this situation. "I appreciate it." She turned her head. "This is Tess Ferguson, my assistant. And unfortunate innocent bystander in this tragedy."

Tess actually laughed. "It's all right. I needed a little excitement in my life."

Dan introduced the others in the room. "Would you like some coffee? A cold drink?"

"I don't suppose you have anything like a tea bag here, do you?"

Troy moved into the kitchen area. "It so happens I'm a tea drinker myself." He gave her a mock frown. "You're sworn to secrecy about this, you understand."

For the first time since that morning Faith relaxed a tiny bit. These men might not be happy to see her—she'd been dropped into their bolt hole, probably put them in a difficult situation. But they weren't going to throw her to the wolves or make her feel like an intruder. And she had the sudden feeling that if anyone could rescue Mark it was them.

"I wish I could give you time to rest," Dan told her but we're getting ready to leave as we speak. I need you to repeat for us everything you've learned from Mark in your...conversations."

Faith sat down at the table, gratefully accepting the hot tea from Troy. "How much has Rick told you?"

"The bare necessities. Why don't you fill in the details?"

So once again she told her story, watching the faces of the men as she laid it out for them, waiting for signs of the usual skepticism. She saw none of this, only an understanding that surprised her. Then she remembered who these men were and why nothing should surprise her.

"So there it is," she finished. "I can tell you, he's badly hurt. Probably tortured. Barely hanging on. And we're his only hope."

Dan and Rick exchanged looks.

She moved her gaze from one to the other. "What?"

"We'll try to make you as comfortable here as we can before we leave," Rick said. "We're not exactly set up for guests but you and Miss Ferguson can share the second bedroom."

"Wait a minute." She stared up at him. "You're leaving me here? Are you kidding?"

"It's the only place you'll be safe." Mike came over to stand by the table. "We have two men coming who'll be on sentry duty at all times. I'd trust my mother with them."

"Plus," Rick added, "This cabin has every kind of security system you could want."

"No." She slammed her fist on the table. "I'm going with you."

Dan shook his head. "Not happening. This mission is dangerous and demands only highly trained people. You'd be a liability."

"But I have one thing you don't," she pointed out. "I can exchange messages with Mark. You might need that to actually pinpoint him. Or find out information about the camp."

They just looked at her, not saying a word.

"You know I'm right," she insisted. "Just tell me what to do. I won't get in the way and I won't be a liability. I can keep up."

More silence, broken only by the snapping of the logs in the fireplace and the sound of the rain against the windows.

"She's right," Troy said at last. "She could be an asset."

Rick turned to Dan. "Did you make contact in Peru?"

Dan nodded. "Cristo knows approximately where the camp is. He gave us enough to at least figure out an insertion point. But he gave us another very valuable piece of information."

Rick reached into the fridge for a cold soda and popped the top took a long swallow. "And that is?"

"DEA has a man in Escobedo's group. Someone they've recently been able to co-opt for personal reasons. He's the one who reported where and when the meeting was going to take place."

Mike picked up another log and threw it on the fire, poking it to make sure it caught. "And why would the government trust someone who's already a traitor to one person?"

Dan's eyes turned cold. "Because he's not a willing participant. He's a field weapons expert and to get his cooperation Escobedo took his sister and won't release her until he proves himself. Uncle Sam promised to help him get her out and hide both of them away."

"Jesus." Mike poked at the fire again. "This

thing gets more convoluted by the minute."

Dan finished the coffee he'd been drinking, rinsed his cup and put it in the sink. "Well, we'd better get to it. We don't exactly have time to waste. We've made the transportation arrangements in Peru so we're set there."

"And me?" Faith asked. "What about me?"

"You'd better live up to your advertising. I'd hate to have anything happen to you but Mark Halloran's our first priority."

"Don't worry about me. I'll be fine."

I hope. Oh, Mark, we're coming. Just hold on a little longer.

And without any warning he was there.

I will. Tidbit...hurry.

*****

"He's doing what?" Winslow held the receiver away from his head and looked at it as if expecting it to turn into a foreign object. He'd been back in his office barely five minutes when he got the call. Suddenly the room paneled in warm mahogany with its thick carpets began to more closely resemble a plush cell.

"You heard me." Digger's voice was harsh. "I approved it so don't give me any shit. We need to find her and get her out of the way."

"Whose idea was this, anyway?" Winslow yanked at his tie to loosen it, unbuttoned his collar and opened the door to the hidden bar.

"I told them to smoke her out." Digger snorted. "I guess they took me literally."

"You don't think burning down her house is a little drastic?"

"I think going to prison would be a lot more radical. At this point we need to stop her from banging on doors. This will either keep her occupied or scare the shit out of her."

"If Phoenix has her they'll never let her out in the open. Even with something like this."

"Don't be so sure. Besides, this might be a way to get at them too."

Winslow laughed but there was little humor in the sound. "Now I know you're crazy. Nobody gets at them. You above all people should know that."

"Still, it's a shot we have to take."

Winslow poured two fingers of bourbon into a Baccarat tumbler, tossed in some ice cubes and tossed a healthy swallow down his throat. "Are you any closer to finding out who gave up the info for the mission to begin with?"

"Another boondoggle."

The silence that drifted along the connection was almost palpable. Winslow finished his drink and poured another one. Before this was over he was liable to turn into an alcoholic.

"No hint?" he pursued.

"My boss knows," Digger said, his voice tight. "I know him well enough to read the signs. But I couldn't blow it loose if I shoved a stick of dynamite up his ass."

Winslow tossed back part of the second drink. "Argentina is beginning to look better all the time."

Digger made a noise. "That may not be far enough."

"So when is this event supposed to take place?"

"Tonight. I'll call you when it's done. You'll be home?"

"I don't know. Call my cell. I'll have it on. And Digger. These guys better know what the hell they're doing."

* * * * *

Faith had asked for the chance to take a
shower, which made her feel marginally better.
When she emerged into the main room of the cabin,
showered and dressed in the warm clothes she'd
brought with her, Rick took her into the bedroom to
meet his brother and she and Joey spent a few
minutes talking. It was obvious to her, though, he
was still in a great deal of pain. She waited until
Troy gave him another dose of pain meds, then
went back to join the others.

"I can hardly believe he lived through that," she
told Rick.

"Latrobes are tough," he told her, his face tight
with anger. "But I promise you the people who did
this to him—to Mark—will wish they'd never been
born."

"Have you found out anything yet about the
email message?"

He shook his head. "Not yet. But I've got
someone working on it." He gestured at the other
men in the room. Normally Mike would do it
himself but as you can see, getting ready for this
mission takes priority over everything."

She looked around the room. Gear was
everywhere, laid out in an obviously orderly
fashion. Mike and Dan sat at the big round table
with an assortment of weapons in front of them and
in a chest to the side, methodically checking each of
them over. Faith had no idea what any of them were
but she was sure they could stage a small revolution
with what they had.

Troy sat on the floor, stacking piles of camo
clothing with wet suits and checking everything for
damage. Rick was on the couch, a variety of
equipment on the low table in front of him. Faith

was able to identify some pieces of the comm gear just from reading she'd done.

Tess was in the kitchen making a fresh pot of coffee and fixing sandwiches for everyone. She grinned at Faith. "You know me. I have to make myself useful."

Faith hugged her. "I have to tell you again how much I hate dragging you into this."

"Are you kidding?" She leaned over to whisper in Faith's ear. "All these hunks in this room? It's like a testosterone buffet." She winked. "And not one of them is married."

"Probably with good reason," Faith whispered back.

"Miss Wilding?" Dan put down the gun he was checking. "We need you for a moment."

"Please call me Faith. I think we're well into the first name stage here."

"Faith, then. Please." He gestured at an empty chair. "Could you sit down for a moment?"

Oh, oh. This couldn't be good.

"What is it?"

"I want to make it perfectly clear to you exactly what's going to happen when we leave here."

"I think I have a pretty good idea," she told him.

"I doubt it. Movies and books romanticize stuff like this. Here are the hard facts. We'll be flying the Gulfstream to Peru. It's too far for the helicopter but we've arranged to pick one up forma...friend. Ed will be flying and he'll drop us at our insertion point. The helo will hover and you'll have to jump without breaking a leg. You understand?"

"Of course." She folded her hands tightly in front of her. They were trying to scare her but her fear for Mark was greater than her fear for herself.

"You'll be wearing gear like the rest of us except

you won't have a rifle. Unless you're very familiar with an AK47, we won't have time to teach you and I don't want to take the chance you might kill one of us by accident."

"Fine." What did they expect her to say?

"You'll have to carry some kind of firepower, however. Just in case. None of us can take the time to provide protection for you."

She glared at him. "I don't expect you to. And by the way, I know how to shoot a gun."

Dan raised an eyebrow, skepticism plain on his face. "Is that right?"

"Yes. It is. Two years ago I took a handgun class and got my license to carry concealed. I practice at the range regularly."

Rick, overhearing, burst into a humorless laugh. "You're just full of surprises, aren't you?"

"Mark insisted on it. He said I travel around by myself too much not to do it."

"I see. And what's your weapon of choice, Annie Oakley?"

Faith resisted the urge to smack him. This wasn't the time to let anger get the best of her. "A Glock nine millimeter. And I'm damned good with it."

"Fine. Here." Dan held out a weapon to her. "See how this feels in your hand. Don't worry, it's not loaded yet."

Faith took the gun and hefted it. "Fine. It's a little heavier than mine but I can handle it."

"All right. Here's a full clip. Mike, take her out on the porch and see how quick she can lock and load."

Faith took the clip and followed Mike out into the cold. She felt like she had the first day at the range, when her instructor looked at her with mixed horror and respect. But she jammed the clip in place, racked the slide and took her stance in three seconds.

"Aim for that target." He pointed to one tacked to a tree, barely visible through the rain.

She looked up at him, he nodded, she shrugged and emptied the clip. Every bullet hit the center of the target. She couldn't help the smug smile on her face.

Mike looked down at her with unwilling respect in his eyes. "Well, well. You're not quite what you seem to be, are you?"

"I don't know. What do I seem to be?"

He led her back inside. "I guess I'm not too old to be surprised," he told Dan, nodding. "She's good to go."

Troy was eyeing her for a fit with camo clothing when Joey, who they'd all thought was asleep, yelled to them from the bedroom.

"Hey. Come here, all of you. Right now."

Flashing looks of concern at each other, they rushed to the room. Joey was sitting up in bed, watching the small television hooked to a satellite receiver. Panic flashed in his eyes.

"Take a look at the news." He pointed to the screen.

Dan stared at the image of a home engulfed in flames.

"A total destruction of the home of well-known author Faith Wilding. Investigators have yet to determine the cause..."

"Shit," Rick ground out.

Faith moved to look at the television. "What...Oh my God! That's my house." She looked up at Rick. "My house is burning down." She turned to push past him but he caught her arms.

"Where are you going?"

"I-I-I have to call someone. Everything I own is

in that house." She tugged at his grasp. "Let me get my phone."

He tightened his grip. "First of all, your cell phone won't work up here. You'd need a satellite phone."

"Which you have, right?" Her arms were upraised her hands curled into fists as she continued to try to free herself.

"Yes, but I'm not letting you use one. Faith!" He raised his voice. "Listen to me, will you?"

She fought back the tears burning her eyelids. This was no time to fall apart. "Please let me go. I have to call someone. My agent. The fire department. Somebody."

"No." Dan had moved to stand beside her. "Faith, this is exactly what they want. This is why they did it."

She stared up at him, shocked. "You mean this was set deliberately?"

"I'd bet on it. They tried to kill you, we made you disappear, now they need to get you out in the open."

"Dan's right," Rick added. "Whoever these people are, they're obviously pretty powerful. Penny ante crooks wouldn't do something as drastic as setting your house on fire."

"And I guarantee you," Dan picked up again, "they've got every place monitored that you might call. They'll trace you and swoop in to get you."

Tess had been standing in front of the set, watching with stunned horror as firemen worked to subdue the flames without much success. She turned to her friend. "Faith, they're right. You've obviously pushed some pretty powerful buttons and now you're a liability. They need to get rid of you before you do any more damage."

Faith couldn't stop shaking, hardly able to

absorb the fact that every personal possession she had in the world was gone. The first editions of her books, her notes, family pictures and mementoes. God, the list was endless. She realized what people felt like who lost their identities.

"Those are just things," Tess reminded her. "Maybe you can't replace them but at least you weren't in the house. Be grateful for that."

Rick led her gently back into the living room, sat her at the table and motioned for Troy to pour some brandy in a glass. He wrapped her hands around the tumbler of whiskey. "Drink this, but just a sip, enough to counteract the shock to your system. . You'll need all your wits about you on this trip.

Shock didn't begin to describe what she felt. Her body trembled all over and she felt as if her veins were filled with ice. She had to use both hands to grip the glass as she lifted it to her mouth. Even then a few drops splashed onto her fingers.

Dan seated himself across from her. "Tell me again who you talked to about Mark."

"Only Major Gregorio and Colonel Ryan. But I asked Senator Winslow to help me get into Fort Bragg. The major wasn't returning my phone calls." She gave them a brief recap of her conversations, shivering at the look they exchanged. "What?"

"I can promise you the leak didn't come from Gregorio or Ryan," Dan said. "That means Winslow is somehow in bed with the devil. He wasn't fooled a bit by your ploy of wanting to write a different kind of book."

"Something you said pulled a trigger with him," Rick pointed out. "My guess is he or someone else had you checked out and found out more about your relationship with Halloran than you'd want them to know. If they're the ones in bed with the

247

enemy, it was decided you were a liability."

If possible she began to tremble even more. She quickly lifted the glass to her lips and took a healthy swallow, sputtering as the fiery liquid burned her throat.

Troy handed her a glass of water and smiled at her. "Try sipping it. Goes down a lot easier."

"Thanks." She drank most of the water, then turned back to Dan and Rick. "So what do I do now? My life was in that house."

"I know and I'm sorry." She could tell he was choosing his words carefully. "I don't mean to make lightly of your loss but things are replaceable. People aren't. But you went through all of this to help Mark. Are you strong enough to put this aside until we do what we need to?"

What she really wanted to do was jump into bed, pull the covers over her head and cry. But overriding it all was the fact that Mark needed her. That she was his only link to a rescue. Rick was right. There was nothing in that house that couldn't be replaced. There was only one Mark. And she'd just realized fully the depth of her feelings for him.

She took in a deep breath and let it out. "I'll be okay." Her voice was shaky, so she swallowed and tried again. "I'm fine. I can do this."

Dan smiled at her. "Good. Now, let me ask you. Do you trust us?"

She widened her eyes. "What a question. Of course."

"Then I'm going to draws up a short document for you to sign giving us power of attorney. Write down your insurance information and anything else you think pertinent. We'll fax everything to our attorney. He'll act on your behalf and you can get this off your mind."

"You'd do this for me?" She looked from one to

the other.

"It's what we do for our friends," Dan told her.

Now she really did want to cry. Then another thought struck her. "My parents. Oh my God, they'll be frantic because they can't reach me."

Rick handed her one of the satellite phones. "Call them but give them no information. Okay?"

She nodded. "I know what to do."

"Okay." Dan rose from the table. "Let's get it done, folks."

The atmosphere in the cabin was noticeably more charged, as if everyone's adrenaline level had spiked. Which, Faith thought, it probably had. The fire, added to the importance and danger of the mission, had everyone just that much more on edge. While the men were going through their routine, she was pulled addictively back to the television, unable to draw herself away from the news reports.

In less than an hour they had Faith set up with their attorney, outfitted her with the gear she'd need and checked her over to make sure she knew how everything worked and gotten themselves rigged out.

"Why the wet suits?" Faith asked, watching as Troy rolled them up into thin bundles.

"Just in case," told her. "If we have to do a water drop we'll need them. But we'll wait on that."

She noticed the men carried .45 caliber handguns, not the nine millimeter like hers.

"Better stopping power," Mike explained. "But more gun than you need. You manage that Glock and you'll be okay."

"And what are these?" She pointed to the one he was working on.

"That, darlin', is LaRue Tactical Peda. The most dependable rifle ever made. Doesn't jam. Doesn't misfire. Easy to field strip. And highly accurate."

"A killing machine," she commented.

Mike looked up at her without a trace of humor in his eyes. "In this kind of situation, that's exactly what you want."

She couldn't help the chill that danced along her spine.

In the kitchen Troy was packing a large knapsack with water and granola bars. "Bullets and beer," he told her.

His jaw dropped. "Excuse me?"

"Two things you carry on a mission like this— ammo so you don't run out and water so you don't dehydrate. We throw in a granola bar just in case." He buckled a wide equipment belt around her waist. "I'll give you your stuff before we land."

She noticed Rick working with a gun different from the AK47 and asked him about it. She needed to keep talking to quell her anxiety and nerves.

"This is a Barrett .50 caliber. It's a long range sniper rifle, the kind my brother uses."

"And you," she added.

"Yes. And me."

"So does this mean you're planning to set up as a sniper when we get there? What will everyone else be doing?"

"Don't worry. Everything's covered." He studied her face for a moment. "You never did tell me how you dug up all this information about me. Or how you knew to call Phoenix."

So she told him about Andy and the things he did for her.

Rick just shook his head. "When we get out of this, bring him to see me. We can sure use a guy like that."

"All right. I will." She was sure Andy would be in hog heaven with a chance like this.

"Meanwhile, I sent your hate email up here for

us to check out. Let's send it to Andy and get him to track it while we do our thing."

"Okay." Using the satellite phone, she called Andy, told him what she needed, then waited while Troy sent the email and Andy let her know he'd received it.

"This shouldn't take long," he told her.

Whatever he found would be one more piece of evidence as they tried to identify the people behind this whole mess.

She tried to put the fire at the back of her mind, despite the awful sense of destruction she was feeling. In spite of her efforts, though, she couldn't stay away from the television, the horror of the scene continued to sicken her.

"It's...devastating." She fought back the nausea that bubbled up from her unsettled stomach. What kind of people destroyed a person's whole life like this?

"The captain..."

Faith jumped, unaware that Joey had awakened. She hurried to bring him some water, which he drank gratefully.

"The captain," he began again. "He'll kill them, you know."

She dredged up a smile for him. "And I plan to make sure he gets back here to do just that."

Finally, realizing she was just getting in everyone's way, she looked for Tess and found her in the second bedroom.

"You doing okay?" Tess's face was filled with concern. "You don't look so great."

"I'm fine." Faith flapped a hand at her. "I'll be doing a lot better when we find Mark."

At the mention of his name she was overcome with an urge to reach out to him, to assure herself he was still alive.

Mark. She waited but there was no response. She focused her mind the way Aunt Vivi had instructed. She also let herself reach back to the circle in Vivi's kitchen, the energy circle where the women had infused her with psychic strength.

Mark, she tried again.

Too late. The voice was deep and slammed into her like a steel wall. In an instant she felt an overwhelming presence of evil pressing into her. Her lungs felt compressed as if they didn't have enough air in them.

Mark! She tried to scream it in her head but what came out was less than a whisper.

Death is waiting for him. Say goodbye.

She grabbed her throat, invisible fingers squeezing her windpipe.

"Faith?" Tess was in front of her, a shimmering image. "Can you hear me? Breathe, okay?"

And then it was all gone. Dispersed, like so much smoke, as if it had never been there.

Faith collapsed back onto the bed, a fine sheen of perspiration on her face, dizziness threatening to engulf her.

"I'm getting Troy." Tess headed for the door.

"No!" Faith shouted at her, swallowed and lowered her voice. "No, please. Do not get anyone."

"But..."

"I'm asking you please. If they see me like this they'll never let me go with them."

"And maybe you shouldn't." Tess's eyes were filled with worry.

"I have to." She forced herself to stand up. "Especially now. But first I have to borrow one of their phones and call Aunt Vivi. I need her help."

Chapter Sixteen

"Let me get this straight." The man known as Digger was pacing in his library, having left his office to conduct business too volatile to be open to detection. "You burned down her house. She hasn't shown up. There are police and fire investigators all over the place. And we're still no further ahead than we were before."

Mr. Green popped a Tums in his mouth. At this rate they'd become the staple of his diet. "It was a calculated risk."

"Calculated risk?" Digger's voice rose at least ten decibels. A vein at the side of his neck bulged and throbbed and his skin color was a dangerous shade of red. "That's what you call this unbelievable disaster?"

"We discussed this with you," Green began.

"No." Digger banged his fist on his thigh as he walked. "You talked. I listened. I told you it was a stupid idea. You explained to me why it would work. Instead we've created a page one news story that could lead to all kinds of other things."

"They won't find any trace of arson," Green assured him, mopping his forehead with his handkerchief.

"They damn well better not." Another silence stretched. "I'm tempted to tell you to get yourselves back here but I think you'd better stay around another day or so, just to see what shakes out. Someone will show up to handle things for the elusive Miss Wilding. I want to know who it is and where they came from."

"We'll handle it," Green promised.

"Better than you've handled everything else so far," Digger warned. "I should have had you eliminated after the first fiasco."

The call disconnected.

ON the other end Green paled as he snapped his own phone shut.

"I take it he's not too happy," Brown guessed.

Green glared at him. "I'd say that's a masterpiece of understatement." He turned back to the television. They'd seen the bit on the fire at least a dozen times. Now the local news was on, giving it full coverage, interviewing everyone who could put two words together. At the moment they had the arson investigator on and Green leaned forward to catch his statement better.

"We aren't finished going through everything," the man was saying. "There are still too many hot spots. But our first determination is faulty wiring was the cause. We have to take a closer look to be sure."

"The police have said no one was home," the reporter commented. "Is that true?"

"At least we haven't found any bodies yet. But we also haven't heard from the owner."

The reporter turned full face to the camera. "Hear that, folks? If anyone knows the whereabouts of famous author Faith Wilding, please ask her to get in touch with the fire department at the number on your screen. Miss Wilding, if you're seeing this, it's urgent that you contact the authorities."

Green punched the Off button on the remote and the images disappeared. Yes, Miss Wilding, where in the fucking hell are you?

"Do we go home, then?" Brown's posture and tone were good signals of how little that prospect appealed to him.

"No. We get one more chance. Come on, let's get out of this room for a while and I'll tell you what we need to do.

* * * * *

Tess looked at the two men who arrived to do sentry duty, rolled her eyes and whispered to Faith, "Take all the time you want. What a couple of hunks."

"Tall, dark and deadly," Faith agreed and indeed they were.

Well over six feet, with jet black hair and eyes the color of coal, they had a grim, lethal look that said, "Don't mess with me."

Rick explained that, like Troy, one of them had been a medic and was well qualified to take on Joey's care.

It took only minutes to load everything into the helicopter, despite the rain that wouldn't let up and then they were lifting off, fighting the winds that came in over the ocean and swept up the cliffs, settling down at last as Ed found a smooth pathway. They'd chosen to have him fly rather than Mike because someone needed to be on point with the copter and Mike was needed in the mission.

Faith found the big Bell Ranger surprisingly quiet considering it had been stripped down inside to a bare shell. None of the acoustical cushioning of the fixtures on the trip up. Instead, the space was taken up with firepower, comm gear, other items like NVGs, which she learned stood for night visions goggles, the wet suits and instruments that could read heat signatures. Faith tried not to look too hard at the stash of medical supplies and the litter stowed at the back of the cabin. She prayed hard that Mark would still be alive when they found him to make use of those things.

It seemed barely minutes had passed before they were back in the hangar where they'd landed and up in the Gulfstream, this time the larger one.

Now they were sitting in the cabin around a table, looking at the maps in the center. Dan had plotted the course to Peru. and he reviewed it for them one more time. "We'll go down the Atlantic coastline," he told everyone, until we get to Panama. There's a place there we can refuel, then cross over to pick up the western coast of South America."

"Can we get ton where we're going in this plane?" Faith asked. "I'm sorry. I', sure that was a stupid question."

Dan cracked a smile. "Not at all. The helo can't go as far as we want without refueling too many times. That's why we're taking the Gulfstream to a place not far from where we figure Mark's being held. There will be a helo there waiting for us." Don't worry. We're fine."

"And after that?" Mike prompted.

"Iquitos is in the very north of Peru, kind of hugging Columbia and Bolivia. It sits right on the Amazon." He poked at a mark on the map. "This is as close to pinpointing the camp as Joey and I could come. We'll cut in at Chiclayo, then pick our way along the Amazon." He folded the map. "Miss Wilding."

"I really think you should call me Faith." Her smile was shaky.

"Very well. Faith. Once we're in the marked area, we're hoping you can make contact with the captain and maybe get a few more clues as to where he is."

"I'll do my best." She wet her lips.

"Did the call to your aunt help?"

"Let's hope." She closed her eyes and called up the conversation.

* * * * *

"Oh, my dear," Vivi had said. "You are so unprepared for this."

"I know, Aunt Vivi, but I don't have a choice. I need your help."

"All right. Let me think a minute."

Faith waited, curbing her impatience.

"All right, you will need to do more visualizing. Is it working for you?"

"So far, until that last episode. I think he tried to build a solid shield between Mark and me."

"Let's work on that, then, because this force of evil will try to stop you. Close your eyes and visualize a row of parabolic shields around you. Can you do that?"

Faith closed her eyes, lulled by Vivi's soothing voice.

"Fine. Now, make sure they're turned away from you, so any energy bounces back to the interloper. Whatever he sends your way will come right back to him."

"Okay." She clasped her hands. "Now what?"

"Next. Remember the stone walls we taught you how to build mentally?"

"Yes, I do."

"Go ahead and build it inside the parabolic reflectors. On the wall is one opening, a narrow pipe hole and you are to imagine Mark right there. Only he will be able to get through that hole."

"It's working!" Faith swallowed her surprise.

"Good, good. Now we'll do one more thing."

"What's that?"

"I will have Emily and Sarah come over and we'll form a docile energy circle, creating an unbreakable ring and transporting it to you."

Faith's eyes flew open. "Can you do that?"

"We're going to try. About what time do you think you'll be arriving at your destination?"

Faith checked with Dan and passed along the information.

"All right, dear. We'll set the alarm to be ready."

"Thank you so much, Aunt Vivi."

Vivi's voice dropped slightly. "Don't be afraid, Faith. The spirits will guide you. I promise. Now start practicing."

* * * * *

Now she sat in close quarters with four men she hadn't even seen forty-eight hours ago, heading off to a country she'd never been to, on a mission some might call hopeless, praying as hard as she could that she could do her part and get Mark out safely. She leaned back in the chair closed her eyes and tried to make everything around her a blank.

Establish your boundary-type shields first.

She heard Aunt Vivi's voice as clearly as if she were sitting in the cabin next to her. She could visualize her aunt sitting at her kitchen table, fiddling with her teabag, dunking it in a cup of hot water. Her brow would be furrowed in concentration but as she inhaled the light fragrance of the lotus tea, it would smooth out and she'd close her eyes, centering herself. For one fleeting moment Faith wished herself back in that familiar kitchen, embraced by the warmth of Vivi's presence. Then she pulled up her mental socks. Mark needed her. More than that, Mark loved her, as she loved him, something they'd only now, in this perilous circumstance, admitted to each other. She had to make sure they had a chance to let it blossom and grow.

Faith called up a remembered image of a parabolic reflector and imagined herself lining them up in a circle, convex side outward, so any negative energy directed toward her would rebound to the sender. Next she visualized dark grey bricks floating to the circle and aligning themselves one on top of the other, row after row, until they reached the top of the reflectors.

In her mind she saw herself sitting down in the middle of the impenetrable circle and focusing on one spot as Vivi had said. The place where only Mark could reach her. In an instant a hole appeared, about the circumference of a household plumbing pipe. In the shimmering light that drifted through it she saw Mark's face as she'd last seen it, smiling, affectionate, sexually replete.

Her heart tripped in its rhythm. This just had to work. She wanted a lifetime with him like that fabulous weekend. She would do whatever it took to help these men pull this off. And now, with her shields in place, the tension gripping her body began to ease.

"Faith?" Rick shifted over to sit next to her.

"Yes?"

"Are you all right? You looked a little spacey there for a minute."

She smiled. "I'm fine. Just following my aunt's instructions and mentally preparing myself."

"I still wish you hadn't insisted on coming along," he grumbled.

"But I did and I'm here." She studied his face. "Don't worry about me, Rick. Focus on Mark. I promise you I won't be a liability."

One corner of his mouth turned up in a half-smile. "No, I don't think you will. But promise me, if things start to get hairy down there, take cover and don't do anything foolish."

"Believe me," she grinned. "You are looking at one bona fide coward."

He gave her a penetrating look that seemed to see all the way inside her. "No, Faith Wilding, I think you're wrong. I think you are one very brave, very courageous lady. Mark Halloran is one lucky bastard."

"Thank you." She didn't know what else to say.

Mike, who had been talking on his headset, looked over at her. "I just had a call patched through from the attorney we sent to San Antonio. He's on site and scoping things out." His expression was grim. "Sorry to tell you this but your house is a total loss."

Faith forced back the automatic tears. "Like you said before, all that burned are things. I'm still alive."

"That's the most important thing. He's got someone else on site with him, nosing around, watching for anything that catches his eyes. Whoever did this is sure to come back to the scene of their crime, especially since you haven't shown up."

"Thank you for taking care of this," she told him.

He shrugged. "It's what we do."

Then he went back to what they'd been doing for the last several minutes, all of them—checking their guns for perhaps the hundredth time. And in the midst of this unbelievable danger, her life falling apart in shreds around her, she suddenly felt very safe.

* * * * *

"I can't believe they burned her damned house down." Gregorio was pacing in his office, a neat trick since the room was barely twelve feet square. "These people are animals."

Frank Ryan sat on a metal folding chair, holding his third cup of coffee of the day. "It also speaks to the fact that someone very high up is pulling the strings. No one else would dare take this kind of chance."

"You're right." Gregorio ran his hand over his military haircut. "But who the hell can it be?"

"Sit down and let's go over this step by step. We'll list everyone who had any knowledge of the mission and check each one out."

They started with Rick Latrobe, the source of the tip but crossed him off at once.

Ryan looked at his watch. "I promise you by now Rick and his band of merry men are on their way to Peru to pull off another one of their miracles."

They checked off each and every person who'd had to be contacted as the information made its way up the ladder. No one got a pass. Ryan wasn't ready to delete anyone else until they had proof positive there was no way they could be involved. That included office staff too.

Finally Ryan sat back and threw his pencil on the pad he'd been writing on. "Do you still have that computer guy attached to you who can even find out where Santa Claus lives?"

Gregorio couldn't help but smile. "You mean Sgt. Delray? Yeah, we couldn't live without him. Why?"

"Get him in here. We'll want him to dig around in some files that aren't actually accessible under normal circumstances. And threaten him with assignment to Easter Island if he opens his yap."

"You realize if some of these people find out you're digging into their personal business, *we* could be assigned to Easter Island."

Ryan's smile was grim. "Better than letting

them get away with it."

* * * * *

Green and Brown had changed from their suits to casual clothes and now were trying to blend in with the gawkers standing in front of the ashes of Faith Wilding's house. The thrill seekers were easy to identify, as were the media and the firemen still spraying hot spots. A man in turnout gear stood to one side, a clipboard in his hand, in heavy conversation with a fortyish man in a dark suit.

"The guy in the gear has got to be the arson investigator," Brown observed, "but who's the dude in the suit?"

"A good question," Green answered. "One we need an answer to."

"Not that we can just walk up and ask him," Brown pointed out.

"He acts like he's in charge of something. Maybe from her insurance company."

They stood there watching, trying to be as unobtrusive as possible, avoiding the attention of the media. Something about the man in the suit bothered Green but he couldn't say just what. Whatever it was gave him an uncomfortable itch. As surreptitiously as possible he took a picture of he man and his license plate with his cell.

"He's leaving," Brown pointed out. "Should we go talk to the investigator?"

Green gave him a pitying look. "And say what? Who's that man you were talking to? I'd guess they're looking for anything or anyone suspicious right now and we sure don't want it to be us." He speed-dialed a number on his phone, spoke briefly to the person who answered and sent the photos he'd taken. "They'll get right back to us. Meanwhile try not to attract attention."

His cell phone rang five minutes later. The conversation was brief and when he hung up his face was white.

"What?" Brown asked. "Who the hell was that guy?"

"His name is Roger Addison." Green wet his lips. "He's an attorney."

"So?" Brown chuckled. "Are you afraid he'll sue you?"

"Listen to me, you asshole. There's no information about him on the web. Our boss had to do some fancy hacking to find out about him. He's related to Dan Romeo."

"And he is?"

"The head of Phoenix. And all the information stops there."

Brown began to sweat. "Digger said he was afraid Faith was with them. You know what that means?"

"It means Phoenix has probably gone after Halloran and plans to finish the job his unit started."

"That's right. It also means we need to get the hell out of here and back to DC. The roof's about to fall in."

* * * * *

"Are you calling Peru?" Winslow asked. He'd switched to brandy, hoping to settle his stomach. Hoping he wouldn't throw up or pass out as he absorbed Digger's news.

"I don't think so."

"Why not? You need to warn them?"

"And then what, you idiot?" Digger was practically shouting. "Let him know how badly we've fucked up? Do you have a death wish?"

"Phoenix will wipe them up," Winslow whispered. "All of them."

"You'd better hope so. Otherwise they'll be coming after us."

Winslow took a healthy swallow of the brandy. "So what happens now?"

"I don't know about you but I'm going to make damn sure my tracks are covered and plead ignorance of anything that comes up."

"But what if they find out...I mean, the money..."

"It would take an unusual forensic accountant to track my money. I hope you're set up the same way. Go through your personal papers and make sure you haven't left any tracks. Oh and Winslow?"

"Yes?" The sound was like a death rattle.

"I wouldn't plan on running for office again, if I were you. Just in case."

Chapter Seventeen

They landed to refuel in Panama with the world still in darkness. Faith took advantage of the opportunity for a potty break and a chance to wash her face and hands. She grimaced at her image in the mirror.

Her face was deathly pale, her hair looked like a rat's nest tied up in a rubber band and dark bruises lay beneath eyes that had a haunted look. Somehow the men had managed to find cammo clothing that didn't fit too badly and two pairs of thick socks took care of the space in the boots. She was very conscious of the Glock in the belt around her waist and the four clips in the pouch.

"All set for the cover of *Vogue*," she whispered to herself.

Out on the tarmac the men were standing next to the plane, Dan in conversation with the man who'd greeted them on landing.

Rick spotted her as she walked up to them. "All set?"

She nodded, shoving her hands into her pockets to keep them from shaking.

"Okay. We're on the last leg here." He handed her what looked like a thin wire loop that he slipped over her head, with an extension he pressed to the hollow of her throat. "This is how you'll communicate. Don't say a word unless we tell you to. Every time Dan asks you to check in, tap this," he touched the piece at her throat, "five times. That's your number. Got it?"

She nodded.

"Okay. It will be light when we land, unfortunately, so we won't need the night vision goggles." He studied her face. "We'll pick up the chopper that's waiting for us and head for the insertion point. Ed will hover when we get there and you'll have five seconds to jump to the ground. Remember to bend your knees."

"Okay." She tried to ignore the flip flops in her stomach.

"Last thing. We've pinpointed the place pretty close to where we think the camp is but we'll need you to reach out to Mark and see if he can give us any clues. Can you do that?"

"I can do whatever I have to."

He squeezed her shoulder. "Good girl. When we land, you stick close to me until I tell you to hide yourself."

"Let's go, folks." Dan motioned to them with his hand.

In less than a minute they were lifting off again, heading away from the rising sun, stars still dotting the fading night sky around them.

I'm almost there, Mark. Please hang on just a little longer.

* * * * *

"I can only stay a few hours," the Wolf said, lighting a cigarillo. His chopper had landed five minutes ago and was waiting in the clearing off to the side. "I have other business that demands my attention. Either get this taken care of or we're done."

Escobedo's smile was nasty. "I know you, greedy bastard that you are. You won't walk away from the money you get from us."

The Wolf's eyes narrowed. "Listen to me, you piece of shit. No amount of money is worth destroying a business it took me years to build up. I won't spend the rest of my life running and hiding because suddenly the wrong people know too much about me."

"Is that a fact?" Escobedo's voice was flat.

"My success has been my anonymity. No one knows my real identity. This can blow it all to hell and I'm not willing to absorb that kind of risk."

"But you're here," Escobedo pointed out. "Are you not?"

"I am here to finish it. Or you. Take your choice."

"Very well. Come. We will have breakfast and then resume the, shall we say, festivities. This time I promise you, we'll get results."

Mark had heard the helicopter land and at first it startled him. Then he remembered the Wolf had left yesterday, saying he'd be back today. Through the narrow slit where the tent flaps didn't quite meet he could see the chopper some distance away, sitting in the clearing. Last time he'd arrived in the trucks with Escobedo's men but today he was on his own.

The men on guard duty would be changing shifts now, he knew. They'd all be having breakfast together, then those on the night duty would head for their cabins to catch some sleep. He marveled that so few men accomplished so much but he supposed when you trained for nothing else you could do whatever it took.

He knew this was probably the last morning he'd be alive to wake up. The Wolf wanted his answers today. If he didn't get them, they'd all cut their losses and that would be the end of Mark Halloran.

He regretted being unable to complete his mission, wiping out this burgeoning band of terrorists and ridding the world of a dangerous arms dealer. But more than that, he regretted never telling Faith how he felt about her. Never letting her know that she was his anchor, his love. How badly he wished they'd had more than that one weekend. More time to enjoy each other, to take this new relationship to the place where he knew it would go—marriage, a future.

What an idiot he'd been. There were plenty of other men doing what he did who had it all. Why had he been such a stiff-necked jerk, thinking he couldn't split his loyalties?

He had long since passed the point where the pain of his wounds was foremost in his mind. Doctors had said it was possible to cross that threshold where pain was so constant it lost its agonizing edge. But that's where he was now. His body was hot with fever and he was sure infection was rampant in his system. He was at the end of his resources.

But the very last thing he could do was resist giving them information. Whatever they did to him, he would simply close his eyes and will himself to die.

Mark! I'm so close now. Promise me you'll hold on a little longer.

His head jerked up. *Tidbit?*

We're almost there. Don't give up now.

He waited but she was gone. But her sweet, sweet voice and her pleading message were enough. Somehow he'd keep it together until help arrived. Because now he believed it was finally on the way.

* * * * *

"Jesus Christ." Frank Ryan looked at the information on the computer screen, refusing to believe what he was seeing.

"That's not possible," John Gregorio said. "I

have a hard time believing this."

"Yeah, me too. But there it is." He turned to the young soldier who'd been doing the work for them. "Thanks, son. I think you'd better leave us alone now. And remember..."

"I know," the young man said. "Zip the lip or it's Easter Island."

"Or worse," Gregorio growled.

"Yes, sir. Sirs." He saluted and let himself out the door.

The two men couldn't take their eyes away from what they were reading. Ryan scrolled up and down on the screen, they switched back and forth between the documents the hacker had found for them. The magnitude of the situation frightened them both.

"We're lucky we aren't in World War Three because of these men," Gregorio said at last.

Ryan nodded. "For men in this position to be consorting with the worst arms dealer in the world is worse than treasonous. The damage they could do scares the shit out of me."

"What made you start him off on this path, anyway?"

"You told me Winslow badgered you into giving Faith Wilding an appointment but ordered you not to give her any information. Certainly we wouldn't tell her anything classified but this would have been a great chance to get some favorable publicity about what our mission is. Why did he want you to kill it?"

"Because he sensed she had an agenda that was less literary and more personal, is my guess. He didn't want anyone digging into what happened to Mark Halloran and his mission."

Ryan swallowed the last of the cold coffee in his cup, made a face and threw the empty cup in the trash. "He'd have been a lot better off if he'd tried to

work with you on this and figured out how to turn
her off."

"I don't think anything could have turned that
woman off. She was like a dog with a bone. I knew
the minute she walked out of here all hell would
break loose."

"And now she's got Phoenix involved."

Gregorio smiled. "Oh, they'd have been on it
anyway. I knew once Rick got his brother out of the
hospital they'd go in for Halloran."

"I wish them luck." He cleared his throat.

"Well. We have to do something with this. I'd
call McLean myself but it will be better coming from
the head of JSOC. He always swears his people are
thoroughly investigated and vetted. And look who
handles that. Ray Frost, his chief of staff. This will
certainly give him something to think about. Along
with a bad case of indigestion."

"No kidding. Right now the Department of
Defense is fielding enough crap as it is."

"All right, then. I'd better get JSOC on the line.
Can you get me a ride out of here? They'll want to
talk to me in person. And we need to find out who's
in the field doing the dirty work."

The major picked up the phone. "Consider it
done."

* * * * *

The Bell Ranger they'd switched to had made a
one-eighty turn and they'd been flying back into the
rising sun for about twenty minutes now.

"All right, folks." Dan made sure he had the
attention of everyone in the cabin. "Five minutes to
go. I wish we were doing this at night rather than
daylight but we take what we can get. Everyone
ready?"

They all nodded in turn, checking their gear and their firepower one last time.

"All set, Faith?" Rick leaned close to her. "This is it."

"I'm ready."

"Just do what I tell you to, okay? Got your earpiece in?"

She nodded.

"Can you hear me?"

"Loud and clear."

"Good. We're dropping close to approximately where we think the camp is. Good thing this looks like just one of the many personal choppers that fly over here. We'll be able to pinpoint things better as we get closer. And we've got top of the line equipment to read heat signatures, so we know where everyone is. Just stay behind me."

"Got it."

The five minutes seemed to rush by. Then Rick was urging her onto her feet and towards the door that Mike had opened. The helicopter went into hover mode and one by one the men dropped to the ground in a crouch.

"Your turn," Rick told her. "I'm right here with you. Remember to bend your knees."

They were less than ten feet above the ground but to Faith it might as well have been five miles. She felt the pressure of Rick's hand on her shoulder, gathered her courage and pushed herself out of the doorway. She remembered about her knees, bending down to a deep crouch. Nevertheless she landed with a thud that jarred every bone in her body and shook the fillings in her teeth. Knowing she didn't have time to worry about aches and pains, she tucked herself and rolled when she hit the ground as she'd seen people do on television and in the movies.

"Good girl." Mike was pulling her to her feet and checking her over for broken bones.

Then Rick was beside her, waving off Ed and the chopper. "Okay, Faith. Time to do your thing with Mark. Can you make it work?"

"I'll try."

They had landed in a tiny area of waving grasses surrounded by tall trees with wide trunks and plants so thick it was impossible to see where one ended and the other began. The scent of the river drifted in the air.

"The Amazon," Rick explained. "We're five or six miles from it but the scent still carries on the wind. Do you need me to do anything?"

"No. Just... If I can be by myself at that tree over there?"

"Go ahead. We'll keep watch."

She leaned against the rough bark of the tree, brushing at the insects crawling up and down the trunk. She used an old trick to center herself, pulling down a mental window shade to blot out everything else. Then she called up the image of Mark's face, the one she'd used building her shields.

Mark!

Silence for a moment, the heavy pressure she'd felt last night (was it only that short a time ago? The creeping miasma of evil began to wrap itself around her.

He is dead. You are done.

No! She wouldn't believe it.

Dead, the voice repeated.

Aunt Vivi, she called out. I need you now. As if they were standing right next to her, she felt the invisible energy shield from the women thousands of miles away. The air vibrated with it. Almost shimmered with it. Then she brought up the image of the circle, the parabolic reflectors, the stone wall and the tiny opening where only Mark could get through.

Again she felt the evil pressing in on her, nearly suffocating her but she concentrated as hard as she could on the circle of protection, drawing on the energy of the women. Little by little the battle of wills turned in her favor and pressure eased.

Mark! she tried again.

More silence.

At last, very faintly *Tidbit...same weekend too.*

Oh, God, you're alive! She felt tears running down her cheeks and swiped at them impatiently. *We're here. Right near you. Not far away.*

Here?

In the jungle. Phoenix is with me. We're coming to get you.

She waited out what seemed another interminable silence.

How...find me?

Later, when we have more time. I need your help.

Funny...me...help...

No. Listen. We're about five miles away. Can you give me any clue about your location? Anything we can spot?

This time the pause was longer and she was afraid she'd lost him.

Chopper...outside tent...landed here...

She tried to keep the exhilaration out of her voice and remain calm for him. *Okay, okay. That's good. I'll tell them. Keep listening for me, my darling.*

She motioned to Rick.

"Something?" His own eyes held a flicker of excitement.

"A helicopter. He said one landed in the camp. Outside a tent. Maybe the one where they're keeping him."

Rick unclipped the remote microphone from his belt. "Ed? We need you to do a circumference search for a helicopter," he whispered. "It should be in a clearing where the camp is." He raised his eyes at Faith and she nodded. "Yeah. Where the camp is."

Faith had a hard time controlling her impatience while they waited for Ed to contact them. She didn't know how the men could stand so calmly but she guessed it was years of training. She forced herself to be just as quiet but her heart was racing.

She held her breath as Rick lifted the comm unit to his mouth again.

"Okay. Got it. Thanks." He unclipped his tiny GPS unit and punched in some numbers. "Come on."

He took Faith's arm and moved toward the other three men. "Apparently a bird landed in their camp just recently. Ed spotted it from the air and gave me the coordinates. We're three miles away. Let's go."

The trek through the jungle was nerve-racking. The men moved like silent ghosts, barely rustling the foliage. Faith tried her best to do the same while still keeping up the pace. Periodically they would stop, listen, then move out again. Three miles had never seemed so long to her.

At the exact moment she was sure she'd drop if she had to take another step, they halted. No one spoke. Dan gestured to the others with hand signals. Rick put his mouth close to her ear. "We're close. Go with Dan. I need to take up my position."

Faith looked at Dan as Rick moved away at an angle. He motioned for her to stand beside him. "We're going closer. I'm going to put you out of the line of fire. Stay there. If I ask for your signal, you know what to do."

She nodded.

"Okay. Let's go."

And then they were within sight of the camp. Mike pulled out a small pair of binoculars and swept them from left to right.

"Four cabins," he whispered. "Campsite in the center. Helicopter off to the left next to a tent."

"Must be where Mark is," Dan whispered back. He pulled out the tiny instrument that registered heat signatures and swept the site as Mike had done with the binocs. "Yup. He's there."

"How many?" Troy asked.

"I count ten, including Mark. Not a large group. Okay. No talking. Everyone ready? Okay, then. Let's move."

Dan boosted Faith up into the crotch of a tree where a thick limb jutted out, nodded and moved away from her. From her vantage point she could see the men move out in different directions, so silent if she didn't know they were there she'd have been unaware of them.

She had no idea where Rick was but he was the sniper so she assumed he'd be someplace up high. Pulling the Glock from her belt, she rammed home a clip and racked the slide. She'd never shot anything but a paper target but she could kill to save her life. Or Mark's. Holding the gun the way she'd been taught, she sat and waited.

* * * * *

"What was that?" The Wolf looked up from the cup of really bad coffee he was drinking. He couldn't wait to get shut of this cesspool. This was the last time he let himself be talked into a situation like this, no matter how much money was involved.

"A helicopter." Escobedo drew on his cigarillo.

"What is it doing here?" the Wolf looked up again. "You don't think that's suspicious?"

"Not at all. Helicopters fly over here all the time. You'd be surprised how many people have them."

"Still. It's possible someone has found us."

Escobedo laughed. "And who would that be? The people around here know enough to stay away from me and everyone else minds their own business."

"If what you say about Halloran and his psychic abilities is true…"

"Pah! True or not, Felix has slammed down a mental shield. In any event, *el capitan* is close to breathing his last. When we are rid of him it will all be over."

"Let's get to it, then. I must leave shortly." He dumped out the rest of his coffee and set the empty tin cup on a rock.

"Fine." He moved into the central part of the camp. "*Hola!* Time for the morning's entertainment. Two of you please bring our guest out here to me."

The two men closest to the tent rose from the log they'd been sitting on and started to get Mark.

Then all hell broke loose.

Chapter Eighteen

At the sound of the first shots Faith flinched and nearly lost her balance but she righted herself quickly, still gripping the gun. From her perch she had a pretty good view of the central part of the camp. She saw the two men heading for the tent pitch forward and fall. Suddenly everyone was running around like crazed chickens. Four men ran from one of the cabins carrying what looked to her like enormous weapons. From the perimeter she heard the sounds of rapid-fire rifles spraying the trees and bushes.

The jungle came alive at the disruption. Leaves rustled in trees and plants as birds of every color flew into the air, squeaking and squawking, flapping their wings in a desperate bid to escape the disturbance. Howler monkeys screeched, their ear-splitting cries piercing notes above the splat of bullets. Faith could hear the sounds of animals crashing through the underbrush as they raced for protection.

A thin, dark man in the center of the camp was screaming at everyone in Spanish, shouting orders to the men, who began indiscriminately spraying the area with bullets. A man dressed in grey slacks and darker grey shirt, an anomaly compared to the jungle attire the others wore, ran from the far side of the camp toward the clearing at the other side, where a helicopter stood waiting. He waved his hand in a circling motion and the rotors began their preliminary whine.

Faith couldn't spot any of the Phoenix men but she knew they were there by the constant chatter of their guns. She focused on the tent where she was sure Mark was being held.

Hold on, Mark. We're here. We're here.

As the man in grey slacks approached the helicopter at a dead run, Faith heard the whistling sound of what she later learned was a rocket propelled grenade and the 'copter exploded in a bright fireball. The man in grey fell back, pushed to the ground by the force of the explosion.

"Oh my God," Faith screamed, forgetting the order for silence in the shock of the explosion.

"La senora!"

She heard the voice from below her and looked down to see a man raising his rifle toward her. She reacted automatically, barely taking time to think, all those hours on the range paying off. Before the man could fire she aimed the Glock at him and emptied the clip into him. He fell back, his face and chest covered in blood, his finger tightening on the trigger one last time in death, the rifle spraying bullets into the air.

Her heart was racing so fast she was sure it would explode any minute.

Think of him as a paper target. Don't think of him as a person.

But she suddenly remembered her promise—*I'll get you out even if I have to kill someone.* She hadn't expected it to come to that but she realized with a shock that she'd do it again if need be.

Suddenly Mike was there, giving her a reassuring smile. "Good girl. You're doing great. Just hang on a little longer, okay? And be sure you put that second clip in the gun. "

When he heard the click of the clip jamming home, he moved away from her toward the camp.

Faith, frozen in her position, trying to make herself breathe, saw bodies everywhere. Only two men were left alive now, the man in grey and the one who'd shouted orders earlier. The latter ran for the tent and moments later Faith felt her heart clench as he dragged Mark into the clearing, a knife at his throat.

She nearly cried out at Mark's condition— filthy, covered in mud, dried blood everywhere on his body, his face twisted in pain. Before she could stop herself she climbed down from the tree and raced toward the open space. At the edge of the clearing a hand grabbed her and dragged her back.

Troy pulled her next to him and shook his head. "Stay here. It's all right."

All right? How could it be all right? They'd come all this way to rescue Mark and now he was about to be killed right in front of her.

"I have your captain," the man called. "Let me leave here in my vehicle or I will slit his throat."

The man in grey had moved to stand next to him, a gun in his hand. "I'll shoot the first person who tries to walk in here," he warned.

Faith tried to tug free of Troy's grip but his fingers were like steal. He shook his head again. "It will be all right," he mouthed. "I promise."

In the next instant a shot split the air and Escobedo's head exploded like a ripe tomato. He fell back, one arm still holding Mark but the knife hand thankfully flopped to the side.

"The next one's for you, Lobo," a voice called out and in seconds the Wolf was nothing more than a pile of grey material next to Escobedo.

Now Troy released Faith and she raced toward the clearing, where Dan was already lifting Mark from Escobedo's grip and stretching him out on the ground. Faith threw herself onto him, ignoring his injuries, ignoring the blood and dirt, ignoring everything except the fact that this man was alive...and in her arms. Still breathing. Still here.

"Hi, Tidbit." His words were edged with pain

but his mouth tried to turn up in a smile.

"Hi," she sobbed. "F-Fancy meeting you in a place like this."

Behind her she heard Dan chuckle, then he reached down to lift her up. "We need to get out of here, Faith. And we need to get Mark on the litter. Come on."

Behind her she heard Mike call for Ed to bring in the helicopter and, as it landed, Rick came running from wherever he'd been, carrying his sniper rifle. She knew he'd been the one to fire the last two deadly shots and she couldn't find words to thank him. He began moving around the camp, leaving something every place he stopped, Mike following behind him with a roll of what looked like heavy twine.

"Hang on a little longer, buddy," Troy said, as he and Mike strapped Mark into the litter from the bird.

As Ed landed, Faith saw a member of Escobedo's group still alive, scrambling out of the foliage where he'd been hidden.

"Grab him," she shouted, then froze as Dan moved forward, hand extended to the man.

"That's Alex," Rick said softly. "The inside man. It's a wonder they didn't figure it out and kill him."

Then they were all on board, the litter locked down, Troy on one side already giving Mark a shot for the pain and beginning the arduous process of cleaning his wounds. Faith sat on the other side, gripping his hand, tears still streaming down her face. The rotors whined, dust kicked up around them and they lifted off. They were maybe five hundred feet above the ground when Rick depressed a button on the tiny mechanism in his hand and the entire camp exploded.

Faith looked over at him, eyebrows raised.

"Just a little precaution," he told her. "Better for them to all just disappear rather than have someone find their bodies. This way we can report a clean kill." He grinned at her. "By the way, nice shooting back there."

"Thanks," she told him, in a shaky voice. "I hope I don't have to do it again any time soon."

His face turned serious. "You'll have a reaction to this when everything settles down and the adrenaline rush is gone. Try not to waste too much time on it. Think of it as taking out the garbage."

"I-I'll try. And thanks." She took in a deep breath and let it out.

"Tidbit?" Mark's words were slurring from the effects of the medication.

"Right here." She squeezed his hand.

"Love you."

"I love you too." Tears were flooding her cheeks again.

His eyes closed and Faith looked up at Troy, frightened.

"He's fine," he assured her. "Just knocked out from the pain meds. He's hot as a pistol from fever. I think all his wounds are infected. I'm going to give him massive antibiotics and then finish cleaning him up. It's better if he's asleep."

"Okay." She lifted Mark's hand to her lips and kissed his fingers, then turned to the other men. "I don't know how to thank you all. I mean, for doing this."

Rick smiled. "Just a walk in the park, Faith. Happy to do it. But you tell that big lug when he wakes up we don't plan on having to do it again."

"I will."

She heard Dan on the radio talking to the men at the cabin, then making a call to someone else to give a terse report on what happened.

"All set," he told everyone over the noise of the rotors. "There are about to be a couple of unhappy people in Washington."

They set down briefly at the edge of Iquito where two men were waiting for Alex.

"Escobedo had his sister," Rick explained to Faith. "These men are going to help him get her away from where they've been hiding her."

Then another stop to switch back to the Gulfstream, carefully moving Mark and getting him set in cabin. Finally they lifted off again and Faith hitched closer to the litter. She sat holding Mark's hand as they flew into the bright glare of the morning sun. They were finally going home.

* * * * *

Trey Winslow had just arrived home and was in his den pouring a before-dinner drink when Georgia came to the doorway.

"Trey?" Her voice sounded thin and her eyes were filled with worry.

"What is it?"

"There are...some people here to see you."

He lifted an eyebrow. "People? I wasn't expecting anyone."

Two men in the full uniform of military police appeared behind her. One of them stepped forward. "Senator, you'll need to come with us."

Trey's hand shook as he set the glass down and his stomach heaved. "Can you tell me what this is about? I'm afraid there's some mistake."

The Attorney General moved into the den, a somber expression on his face. "I'm afraid not, Trey. I came along myself so we can do this with a minimum of fuss. But I think you know what this is all about."

"Trey?" Georgia looked at him. "What's happening?"

He picked up his jacket from the chair where he'd dropped it. "It's all right, sweetheart. Just a little misunderstanding. But you might call Sam Morgan and tell him his legal skills might be needed."

He buttoned his jacket, tightened his tie, kissed his wife and walked out of his house for what he was afraid was probably the last time.

* * * * *

Mr. Brown and Mr. Green sat quietly in their seats as their plane landed smoothly at Ronald Reagan Airport. They'd said little to each other since the call came to get their asses back to Washington. Things were falling apart. They knew it.

All they wanted at this point was to finish up their business, get the hell out of Dodge and take their money with them. How bad could hiding away on an island be, anyway?

As the plane rolled up to the gate, the co-pilot exited the cockpit and walked purposefully into the cabin until he reached their seats. He motioned for the passenger in the aisle seat to stand and took his place.

"Please wait until all the other passengers have deplaned," he said in a quiet voice. "I'd appreciate it if you didn't cause a problem."

Mr. Green tried to bluff his way through. "What's going on? What's the meaning of this?"

The co-pilot just looked at them. "I think you know that. If it were up to me, I'd just shoot both of you and be done with it but we all have rules to follow.

Mr. Brown looked as if he were about to throw up and Mr. Green broke out in a cold sweat. They sat wedged in by the co-pilot until the plane was empty of all the other passengers. Seconds later three men in the uniforms of the military police entered, their faces grim. One of them stepped forward.

"Lloyd Brannigan? George Harris? As employees of he United States Department of Defense, it is my duty to tell you that you've been charged with treason."

"There must be some mistake." Brannigan, aka Green, tried to bluff. "Do you know who we report to?"

The man looked at him his face rigid with distaste. "We do. The chief of staff to the Secretary of Defense, who at this moment is also being arrested."

Brown and Green looked at each other.

"Shit." Brown (Lloyd Brannigan) said the word softly.

"Double shit," Green (George Harris) agreed.

"You need to come with us," the man announced. "You won't want to cause a disturbance. Any one of us would be more than happy to shoot you, given the chance."

Mr. Brown and Mr. Green looked at each other. It was truly over and the jaws of hell yawned before them.

* * * * *

Secretary of Defense Howard McLean walked into the office of his chief of staff, Raymond "Digger" Frost, his face tight with anger. The telephone call from JSOC had been like a pistol shot to the head. If the proof hadn't been sent to him on

284

his very private email, he'd have vigorously denied it. But he couldn't dispute the facts.

Shit. This was all he needed right now.

Digger was on the phone but at the look on his boss's face he hastily said, "Call you back," and hung up. "What's up?"

McLean stared at the man in front of him, wondering how he could have misjudged him so badly. "I've known you a long time, Digger," he said slowly. "We've been through a lot together."

Digger's smile disappeared. "Is something wrong, chief?"

McLean shoved his hands in his pockets. "You think you know someone and one day something happens and you realize that person is a stranger. Someone you don't even understand."

Sweat popped out on Digger's forehead. "Mind telling me what this is all about?"

"I think you know what I'm talking about. It's about being a traitor. About selling out your country to make money. About turning your back on everything good and decent."

"Chief, I—"

"They rescued Mark Halloran this morning," McLean said.

Digger paled. "I beg your pardon?"

"It isn't my pardon you should beg. It's the souls of those brave men killed because you sold them out." He turned toward the door and waved two military police into the office. "Get this garbage out of here."

He could hear Digger protesting all the way down the hall and a terrible sadness settled over him. It would be a long time before he ever gave anyone that kind of trust again.

* * * * *

The rain had stopped by the time the chopper landed on the bluff next to the cabin. The wind, however, was still strong but Ed battled it skillfully as he set them down. The door to the cabin banged open and Tess, clad in an oversized sweatshirt and rolled-up jeans raced out to the clearing. She stood impatiently to the side as Troy and Rick leaped down, then lifted the litter out. When Faith followed them Tess threw her arms around her.

"Thank God, thank God." She hugged her friend. "I was so worried. Even though Dan called to tell us you were all okay, I had to see you with my own eyes."

Faith hugged her back, then tugged loose. "Let's go inside. It's freezing out here."

The men had carried Mark into the second bedroom and moved him onto the bed. Troy was busy shifting the IV bags and setting up equipment. He turned as Faith came in the door. "I could only do basic first aid on the chopper," he told her. "Give me about a half hour, okay? Those wounds really need better cleaning, some of them need packing and others may need stitching. And it won't hurt for me to bathe him. He's got twenty layers of jungle dirt on him."

"Can I help? Please?"

Troy studied her face, then nodded. "All right. I can use the help. Find something clean to change into and wash up real good. I'll get everything ready."

It took more like an hour and Faith had to bite her lip to keep from crying again at Mark's condition. How he'd managed to stay alive was a miracle in itself. Finally they had him thoroughly cleaned, stitched, bandaged and medicated. Faith pulled a little wooden chair up to the bed and sat down.

"I'll stay with him."

"All right. I'll bring you in a better chair, though."

She gave him a watery smile. "It doesn't matter. I could sit on nails and not feel it."

"I'll bet you could," he grinned.

The others came in to check on Mark and Tess brought her a mug of tea, having found more teabags in the cupboard.

"You should eat something," she said. "You can't live on tea."

"Later. But thanks."

She reached for Mark's hand—the one without the IV in it—leaned forward to touch her forehead to his body and finally, now that it was done, gave in to the flood of tears.

* * * * *

It turned out, of course, to be the scandal of the year. Maybe of the decade. A member of the Senate Armed Forces Committee and the chief of staff to the Secretary of Defense selling information to the world's most notorious arms dealer. Selling out the men and women fighting to preserve the very freedom those men enjoyed and putting the country they served at risk. Secretary McLean looked as if he'd aged twenty years and Georgia Winslow went into what could only be called seclusion.

The Department of Justice was ruthless in rounding up everyone who had ever been involved with them. And thanks to the efforts of Major Gregorio and Colonel Ryan, they had the information on the money trail and scooped up everything in their accounts.

At the cabin in Maine the men of Phoenix monitored the television reports, angry at the callousness and greed of two men who had jeopardized so many lives, not to mention the security of the country. Joey improved daily, excited that his captain was actually safe and alive and even managed to visit Mark's room.

Dan, Rick and Mike left, heading back to Baltimore where they would operate out of Dan's condo, although they checked in daily. Only Troy remained behind to take care of his two patients.

Major John Gregorio had flown up on a sunny morning and brought them further information. He spent an hour with Mark, visited with Joey, quietly thanked Troy and asked him to pass along his gratitude to the others.

He shook Faith's hand firmly before he left, a look of admiration in his eyes.

"You're a courageous woman, Miss Wilding," he told her. "You've got guts and determination. Captain Halloran's a lucky man."

The Phoenix attorney had taken care of Faith's situation with startling efficiency. She already had a check from the insurance company and an offer from her publisher to replace her materials. She'd spoken to her parents and assured them she was fine, Mark had called his folks and Tess had gone back to San Antonio to begin rebuilding the materials Faith would need to go back to work.

By the following week Joey was stashed someplace else and everyone else had tactfully removed themselves. Troy had agreed that Faith could handle whatever care Mark needed and Ed had flown some supplies up to them. Faith stood with Mark outside in the fresh air and sunshine as they watch the helicopter lift off Then they headed back inside.

"I insist that you lie down," she told Mark. You've been up a lot today."

"Only if you join me," he grinned.

She gave his arm a playful swat as he dropped onto the bed. "You're in no shape for any funny stuff, soldier."

"You'd be amazed at what I'm in shape for." He smiled, but his eyes were dark with need.

"Mark." Faith busied herself taking off his shoes and socks, tugging down his jeans, pushing him under the covers. "I'm serious."

"So am I." He reached up and pulled her down on top of him, then rolled her to his side. "I'm a sick man. You have to do what I tell you. And what I'm telling you is to get under these covers with me right now."

"I don't think..."

"Right. Don't think." The smile left his face. "Please, Faith. It's been so long. I need to hold you next to me. Naked."

Biting back further protests, Faith kicked off her shoes and pulled off her socks. Removed her clothes and dropped them on the straight-back wooden chair. Gave him an assessing look as if to assure herself he was really okay for this kind of activity, she reached into her large tote and pulled out a box of condoms.

Mark's eyes lit with amusement.

"A woman who comes prepared. I like that."

She took one foil packet out and tossed it on the night stand. By the time she pulled the covers back to slide in beside Mark he'd gotten himself out of his shorts and t-shirt. His arm came around her to pull him next to her. She'd thought he'd be cold but when she touched him his heat was rising from his body.

She took a moment to indulge herself, running

289

Jungle Inferno

her hands over him, exploring him, assuring herself he was really here and alive. He was thinner, leaner, still recovering from near-starvation. And when she touched the bandage still covering the wound on his leg she wanted to cry.

"It's okay, Tidbit." He stroked her back. "I'm fine. It's over and done and I'm home."

"I could have lost you." She buried her face against his shoulder.

"Not a chance."

He tunneled his fingers in her hair and pulled her head toward him. They'd had a lot of kisses since the rescue but none as hot and searing as this one. His tongue probed inside her mouth at once, touching every slick surface, dueling with her own tongue. She was so hungry for him she wanted to just devour him. He ate at her mouth, his tongue everywhere, his lips still rough welded to hers.

He shifted slightly so she was lying more on her back, his mouth still glued to hers, and traced her body with his free hand.

"When I was in that tent," he told her, breaking the kiss, "I thought about this all the time. Touching you. Feeling the weight of your breasts in my hands. The swollen tautness of your nipples. Your skin that feels like rich satin."

Faith rested her hand on his chest, running her fingers over the soft hair against the hard wall of muscle. Scraping his nipples with her fingernails and smiling when he sucked in a breath.

"Feel my cock," he whispered, his voice husky. "Feel what just your touch does to me."

She slipped her hand down his flat stomach to find his shaft hot and rigid and very swollen. And erect. Curling her fingers around it she pumped up and down, once, twice.

"Not too much," he cautioned. "I dreamt about

this all the time I was in that stinking jungle. I want to last more than five minutes."

"No worries," she promised. "Tell me what to do to make it easier for you." She knew he was still fighting residual pain and some difficult with movement.

"Straddle me," he said. "Climb on my chest. I want to see and taste that delicious pussy of yours."

Lithely she moved herself so her thighs were on either side of him and her sex was barely an inch from his mouth. He opened her with his fingers and for a long moment just stared. She knew she was very wet. Had been from the moment she felt his naked body next to hers.

Very slowly he brushed the tip of one finger back and forth over her clit and her cream gushed onto his chest, making him smile.

"Damn. You're really ready for me, aren't you."

"I've been ready for weeks."

He worked her clit, watching her face, his eyes dark with passion. She rocked back and forth, his soft chest hair rubbing against the wet lips of her pussy. She felt his hands on the cheeks of her ass as she moved her that final inch closer to him and then his tongue was on her, licking her, tasting her, and fire streaked through her everywhere.

Mark was afraid *he* wouldn't last long? She had her doubts about herself.

He lifted his mouth, gripped her hips and slid her backwards.

"I think we need that condom about now." She almost didn't recognize his voice.

Faith moved off of his body but before she got up from the bed pulled the covers back and let her gaze sweep over him. His cock stood proud and erect, waiting. Yup, he was ready.

"You're going to have to do most of the work,

Tidbit," he cautioned.

"My pleasure," she assured him.

She ripped the foil packet open, climbed back onto the bed and slowly, slowly rolled the latex onto him.

"Can you possibly hurry it up a little?" he asked through gritted teeth.

She gave a tight little chuckle. "I want to make sure you enjoy every minute of this."

"Believe me, I'm enjoying it. Come on, Faith, I want to be inside you. Right now."

She positioned herself over him, her thighs on either side of his, and slowly lowered herself onto that thick shaft. When he was all the way inside her she leaned her head back and closed her eyes, letting the sensation of him sweep over her. This was it. This was where she belonged. This was what life was all about. Mark so deep inside her they were almost one person.

And then she moved, slowly at first, then increasing the tempo, watching his face, his eyes, seeing the flush of desire on his cheeks. His hands gripped her waist and he pushed her to increase her pace.

"Faster," he told her. "More."

This wasn't the erotic fireworks or sizzling combustion of previous couplings. This was slower, sweeter, deeper. This was so much more than sex. It was love. It was forever.

Faith rocked back and forth then sped up her tempo again. When the orgasm hit them it was slow and long and sweet, starting low in her belly and rising like an encroaching tide to sweep through her body. Mark's hands tightened their grip on her and his cock flexed inside her as he spurted into the sheath. Her muscles pulled at him tighter and tighter, drawing every drop from him as her climax continued to roll through her. She was stretched out on an endless rack of pleasure and Mark was right there with her.

She had no idea how long the pleasure gripped them, but at some point it eased and she fell forward on his chest, her breath was trapped in her throat and her heart hammered fiercely against her ribs. She looked up at Mark's face and saw him staring at her, so much emotion in his eyes it made her want to cry. She smoothed her fingers over his lips.

"I love you," she whispered.

"I love you more," he said.

They lay like that for a long moment before he spoke again.

"Help me get this condom off and then I think I need a nap."

"Right there with you," she grinned.

For so long she'd been afraid she'd never be able to sleep next to him again. Now she cuddled close, spooned against him, the steady beat of his heart thudding against her back in a comforting rhythm. She closed her eyes and gave thanks.

*****

Later, after soup and hot bread, they sat out on the porch to watch the sunset, side by side on the wooden settee. Mark picked up Faith's hand, playing with her fingers.

"We wasted time, Tidbit. Far too much time."

"You didn't know," she started.

He placed a finger on her lips. "I was too rigid. Too set on what I should and shouldn't do. Lying in that tent, afraid I'd never see you again, I made a promise to myself."

"Oh?" Her lips curved in a smile. "And what

was that?"

"The minute I could stand up before a justice of the peace, or a minister, or whatever you want, we'd get married. Now I'm ready and I don't want you to argue with me about it."

She felt tears starting again. For days now she'd felt like a leaky faucet. "Are you sure you want to make that kind of decision now? You've been through so much."

"That's the very reason I want to do this." He placed a fingertip under her chin and turned her to face him. "I love you, Faith. I've wasted enough of my life putting it off. You're going to have to rebuild your house. I want us to do it together."

"I don't want you to give up what you're doing," she insisted. "It's dangerous but I know how committed you are to it."

"Yes, I am. What I do is important to me and I couldn't live with myself if I turned my back on it. But I'll do it a lot better knowing you're in our home waiting for me. Anyway, I only have a year left and then I'm out. Say yes, Faith, and let's get this show on the road."

"Oh, Mark." She leaned over and hugged him. "Of course I'll marry you. Just as quickly as we can."

"You are the anchor in my life," he told her.

"As you are of mine." She gave him a watery smile.

"But remember. No matter where I am, no matter how remote or isolated my location, I'll always be able to tell you how much I love you. You'll always be able to hear my message."

"Same goes, my love."

"And those messages will be the bond that ties us together. No matter what."

He kissed her then, a kiss so full of love and promise her heart swelled. A kiss that sealed a future as bright as the sun shining on their faces.

**Other romantic suspense
by Desiree Holt**

The Phoenix Agency
Extrasensory (Preorder July 2017)
Scent of Danger (Preorder August 2017)
Freeze Frame (Preorder August 2017)
Feel the Heat (Preorder August 2017)

Vigilance
Hide and Seek October 2017
Without Warning 2018
Hostage 2018

Strike Force
Unconditional Surrender
Lock and Load (Available November 2017)
Retreat to the Rear (Available 2018)
Take No Quarter (Available 2018)

Corporate Heat
Where Danger Hides (Early download May 30)
Double Deception (Available Fall 2017)
Book #3 Available 2018
Book #4 Available 2018

About the Author

USA Today best-selling and award-winning author **Desiree Holt** writes everything from romantic suspense and paranormal to erotic, a genre in which she is the oldest living author. She has been referred to by *USA Today* as the Nora Roberts of erotic romance, and is a winner of the EPIC E-Book Award, the Holt Medallion and a Romantic Times Reviewers Choice nominee. She is a USa Today bestselling author, has been featured on *CBS Sunday Morning* and in *The Village Voice,* The Daily Beast, *USA Today, The (London) Daily Mail, The New Delhi Times* and numerous other national and international publications.

Desiree Holt has produced more than two hundred titles in nearly every subgenre of romance fiction. Her stories are enriched by her personal experiences, her characters by the people she meets. After fifteen ears in the great state of Texas she relocated back to Florida to be closer to members of her family and a large collection of friends. Her favorite pastimes are watching football, reading, and researching her stories.

Learn more about her and read her novels here:
www.desireeholt.com
www.desiremeonly.com
www.facebook.com/desireeholtauthor
www.facebook.com/desireeholt
Twitter @desireeholt
Pinterest: desiree02holt
Google: www.desiree02holt

LinkedIn: **www.LinkedIn.com/desiree01holt**

Follow her on Bookbub
http://support.bookbub.com/customer/en/po
rtal/articles/2252078-what-are-new-release-
alerts-?b_id=4259

Keep up with her on her newsletter

http://eepurl.com/ce7DeE